KILL HER AGAIN

Robert Gregory Browne is the winner of the prestigious AMPAS Nicholl Fellowship in Screenwriting and has optioned and developed material for numerous production companies. He lives in Ojai, California. *Kill Her Again* is his third novel.

Also by Robert Gregory Browne

KISS HER GOODBYE
WHISPER IN THE DARK

KILL HER AGAIN

ROBERT GREGORY BROWNE

PAN BOOKS

First published in Great Britain 2009 by Pan Books
an imprint of Pan Macmillan Ltd
Pan Macmillan, 20 New Wharf Road, London N1 9RR
Basingstoke and Oxford
Associated companies throughout the world
www.panmacmillan.com

ISBN 978-0-330-45702-6

1 3 5 7 9 8 6 4 2

A CIP catalogue record for this book is available from
the British Library.

Typeset by Set Systems Ltd, Saffron Walden, Essex
Printed and bound in the UK by
CPI Mackays, Chatham ME5 8TD

Visit **www.panmacmillan.com** to read more about all our books
and to buy them. You will also find features, author interviews and
news of any author events, and you can sign up for e-newsletters
so that you're always first to hear about our new releases.

For Mother,
who always played Beethoven

Acknowledgements

Once again I'd like to thank the usual suspects, including Peggy White, who listened to a good idea and suggested the twist to make it an even better one;

Kathy Mackel, cheerleader extraordinare;

Scott Miller of Trident Media Group, world's greatest agent at the world's greatest talent agency;

Marc Resnick of St Martin's and Stefanie Bierwerth of Macmillan, the best editors a guy could ask for;

Brett Battles, Bill Cameron and Tasha Alexander, who keep me sane during the daylight hours;

My lovely wife, Leila; and

Lani and Matthew – no longer children – who always make their father proud.

Part One

PRESENT TENSE

1

The little girl was about to die.

She knew this instinctively, even though the man in the red baseball cap had never uttered so much as a word to her. It was as if she had crawled up inside his brain and could read his innermost thoughts.

Thoughts of darkness. And dead things.

Lots of dead things.

The little girl wasn't a stranger to death herself. She'd seen it first hand, at six years old, when Mr Stinky got hit by a bus. A lot of the details were hazy now, but she remembered she was playing hopscotch with Suzie at the time, Mr Stinky running circles around them on the driveway, barking like crazy.

Then, for some reason, he had decided to dart out into the street. Saw a cat or something. And the city bus that usually came down their block at nine o'clock every morning came late that day, showing up out of nowhere as if it had been waiting for Mr Stinky to make his move.

The little girl had been waiting too, waiting for Suzie to finish her turn, watching her friend skip from

3

square to square, when she heard the roar of the bus and looked up to see its front bumper smack Mr Stinky right in the head. It knocked him into the air like one of her old stuffed animals, his legs flopping as he did a kind of slow-motion somersault, then landed on the blacktop.

He didn't move after that.

And the bus driver didn't stop.

The little girl screamed and ran into the street, even though she knew her mother would yell at her. And there was Mr Stinky, lying on the ground like a bag of broken toys, his glazed eyes staring up at her, as lifeless as the two black buttons on her favourite Sunday-school dress.

There wasn't any blood, but she knew he was gone, knew he was dead, and he would never come back to her, no matter how much she begged him to, as she cradled him in her arms and cried and cried.

That had been four years ago.

But she still missed Mr Stinky and sometimes wished she could be with him again, to feel him press his head against her arm, or put his paw on her knee, whenever he wanted her to pet him.

Maybe she'd get that wish.

Maybe he was up there in heaven somewhere, waiting for her.

Lying in the back seat of the car, her wrists and ankles bound, her mouth taped shut, the little girl stared up at that greasy red baseball cap and wondered where the man was taking her.

The road bumped beneath them, tree shadows flickering across the ceiling, and from what little she could see of the darkening sky, she thought they were headed into a forest of some kind. Not like the forest she'd camped in with her mom and dad, with the sun and a lake and fishing poles, but a dark and scary Hansel and Gretel kind of place, where kids like her were cooked and eaten.

The little girl's stomach burned something awful, like that night not long ago when she ate too much lemon meringue pie. She wanted to throw up, wanted to release it all over the back seat, because she knew, without a doubt, that her time was almost up. The end was near.

That, just like Mr Stinky, it was *her* turn to—

'**H**ey, McBride, you awake?'

Anna McBride blinked, then turned from the passenger window to look at her new partner. Ted Royer. He seemed to be speaking to her from the far end of a long, dark corridor.

She blinked again and shook her head slightly, trying to clear her mind, a deep sense of dread bubbling in the pit of her stomach as the corridor finally widened, then disappeared altogether.

The darkness, however, didn't. It was a little past one a.m.

'Is that yes or no?' Royer asked.

'Yes,' Anna said, clearing her throat. 'I was thinking, is all. Daydreaming.'

But that wasn't exactly the truth. The truth was much deeper than a simple daydream. And certainly more frightening.

Special Agent Anna McBride was losing her mind.

'Let's get something straight right up front,' Royer said. He was seated behind the wheel of their Bureau transport, a black Ford Explorer. He drove with the casual self-assurance of a career brick agent, a man who had spent many years in the field. 'If we're gonna be working together – and from all appearances it looks like we are – then I'm gonna need you to stay alert and keep focused. You think you can manage that?'

There was an edge of impatience to his voice. Anna knew that this new partnership had not been his choice, that it was merely the luck of the draw that had thrown them together. And she was pretty sure Royer considered it *bad* luck.

But she didn't care about that right now. She had more pressing things to think about than an unstable work relationship.

Like an unstable mind.

As much as she wanted to believe that she'd fallen asleep for a moment, had let the hum of the engine lull her into the Land of Nod, she knew she'd been wide awake, and that what she'd just experienced had not been a dream at all. Not this time.

The question was: what exactly was it?

'Yo, McBride. Am I getting through to you?'

Anna nodded. 'Message loud and clear.'

Royer gave her a sideways glance. 'You're not gonna be one of those, are you?'

'One of what?'

'Smart-asses.' He returned his gaze to the road, which seemed to stretch out forever into the desert darkness, all prairie brush and cactus. The view was as foreign to Anna as a lunar landscape. 'I'll tell you right now, I've had my fill of smart-ass partners, always trying to be clever, but usually at the expense of good investigative work. Too busy listening to their own bullshit to notice anything else.'

Anna was tempted to tell him she thought this might be a case of the kettle and the pot, but stopped just short of letting the words fly. Instead she said, 'You don't have to worry about me. No bullshit. And I'll stay focused.'

This was an outright lie, of course. Staying focused was not her strong suit these days.

'I'm not gonna kid you,' Royer said. 'The truth is, none of us really want you here.'

'I'm beginning to see that.'

Another sideways glance. 'There you go with the smart-ass shit again. I'm surprised they didn't ship you straight to South Dakota. Who'd you have to blow to get this assignment, anyway?'

Anna bit her tongue. Anything she said right now would only egg Royer on, and all she wanted to do was shut him the hell up. The Glock 9 on her hip was calling out to her, but she resisted the urge to put a bullet in his brain. A feeling she'd been fighting since the moment she met him.

She had arrived in Victorville two days ago, less than a week after the doctors had proclaimed her fit for duty, and a little over a month after the blow-up in South San Francisco.

She didn't like thinking about that night, had known the moment it exploded in their faces that she would be the designated scapegoat, as she should be. It was all her fault.

But thinking about it had not turned out to be the problem. Ever since she'd jolted awake to a dark hospital room, a nasty set of stitches on the side of her face to remind her of the mistake she'd made, the majority of her mind's real estate had been occupied by only one thing:

The vision. The dream. Nightmares so vivid they had her waking up in a cold sweat every night. Fleeting thoughts and images that all but disappeared the moment she opened her eyes.

A little girl in trouble.

A little girl who was about to die.

'Here's the drill,' Royer said. 'We get to Ludlow, you stand there and keep your mouth shut. These jurisdictional disputes can get a little tricky, so I'll do all the talking.'

'I thought they invited us in?'

'They did, but the request came from the County Undersheriff himself, so it's unlikely the rank and file are gonna be too thrilled about a coupla feds sticking their noses in the pond.'

'I've seen my share of pissed-off locals. I think I can handle myself.'

'Yeah,' Royer said, wagging his finger at her scar,

which, despite several sessions with CoverGirl, had proven impossible to hide. 'I can see that.'

This silenced her. It was her turn to shoot *him* a glance, but his concentration was centred on the road ahead and he didn't seem to notice.

Or did he?

Was he baiting her? Hoping she'd give him an excuse to send her packing?

The Victorville Resident Agency – one of the bureau's LA satellite stations – wasn't any paradise, but Royer was right, she *should* be in South Dakota. She'd only managed to stay in California because Daddy dear had connections in the Justice Department.

But it was doubtful even South Dakota wanted her.

Nobody did.

'I'll keep my mouth shut,' she said, surrendering to Royer's contempt, knowing she'd have to swallow a lot of pride to make this partnership work. She'd spent a lifetime ramping towards a career that had unravelled in just a few short minutes, so she wasn't about to squander what was likely her one and only second chance, no matter how much it pained her.

Besides, pride was the least of her concerns at the moment. The visions had obviously begun to escalate. They were coming during her waking hours now. And despite what the doctors had told the Victorville Agent in Charge, she knew she wasn't even remotely fit for duty yet.

And until she was, she'd simply have to fake it.

'Looks like we're here,' Royer said, and sure enough the lights of Ludlow, California twinkled in the distance ahead, a dusty oasis in the middle of the Mojave Desert.

Anna wondered how people lived out here, wondered what compelled them to seek out the isolation and the dry, oven-like temperatures. Places like this were scattered throughout Southern California, with no apparent connection to the rest of the world.

Maybe that in itself was the attraction.

'You might want to brace yourself,' Royer said. 'I'm told the scene is pretty grisly.'

Anna didn't mind.

Maybe grisly was just the distraction she needed.

2

It was small as houses go. A worn, two-bedroom box made of brick and stucco, surrounded by a low, sagging wooden fence and fronted by a tiny patch of earth that had never held much more than a few desert weeds.

Anna had always harboured the notion that everything looked better at night. More stylized. Romantic. But there was no romance here. The house was a desolate and dreary reflection of the neighbourhood – and town – it occupied.

A half-dozen County Sheriff's vehicles were parked haphazardly in the street out front, a coroner's van backed into the driveway, its rear doors hanging open.

Several neighbours stood watching from across the street, a mix of old and young, fat and thin, clothed and half-naked, every one of them with leathery, sun-baked complexions that added a good ten years to their appearance.

The first thing Anna noticed as she climbed out of the cool interior of the Explorer was the oppressive summer heat. Middle of the night and it had to be over a hundred degrees. She felt as if someone had thrown a thick, wool blanket around her and she wanted desperately to take off her coat. That, however, wasn't about to happen unless Royer took his off first, and Anna wasn't holding her breath.

Good thing, too, because Royer actually *buttoned* his coat before flashing his creds at a nearby deputy. Ducking under the yellow crime-scene tape, he headed for the open front door.

Anna followed, but before they reached the porch, a sinewy guy in a western shirt, jeans and cowboy boots stepped into the doorway.

'Agent Royer?'

His voice was a deep, sombre baritone, but there was no hint of hostility on his face as he moved forward and held out a hand to shake.

Royer shook it, looking mildly surprised by the man's courtesy.

'That's right,' he said. 'Deputy Worthington?'

Worthington nodded. 'Sheriff's Homicide. But call me Jake.' His gaze shifted to Anna, lingering briefly on the scar before finding her eyes. 'And you are?'

Royer cut her off before she had a chance to respond. 'This is Agent McBride.'

'Welcome to Ludlow,' Worthington said, as Anna grabbed his outstretched hand.

She'd always hated shaking hands with a man, feeling awkward whenever she did it, wondering how to negotiate the task. Squeeze too hard and she might come off as some desperate female trying to prove herself, while not hard enough painted her as weak and ineffective. Finding a balance was tough, and the moment was usually stiff and uncomfortable.

Anna managed to get through this one with a minimum of fuss, however, and was relieved when Worthington didn't hang on longer than necessary.

'I've gotta warn you both that what you're about to see isn't pretty. We've got more than one deputy almost lost his dinner over it, including me.'

'The minute it stops bothering you,' Anna said, 'you'd better start thinking about a change of careers.'

Royer shot her a frown, but Worthington nodded solemnly, then handed them each a pair of latex gloves and gestured for them to follow him inside. 'Let's get to it.'

Royer didn't wait for Anna or offer her the chance to go in first. She was, she realized, merely an accessory here. A show of force that didn't really translate into action. This was Royer's party and she was the annoying little sister whom mom had foisted on the big kids.

Her only sense of satisfaction came from the fact that Royer had been wrong about the reception. Worthington seemed genuinely glad to see them.

Pausing at the doorway, she turned as she snapped on the gloves, taking another look at the neighbourhood, at the ramshackle houses that lined the street. She had a feeling that even out here in the desert, a street like this was no stranger to violence. There'd have to be something extra special going on inside to gather such a crowd at one-thirty in the morning.

Grisly, Royer had warned her. Not pretty.

Turning back towards the house, Anna stepped past the threshold and took it all in.

The first thing she noticed was the blood. It was hard not to, considering it was everywhere, arterial spray all over the furniture and walls. She didn't need gloves, she needed a haz-mat suit.

A split-second after the blood registered in her brain, the smell hit her, the same smell that accompanied too many of the homicide scenes she'd been to.

Urine and faeces.

It's the thing they never tell you about in movies and television. That when some people die violently, they evacuate their bladder and bowels. From rock stars to anonymous paupers, it isn't unusual to find them swimming in their own waste.

Mix that with the scent of the blood and rotting entrails and you've got the smell of death.

A smell you never get used to.

Royer and Worthington were standing over a body on the right side of an unkempt, standard-issue living room. A couple of coroner's men stood nearby, waiting to bag it.

The victim was female, possibly thirty years old, although it was hard to tell, thanks to the way the body had been carved up. The killer had been quite liberal with the use of his weapon, which had been sharp enough to cut very deep.

More blood soaked the sofa cushions just above the spot where the body lay, and Anna figured this was where the victim had been killed. She felt the Lean Cuisine meat loaf she'd scarfed for dinner start to back up on her, but forced it down. She wasn't about to give Royer any more ammunition against her.

Not that he needed any.

When she joined them, he said, 'What took you?'

She ignored the question and stared down at the corpse, feeling a sudden sense of sadness wash through her. She didn't know this poor woman, didn't know anything about her, but nobody deserved to be displayed like this to a room full of strangers.

Anna looked at Worthington. 'Who is she?'

'Rita Fairweather. Twenty-seven-year-old single mother of two.'

Christ, Anna thought. Only a year younger than me.

'She worked at a bar in town, place called The Well. Was there until about eleven p.m.' He gestured to the blood on the walls. 'Near as we can figure it, it was pretty much a blitzkrieg attack. They never saw it coming.'

'They?' Royer said, raising his eyebrows.

Worthington hitched a finger and they followed him across the room through a doorway that led to a small, dingy kitchen. Lying on the faded linoleum in a sticky pool of blood was a man of indeterminate age, multiple stab wounds to his chest. An unopened can of Colt 45 lay at his feet.

'One of her boyfriends from the bar,' Worthington said. 'John Meacham. Poor son of a bitch picked the wrong night to get horny.'

Anna noticed something on his neck and crouched down for a closer look. The flesh was slightly pink, with two fresh, reddish marks about half an inch apart.

'Looks like he used a stun gun on this one,' she said.

Worthington nodded. 'That's what we're thinking. We'll know for sure once the ME gets him on the table.'

Anna stood up. 'You say Fairweather has kids. Where are they?'

'Ahh,' Worthington said. 'The reason you two are here.'

He turned again, crossing through the living room to a narrow hallway. As Anna and Royer followed, she began to get a vague feeling of déjà vu.

There was a bathroom at the far end of the hall, and two bedroom doors on either side, facing each other. Worthington led them to the one on the left, to yet another body – a teenage girl, her mouth taped shut, her wrists and ankles bound, more stab wounds.

An image flashed through Anna's mind—

—the little girl, bound and gagged in the back seat of a car—

Anna blinked it away, forcing herself to concentrate on the room, which was largely occupied by two twin beds and a parade of stuffed animals and action figures. One of the beds sported Los Angeles Dodgers bedsheets, while the other carried a pastel-pink comforter covered with a throwback to Anna's own childhood: My Little Ponies.

A bookshelf to her right held dozens of children's books, including some of Anna's own favourites. *Little House on the Prairie. Through the Looking Glass. The Wonderful Wizard of Oz.*

She remembered many a night, her mother perched on the edge of her bed, reading aloud to her, and she wondered if Rita Fairweather had ever had the chance to do the same.

Worthington gestured to the body on the floor.

'Tammy Garrett. The family babysitter. She looked after the kids three nights a week.'

She couldn't have been more than fifteen, sixteen years old. Plump. Baby-faced.

'And the kids?' Anna asked, already knowing the answer.

'Like I said, the reason you two are here.'

Worthington moved to the nightstand between the two beds and with his gloved right hand picked up a small digital camera, pressed a button and handed it to Anna.

'Evan and Kimberly.'

Anna looked down at the photograph on the tiny LCD screen. A woman whom she assumed was Rita Fairweather stood with her two young children, a boy and girl, on the grounds of what looked like a carnival. There was a Ferris wheel in the distance and, directly behind them, the black hole of a doorway led to what

17

a gaudily painted sign said was DR DEMON'S HOUSE OF A THOUSAND MIRRORS.

Something stirred at the periphery of Anna's brain – another image flash, too fast to decipher, accompanied by a sudden unexplained rush of vertigo.

Acutely aware that the deterioration of her mind was still in progress, and that the distraction of blood and faeces and dead bodies had been temporary at best, she waited for the dizziness to pass.

'You all right?' Worthington asked.

She knew her face must be showing her distress. 'Fine,' she said. 'Just a little touch of nausea.'

He nodded, offering her a grim smile. 'Like you said, the minute it stops bothering you, you'd better start thinking about a change of careers.'

Anna managed a smile in return, but Royer was having none of it. Giving her an impatient scowl, he snatched the camera out of her hands and stared down at the image of Rita Fairweather and her kids.

'Where was this shot?'

'High-school football field. Carnival comes through town every year. Still here, as a matter of fact, so the photo is recent.'

'I take it they're missing?'

Nothing like stating the obvious.

'No sign of 'em,' Worthington said. 'And being so close to Nevada and all, we figure there's a fairly good chance they were taken across the state line.'

There was no guarantee that this had happened, of course, but Worthington had been smart enough to hedge his bets and call in the FBI. Crossing state lines automatically made it a federal case, and the Ludlow County Sheriff's Department was undoubtedly ill prepared for a crime of this magnitude – which explained the complete lack of hostility towards a couple of federal outsiders. They were anxious to hand it off.

'What about the father?' Royer asked. 'He still in the picture?'

'Dead two years, according to the neighbours.'

'Is there a ransom note?' Anna asked.

It seemed like a ridiculous question. Who was left to pay ransom? And even if she were still alive, Rita Fairweather obviously wouldn't be able to afford one.

But you never knew whether there was a rich relative somewhere in the picture and, for all of her faults, Anna believed in being thorough.

'No notes, nothing,' Worthington said. 'I figure we're dealing with a predator – and not just any predator at that.'

'What do you mean?'

'This'll sound a little crazy, but you work a crime scene long enough, the victims start to talk to you.'

'And what are they telling you?'

'That whoever did this, it wasn't his first time. He's had practice, and a lot of it.'

Anna thought about the serial perps she'd studied back at Quantico. Sociopathic savages who brutalized and tortured their victims, treating them with less sympathy, less mercy, than they would a bug on a wall. It was true that many of them had been victimized themselves, but this was a reason for their behaviour, not an excuse, and she knew that should she ever encounter one in the wild, she wouldn't hesitate to blow him away.

Just as this thought entered Anna's mind, her gaze fell to the camera in Royer's hand, to the photograph still onscreen. But it wasn't the children she saw, it was the Ferris wheel, the house of mirrors.

Then, all at once, a rush of images came at her as if they were being poured from a box full of puzzle pieces, flickering past her mind's eye so rapidly that she was once again overcome by vertigo, a dizziness so strong she had to grab onto Worthington's arm for support.

'What is it?' he asked. 'What's wrong?'

But the onslaught was so overpowering that her brain couldn't form the words to answer him, the images continuing to assault her—

—a spray of blood—

—the bound little girl—

—the man in the red baseball cap—

—tree shadows flickering across a tattered car ceiling—

—an ornate locket swinging from a rear-view mirror—

Anna stumbled back, nearly losing her footing as she turned and hurried through the doorway. Stepping quickly down the hall, she crossed the living room and went outside, pulling her coat off as she moved, trying to get some air, trying desperately to purge her brain of these terrible images—

—a dark corridor of trees—

—a remote clearing—

—a suitcase full of bloody knives—

Then finally, thankfully, the last of them flitted by as she leaned a hand against the wall and closed her eyes, wondering what the hell was happening to her, wondering if she was indeed going mad.

3

'What the fuck is the matter with you?'

Anna was at the rear of the house now, seated at an old patio table with a tattered umbrella. Beyond the low wooden fence, across a barren field, was the back side of a junk yard, mountainous piles of debris laid out in neat rows and bathed in moonlight.

Old tyres. Car parts. Rusty washing machines. Scrap metal. All caged in by a chain-link fence.

Anna had been staring at it for a long time, thinking that if there was a junk yard for demoted and disgraced FBI agents, she'd surely be at the top of the pile.

She looked up at Royer, saw the fury on his face. They'd been working together for a total of four hours now and she already knew the partnership was doomed. He'd be filing a complaint against her as soon as they were back in Victorville.

'Well?' he said.

'I got nauseous.' She wasn't about to tell him the truth. 'You've never gotten sick at a crime scene?'

'Never,' he said. 'And if I did, I sure as hell wouldn't show it.'

Anna glared at him. 'Is that what this is about? Macho pride? Did I embarrass you in front of the deputy?'

'All I asked you to do was keep your mouth shut and focus, and you can't even do that.' His cheeks were red with anger. 'You're a disgrace to the Bureau, you know that? Must be nice to have a daddy with connections.'

Anna felt the heat rise in her own cheeks. But it wasn't anger that caused it. It was humiliation.

After the fiasco in San Francisco, if *she'd* been the one making the decisions about who could stay and who needed to go, she would've ignored the political pressure and booted her ass right out the door. Permanently.

But Daddy was an influential man and *had* been for as long as she could remember. And in her desperation to keep her career from completely caving in on her, she had called him and asked for help.

But the truth was, she hadn't deserved his help.

A man was paralysed, had almost died, because of her inability to lead. She had let down her own partner. Had let everyone down. Including herself. And maybe that was the reason for these strange visions. The vertigo.

Maybe it was the guilt that was driving her mad. Maybe it all came from some inner darkness she harboured, a subconscious need to be punished for what she'd done.

But why the little girl?

Why that particular scenario?

Was she someone Anna knew?

From somewhere far off Royer said, 'You're not even listening to me, are you?' But the words barely registered and, when she looked up again, he was gone. Headed back to the house.

She watched him slide the glass rear door open, angrily flick the curtains aside and disappear behind them.

Anna turned, looking out across the field at those giant piles of junk, thinking she might as well get it over with and crawl on top of one right now. Her career was done. Kaput. Pump her full of morphine, Doc, then pull the plug.

But then she paused, drawn out of her rendezvous with self-pity by movement across the field:

A shadow near one of the junk piles.

A silhouette, low to the ground.

Was it an animal?

A junk-yard dog?

She rose from her chair, moving closer to the wooden fence. And as she moved, the silhouette moved also, retreating.

But it wasn't a dog at all. As it hurriedly crawled backwards, it crossed into a pool of moonlight, exposing feral eyes in a small round face—

—the face of a young boy.

And even from this distance, Anna was sure she recognized him.

The boy in the amusement-park photograph. Evan.

Rita Fairweather's son.

Climbing quickly over the fence, Anna started towards him, calling his name. 'Evan?'

But the boy picked up speed, standing now, turning towards the darkness between two piles of junk. As he disappeared between them, Anna ran, calling out for back-up, hoping one of the deputies would hear her.

The field was made of rutted, sun-baked dirt, and navigating it in the pale moonlight without falling on her face was tricky, but she managed to get across, then leapt onto the chain-link fence, using the momentum to pull her up and over it.

As she jumped down to the other side, she landed wrong, tweaking her left ankle. Biting back the twinge of pain, she reached for her flashlight, only to realize she wasn't wearing her coat, had left it hanging over her chair in the back yard.

She could run back for it, but the boy might be gone by then. Hesitating only a moment, she looked up at the rusty mountains of junk that loomed above, then moved into the darkness between them.

'Evan?'

Nothing in return.

'Evan, don't be scared, I'm a friend. A friend of your mommy's.'

Still nothing. The darkness was nearly impenetrable here, the junk piles blocking out the moon. It suddenly occurred to Anna that Evan might not be alone, that the predator or whoever had killed those people back at the house might have been watching all this time.

Watching and waiting.

But for what?

She reached to her holster and released her Glock, bringing it up in a two-handed grip, resting her finger against the trigger guard. Moving forward cautiously, she decided not to call out again. If the boy *wasn't* alone, she saw no point in telegraphing her position.

A sound spun her to the right. It was little more than a creak of metal that could simply have been caused by a shifting of the earth.

But Anna didn't think so.

Turning, she wound her way around the large silhouette of what looked like the remnants of an old school bus. There was a moonlit clearing up ahead. Hearing the creak again, she gauged its direction and picked up speed, deciding to skirt the edge of the clearing to keep her exposure to a minimum.

Then, just as she was edging closer to the moonlight, there was a burst of movement from inside a nearby pile of rubble as the boy, Evan, flew across the clearing and disappeared into the darkness on the other side.

'Evan, wait!' she shouted, but he didn't slow down.

Quickly holstering her Glock, she ran for all she was worth, pain shooting through her ankle as she moved out into the open, knowing she was taking a risk exposing herself like this. But her instincts told her she was safe, that the boy was alone out here. Alone and afraid.

She didn't know what he'd seen back at that

house, but suspected the worst, and all she wanted to do was catch up to him, to let him know that he *wasn't* alone, that there were people who wanted to help him.

'Evan!' she shouted, as she moved again into darkness, wishing she had her flashlight.

Hearing a whimper, she froze, knowing she was close. And, despite the lack of illumination, she sensed that the boy had miscalculated and had hit a dead end of some kind, a wall of junk that held no escape.

She heard him struggling for breath. Raw and ragged. Frightened out of his wits.

'Evan? Are you there? It's okay, I won't hurt you.'

Then, as her eyes began to adjust, she could see the small, pale oval of his face, low to the ground, eyes wide and terrified. He was lying inside a warped wooden cabinet with one of its doors missing, the other hanging by a single hinge.

Moving closer, Anna crouched down, peering in at him.

'It's okay, hon. It's gonna be—'

The vicious bark of a dog cut her off and spun her around. Anna reached for her Glock, but a shotgun blast to the sky stopped her cold as a flashlight beam shone directly in her face.

'Keep your fuckin' hands right where they are, Missy. You wouldn't be the first trespasser I've shot.'

4

Daniel Pope was watching himself on TV when he got the call.

He did that a lot. Watched himself.

Not out of any sense of vanity – that was one human failing Pope couldn't claim – but simply because he found that studying his performances allowed him to improve his craft. Such as it was.

While Pope didn't take much pride in his personal life these days, he'd always been proud of his work. Something to cling to.

And Pope desperately needed something to cling to.

So there he sat, in the dim light of his hotel room, smoking a bowl of White Widow as he watched the DVD of last night's show. The same DVD they sold to tourists in the casino lobby for fifteen bucks a pop.

Then his cellphone chirped.

Pope grabbed the remote, hit the pause button, then snatched the phone up off his nightstand and squinted at the screen.

Just what he was afraid of.

Sharkey.

Pope debated letting voicemail pick it up, but knew that would only stall the inevitable, forcing him to call Sharkey back. And he certainly didn't want to have to do that.

He stared at his image on the television screen, saw himself frozen in motion, wearing that ridiculous glittery black tux, thinking he should seriously consider revamping his wardrobe. Flashy costumes were more or less cultural de rigueur in a Vegas-style lounge show, even a low-rent show like his. But why not let his assistants, Carmen and Feather, handle the glitter? A good half of the tourists only came to stare at their tits anyway.

Pope sighed, then finally clicked the phone on and put it to his ear. 'Hey, Sharkey, what's up?'

'You're actually awake at this hour?'

'You must've figured I would be.'

'Nah, I was just gonna leave a message. But I like this better. I always feel like I have to be polite on voicemail.'

'I don't think anyone would ever accuse you of that.'

Sharkey barked. It was supposed to be a laugh, but didn't quite qualify. 'You're a funny guy, Danny. Maybe you should consider a change of format. Put a little comedy in your act.'

'It's already got some,' Pope said.

'Yeah? Colour me stupid, but I don't think a bunch of idiots bouncing around onstage is all that funny.'

'Did you call to offer me a critique, or is there a point to this conversation?'

Sharkey got quiet a moment, then said, 'Troy wants to see you. And he's pretty upset.'

'About what?'

'About you, that's what.'

Pope quickly ran a list of possible fuck-ups through his slightly stoned brain, but only came up with one likely suspect.

'The session?'

'Bingo. He's thinking maybe you got something wrong. Got some wires crossed, made a mistake.'

'It doesn't work that way,' Pope told him, staring again at the TV screen, looking at his face, noticing that his expression was frozen in a grimace – an accurate reflection of how he felt about the subject of Anderson Troy.

'I won't even pretend to know how it works,' Sharkey said. 'But then I'm not paid to be curious. The man gets pissed, I gotta do what I can to calm him down. Even if it means dealing with a bullshit artist like you.'

'What's the matter, Sharkey? You don't believe in hypnosis?'

'I don't believe in anything.'

That made sense. But Sharkey wasn't Pope's concern at the moment. 'So Troy's not happy with last night's little rendezvous. What does he want me to do about it?'

'Get your ass up there, that's what. Pronto.'

Wonderful. Just the good news he needed at two

in the morning. 'Why? It won't change anything. The past is the past.'

'Right now you'd better start thinking about the future,' Sharkey said.

Then he hung up.

The elevator in the residential section of the Desert Oasis Hotel-Casino had to be the slowest in the world. But then everything was a little slower out here, and Pope liked it just fine that way.

Forty miles outside of the city proper, a last-chance gas and gambling stop near the California state line, the Oasis didn't even attempt to capture the high-gloss hustle and bustle of the 'new' Las Vegas.

Walking into the casino was like stepping through a time warp. The 1970s all over again, only a little grungier and faded this time around. The booze and cigarette-stained carpet and dusty-looking wallpaper hadn't been changed in decades and the slot machines could actually be cranked by hand.

Anyone who was used to the glamour of the Strip, or even the refurbished beauty of the Nugget downtown, would take one look at the Oasis and immediately start reaching for the Sani-wipes.

It was what the tour brochures called *charm*.

All this changed, however, once you got to the fourteenth floor. Anderson Troy's private domain was as immaculate as a biological clean-room and just about as welcoming.

After a long, slow ascent, still slightly hazed by the killer pot, Pope stepped off the elevator and looked down at the spotless white carpet. Not a stray cigarette ash or splash of bourbon in sight.

'Good morning, Daniel.'

Pope looked up to find Troy's personal assistant, Arturo, standing before a set of double doors. To one side of the doors was a neat row of shoes.

'Morning, Arturo.'

Knowing the routine, Pope slipped off his loafers and lined them up next to the others. Anderson Troy was neither eccentric nor germaphobic, but he did like to keep his carpet clean, especially after his staff and visitors had been traipsing around the casino below.

Pope had once asked him why he hadn't renovated the entire hotel rather than just the fourteenth floor, and Troy had told him that he was afraid it would scare away the locals and budget tourists who made up 90 per cent of his trade.

'Besides,' Troy had said, 'it would cost too much. And you know how fond I am of money.'

Pope did indeed. In fact, his own current lifestyle was, in part, the result of that fondness. But he also knew that the Oasis, just as it stood, was the perfect under-the-radar cover for Troy's other, less legitimate, activities.

Anderson Troy was not your typical casino owner. For that matter, he wasn't your typical *anything*.

He was, however, a dangerous man.

Once Pope's shoes were in place, Arturo handed him a pair of disposable foot covers, which he dutifully slipped on over his socks.

He felt like a toddler wearing bunny pyjamas.

'Go on in,' Arturo said. 'He's expecting you.'

No shit, Sherlock.

Pope almost made the remark out loud, but restrained himself. What was the point? Arturo was a simple working man who did his job and seemed to bear no grudges against anyone. Even when he was killing them.

Instead, Pope nodded and pushed through the double doors into the now-familiar lair of one of the youngest self-made multi-millionaires in the world. A man who had made those millions in DVDs and video games, among other things. Not creating them, mind you, but hacking their copy protection, pirating and selling them overseas.

Only a select few knew that Troy was worth so much. And since making his first several million, he had branched out into a variety of Internet schemes that could potentially land him in prison for life, if he weren't so good at remaining anonymous.

A self-styled gangster, he was really nothing more than a thirtysomething computer geek with a lot of hired muscle. And, of course, the will to use it when necessary.

He was sitting on the sofa, which was a soft grey puff of nothing that blended in beautifully with the muted greys and whites that dominated the room. Looking like a stain on the fabric, he was hunched over a laptop computer, wearing a faded GOT ROOT? T-shirt and frayed, cut-off maroon sweats, his stringy wannabe rock-star hair hanging in his face.

He didn't bother to look up when he said:

'A fag?'

These were the last words Pope had expected to come out of Troy's mouth at that particular moment, so he responded with a simple, 'What?'

Troy tore himself away from the computer screen and made eye contact. 'You want me to believe I was once a faggot? A homo?'

'I think the politically correct term is gay,' Pope said.

'I don't give a fuck how you candy-coat it. This Nigel Fromme guy? I just did a Google on him and found some very disconcerting information. Turns out he was an artist. One of the hottest painters of his time.'

'What's wrong with that?'

'Not a thing,' Troy said. 'It's his sexual orientation that concerns me.'

'I take it he's gay?'

'Gayer than a bucket full of butterflies.'

'So? What difference does it make?'

'Difference?' Troy closed his laptop, got to his feet. He was high-school basketball tall. 'Let me explain something to you, Daniel. I come from a long line of God-fearing, gun-loving homophobes. Now, personally, I'm a little more progressive in my thinking. I don't have an axe to grind when it comes to people's choice of bed partners. You're a guy, you want to bag another guy – shit, you want to bag a gerbil – that's your choice. Whatever you do in the privacy of your home is your own business. But do me a favour and make sure it stays that way. I've got no interest in you unless you're a big-titted blonde with no sudden surprises dangling between your legs.'

He moved towards Pope now. 'So when I find out this Nigel Fromme guy was a full-on flamer, you can understand my concern.'

'Not really, no.'

Troy sighed. 'If I believe all this stuff you've fed me about past lives—'

'*I've* fed *you*?'

'—then I have to believe that my soul once occupied Nigel Fromme's body, right?'

Pope shrugged. 'That's the theory.'

There had long been a debate in the hypnosis community over past-life regression therapy. Was it real, or was it, as Pope's grandfather, an old jazz musician, used to say, pure bushwa?

A lot of people in the field believed that even simple childhood regression therapy was bullshit. Nothing more than a combination of recall and imagination. But, to Pope's mind, that didn't necessarily negate its usefulness as a therapy. Recall and imagination could reveal quite a bit about a person.

For the record, however, it was *Troy* who had originally brought up the subject of reincarnation, after reading an article about it online. Pope's own feelings about the matter remained non-committal. He didn't really give a damn.

'So if this Nigel guy liked to bat for the home team,' Troy was saying, 'then my soul was batting right along with him. The same soul that occupies *my* body, right here, right now.'

Pope said nothing. Figured it was better to let that one go.

'In other words, you're telling me I'm a fag.'

Pope stared at him, wondering if this was a joke of some kind. Troy having fun. Was Sharkey standing behind the door to the kitchen, laughing his ass off at Pope's expense?

He didn't think so.

Troy wasn't the kind of guy who joked around. And computer geek or not, the man was unpredictable when he got angry.

'I'm not telling you anything,' Pope said. 'That's not how it works.'

'Oh? Then how *does* it work? Because the way I see it, either I'm a fag or you made a mistake. Which is it?'

There was a sudden chill in the room. Real or imagined, Pope couldn't be sure. Feeling a presence behind him, he turned to find Arturo standing quietly in the doorway.

Not a good sign.

What had begun as an off-the-cuff, semi-stoned conversation during a late-night poker game had turned into an impromptu, after-hours hypnosis session that had now somehow morphed into a deeply offended and lethally angry Anderson Troy. And the only one Troy could find to blame for the insult was the messenger. The hypnotist. The guy who had put him under.

That, of course, would be Pope. Star of the Desert Oasis Hotel-Casino's ever-popular late-night lounge show, *Metamorphosis*. Twenty bucks and a drink. Discount coupons in the hotel lobby.

'You know,' Pope said, offering Troy his million-dollar stage smile, thinking he needed his glittery black tux to make it official, 'this isn't an exact science. Maybe I did something wrong, got some wires crossed somehow. If you like, we can try again, see what happens.'

Troy nodded to Arturo, who quietly returned the nod and left the room.

'I'm glad you see it that way, Daniel. I was hoping I wouldn't have to replace this carpet again.'

5

The boy couldn't remember any of it.

After Anna identified herself as FBI, the owner of the junk yard stowed his shotgun and muzzled his German Shepherd, letting Anna pull Evan out of his hiding place and carry him back towards the house.

They were greeted at the chain-link fence by Royer, Worthington and half a dozen sheriff's deputies, who had come running, weapons drawn, at the sound of the shotgun blast.

The boy, trembling, kept his face buried in Anna's neck. Rather than deal with the logistics of getting him up and over the fence, one of the deputies ran back for a pair of wire cutters and they simply made a hole big enough for Anna to step through.

She carried him across the rutted field, through the back yard, past the house and on out to the Ford Explorer, where she waved the others away and deposited him on the back seat. He was crying, tears streaking his dirty face, and she could see that he was in shock, a shock that might be too deep to penetrate.

'It's okay, Evan. Everything's okay now.'

But it wasn't okay and the boy knew it, and he continued to tremble as the tears flowed. She figured he had to be close to seven years old, but his reaction to the trauma of this night made him seem much, much younger.

'I want my mommy,' he said in a small, shaky voice.

Anna's heart seized up in her chest. 'I know you do, hon, I know. But your mommy's been hurt and she can't be with you right now.'

'I don't want her to go away. I want her to come back.'

'I know,' Anna said.

She'd lost her own mother to cancer when she was about his age. Remembered the feeling of helplessness, the disbelief. The ache.

'Bring her back,' the boy cried, then flew into her arms again, pressing his face against her chest, sobbing uncontrollably.

Anna held him, wishing she had a magic wand she could wave to make his pain vanish. But she had learned long ago that there was no magic in this world. There were no miracles. No do-overs.

Dead was dead and resurrection was the thing of fairy tales.

Anna's biggest failing as a federal agent was her tendency to become emotionally involved in a case. She knew it could only lead to trouble – and certainly had in San Francisco – but she never hesitated to allow herself to empathize with the victims of crime. If a situation called for her to be a friend, a confidante, or even a surrogate mother, she was more than happy to fulfil that need.

If she had a calling, that was it. Which sometimes prompted her to think she should have continued with her education, rather than allow herself to get side-tracked into law enforcement.

She might be better off now, if she had.

Might even be sane.

As the boy cried against her chest, she pulled him close, rocked him and quietly sang her favourite lullaby, the song her mother sang to her nearly every night of her life before she was too weak to sit up:

> *Every little star*
> *Way up in the sky*
> *Calls me*
> *Heaven in my heart*
> *Wishing I could fly*
> *Away*
> *Drift off to sleep*
> *Into a dream*
> *My soul to keep*
> *I do believe . . .*

Her mother had written the song, playing it on a cheap ukulele she kept on a shelf next to Anna's bed. A simple, almost melancholy tune that, to Anna, now seemed prophetic. As if her mother had known, even before the illness, that death was approaching.

As she sang the last bar, Anna noticed that the

boy, Evan, had grown quiet. Was lost in his own moment, his own memory.

She hoped it was a good one.

'You question him?' Royer asked.

'As much as I could.'

'And?'

Royer and Worthington were huddled in the front yard, several feet from the Explorer, as Anna approached. The boy was asleep on the back seat.

'He's in shock. He doesn't remember anything.'

'Nothing at all?' Worthington asked.

'He knows his mother is dead, but can't or won't tell me what he saw. And he has no idea where his sister is. He's a complete blank, as far as I can tell.'

'As far as *you* can tell.' Royer didn't bother to hide his contempt. Despite this turn of events, his anger had obviously not dissipated. 'Maybe somebody else needs to take a shot at him. Somebody qualified.'

Anna looked at him. She'd never been the type to flaunt credentials, but she'd had about enough of this jerk. 'You're probably right, but just for the record, I have a Masters Degree in applied psychology. I was working on my PhD when the Bureau recruited me.'

'Is that supposed to impress me?'

'I'm merely stating a fact. And it seems to me the only thing you're qualified to do is bitch and moan.'

Royer said nothing for a moment, cycling through three or four different facial expressions before finally settling on what Anna could only describe as a murderous glare. 'That's it, McBride. You're done. As soon as we get back to Victorville, your ass is—'

'Hold on, now,' Worthington said, throwing his hands up. 'As entertaining as this little squabble may be, I'd appreciate it if you two would stow the bullshit and get back to the matter at hand. I've got my men scouring that junk yard, but there's still no sign of the girl.' He looked at Anna. 'You think if we bring an expert in here, we might be able to get Evan to open up?'

Before she could respond, Royer said, 'If you have any questions about how to proceed, Deputy Worthington, direct them to me.'

Worthington frowned. 'Nobody's given you the keys to the car just yet.'

'The Ludlow County Undersheriff might disagree.'

'The Ludlow County Undersheriff is one of my best friends, and he called you people because I asked him to. And until we establish that there's actually been a federal crime committed here, let's consider this a cooperative effort and keep the drama to a minimum.'

Royer cycled through another set of facial expressions, and was still looking for a suitable response when Worthington turned again to Anna. 'I assume the Bureau has somebody they can call for this?'

'Down in Victorville. But it'll take a while to get him out of bed and bring him out here.'

'We don't have the luxury of time.'

'You have somebody local in mind?'

'Unfortunately, the only head doctor we've got within spitting distance is currently out of the county. Around here, most people's idea of therapy is shooting at junk-yard rats.'

'Do I hear a "but" in there somewhere?'

Worthington nodded. 'The thing you said about the boy being a complete blank brought something to mind. There's a guy I know, lives just over the state line, maybe a twenty-minute drive. He hasn't worked with the police in a couple years, but when he did, he was considered one of the best. He might just be able to help Evan remember.'

'A psychologist?' Anna asked.

Worthington shook his head. 'A hypnotherapist. Specializes in forensic hypnosis. Or at least he used to.'

'Used to? What's he doing now?'

For the first time, Worthington's confidence faltered a bit. He seemed almost embarrassed. 'He has a lounge show at one of the state-line casinos.'

Royer broke his silence with a loud snort. 'You gotta be fucking kidding me. You want to bring in some sideshow psychic?'

'Hypnotist,' Worthington said. 'Not psychic. This guy has all the right credentials, is fully trained. Even has a DCH.'

'What's a DCH?'

'Doctor of Clinical Hypnotherapy.'

Royer snorted again. 'Sounds like a complete load of crap to me.'

Anna had to admit she shared Royer's scepticism. The Bureau was no stranger to clinical and forensic hypnosis, but the hypnotherapists they utilized were either psychologists or highly trained agents.

Bringing in some Vegas phoney to work with Evan seemed liked a complete waste of time. But then who was she to judge anyone at this juncture in her life?

Worthington must have read her expression. 'Look,' he said. 'I know it sounds iffy, but the stage gig is only a recent development. He's had some tough breaks the last couple years.'

Anna shook her head. 'We're talking about a child who's extremely fragile right now. There are specific guidelines we have to—'

'I don't give a damn about guidelines,' Worthington said. 'We've got three people dead and a missing girl, and time is our enemy. I know this sounds unconventional, but like I said, we're talking about somebody who was once the go-to guy in Nevada law-enforcement circles.'

'So why did he stop?'

'You more than likely already know.'

Royer's eyebrows raised. 'What's that supposed to mean? Who the hell is this guy?'

Worthington hesitated, and Anna was suddenly struck by the notion that there was something more going on here, something deeper. That the man Worthington was recommending might be more than just a colleague. They were connected somehow.

'His name is Pope. Daniel Pope.'

Anna felt a sudden prickle on the back of her neck. Had she heard him right?

'*The* Daniel Pope? The same Daniel Pope whose wife—'

'That's the one,' Worthington said. 'But when you meet him, you might not want to bring that up.'

6

It was still dark when Pope got back to his room.

The crisis with Anderson Troy, as petty as it was, had been artfully averted. While most practitioners of his craft were loath to admit it, it was often possible for a skilled hypnotist to manipulate a subject's thought processes through visualization and guided imagery.

After putting Troy under again, Pope managed to feed him just enough details to get him to believe that the Nigel Fromme he'd Googled was an entirely different person. That *Troy's* Nigel Fromme – whom Troy himself had eagerly conjured up – was a bad-ass London gangster whose untimely death had been the result of a hail of bullets fired almost point-blank as he was bedding a beautiful blonde Sunday-school teacher.

With very large breasts. And no surprises, dangling or otherwise.

Recall and imagination. A 10/90 mix.

Pope walked away from this adolescent fantasy session feeling like a fraud, knowing he had broken nearly every tenet of his profession, but secure in the belief that Arturo wouldn't be shoving a knife into his ribcage anytime soon, thus maintaining the sanctity of Troy's plush white carpet.

The things we do to stay alive.

Not that Pope really had much of a life these days. But he did like *being* alive.

Standing at his window now, he looked out at the desert darkness and at the distant cluster of squat grey buildings that had kept him company nearly every morning in recent memory:

The Nevada Women's Correctional Facility.

Who in his right mind, he wondered, would think to build a hotel/casino so close to a prison compound?

Then again, he couldn't be sure which had come first. And it was almost as if the marriage had been arranged just for him, so that he could stand here on dark mornings, stare at those distant buildings and wallow in his misery.

He wondered if Susan was awake in her cell, thinking about what she'd become and how she'd gotten there.

Thinking about Ben.

Thinking about Pope.

He was just coming out of the shower, finally ready to crawl into bed, when his cellphone chirped again.

Hoping to Christ it wasn't Sharkey, he snatched it up off his nightstand and checked the screen, surprised by the name he saw.

J.T. Worthington.

Cousin Jake.

The two hadn't spoken in months. Pope had

47

half-heartedly invited Jake and Veronica out to the casino when the show first opened, but they'd never been able to make it. And in that last call, Pope had sensed a trace of disappointment in Jake's voice. As if he thought Pope could do better. That the show was a frivolous enterprise. A waste of Pope's time and talent.

All of which were probably true.

But then Pope wasn't much interested in Jake's opinion. He had little use for friends and family these days.

After the tragedy hit the news, followed by the trial, the sentence and all the nastiness that accompanied them, the people in his life had slowly begun to drift away.

Thanks to the skewed logic of the many graceless television pundits who chimed in, uninvited, with an opinion about Pope's life (not to mention the lurid sensationalism of the tabloid press), some of his so-called friends had actually blamed *him* for the events that had started it all.

And, who knows, maybe they were right.

But he suspected that for those who really knew him, there was no ill will behind this gradual abandonment. After a while, trying to console the inconsolable simply becomes too much of a burden. And in the aftermath of that terrible ordeal, Pope had not exactly been the easiest guy to get along with.

He was scarred. Tainted. A man addicted to distrust and personal failure.

And as much as he'd like to blame it all on Susan,

on what she'd done, he knew that a better man would have faced up to this particular challenge rather than try to bury it with dope and cards and women.

He was as much a prisoner as Susan was. A prisoner by choice, who had turned this room, this hotel, into his own private cell.

He hadn't been outside its doors in over a year.

The phone kept chirping, reminding Pope that he had a call to answer.

He clicked it on, said, 'This must be serious, you're calling me at three in the morning. Is Ronnie okay?'

'She's fine. How are you, Danny?'

'You know how many times I've been asked that question in the last two years? The answer never changes.'

'You staying sober?'

'I don't drink.'

'You know what I mean,' Jake said.

The two of them had spent half their childhood in Ludlow County, California, smoking dope and experimenting with various recreational drugs. There's not much else to do in the desert. But both had eventually lost interest in the stuff as life became more complicated. Careers and family will do that to you.

When Pope lost both, however, the first woman whose company he sought was the blessed White Widow.

'Are you asking me as an officer of the law, or a concerned relative? Although I'm not sure it really matters at this point.'

'Come on, Daniel, knock it off. It's me.'

He and Jake had once been closer than brothers, but time and distance – whether it's physical or emotional – have a way of eroding even the tightest relationships.

Jake, however, was one of the few people who hadn't given up on him.

Pope sank to the bed, hearing the springs groan, letting himself relax a little. 'Sorry, man. Being an asshole is a tough habit to break.'

'Doesn't have to be.'

Pope shrugged. 'Use it or lose it, I always say. What can I do for you?'

'I wasn't just asking before. I need to know if you're straight.'

'Why?'

'You won't like this, but I've got a case here I need some help with.'

Pope sighed. He should have known. This wasn't the first time he'd heard such a request, and he hated it whenever Jake tried to drag him back into his old life. That had been its own kind of prison.

After the murder he'd tried to fit in, to resume his work at the clinic and with the Las Vegas Metropolitan Police Department, but had felt like a man who had gained too much weight and was still trying to wear his old clothes.

'I'm not interested,' he said.

'Come on, Danny. It's important. I wouldn't ask if it weren't.'

'Sure you would. You've been trying to save me from myself since I was twelve years old.'

'Obviously I've failed.'

Pope smiled. 'Now look who's the asshole.'

'You need to snap out of this, my friend. Start circulating again. Use that big brain of yours.'

'I do, twice a night, starting a nine p.m. Not that you'd know.'

'Actually, I would,' Jake said.

'Oh? How so?'

'One of our deputies, a kid named Sanchez, drove out to see your show a while back, brought us a DVD of the night's festivities. You had him up on stage, howling like a goddamn coyote.'

'That one always goes over big with the tourists.'

Now it was Jake's turn to sigh. 'What the hell are you doing with yourself, Danny?'

'Surviving,' Pope said.

'Existing,' Jake countered. 'You can't let this thing rule you forever. There's a saturation point.'

'Then I guess I haven't reached it yet. How many times do we have to do this before you finally get the message?'

'And how many times do I have to ask before you finally say yes? This is a bad one. Three people dead, a little girl missing and a brother who's in a bad way. I hate to tell you who he reminds me of.'

Pope stiffened. 'Then don't.'

'He's about the same age, Danny. Got the same eyes.'

51

'Fuck you,' Pope said, shifting his thumb to the kill button—

'Don't hang up. I know you want to, but don't do it.'

Pope hesitated, not sure why. He had every right to drop the hammer on this conversation. Jake knew this was a touchy subject.

'He may be the only one who can tell us what happened to the girl, but he's in shock, having memory problems. We need somebody out here as quickly as possible and I figured you'd be awake. And I definitely know you're the best man for the job.'

'Not any more,' Pope said.

'I don't believe that. I know the old Danny's in there somewhere. We just need to wake him up.'

'So . . . what? Poke him with a stick and hope he doesn't snap at you? That's expecting too much, Jake.'

'For Christ's sake, all we're talking about is a couple hours of your time.'

Pope hesitated again, trying to push back the image that was suddenly crowding his mind: Ben giggling at the breakfast table as he purposely dribbled milk down his chin.

Every instinct Pope possessed told him to turn Jake down, just as he had a dozen times before. But that image seemed to have grabbed hold of him and wouldn't allow him to form the words.

Finally he said, 'I won't come to you. You'll have to bring him here.'

'Come on, Danny, I've got an investigation to run and a restless Feeb up my—'

'Take it or leave it,' Pope said. 'And all you get is two hours.'

'All right, all right, hold on.'

Pope heard the sound of a hand muffling the receiver. After a long moment of silence, Jake came back on the line. 'You've got a deal. The medic is checking him over right now, but somebody'll be out there with him as soon as possible. I'll call you back with the details.' He paused. 'And Danny? Thanks for this.'

Pope pressed the kill button.

7

'I gotta tell you,' Sanchez said. 'The guy's pretty freaky. Lotta people go to the show because of the tabloids and all, but he's definitely the real deal. Had a bunch of us up onstage doing all kinds of crazy stuff.'

It was close to four now and they were rolling along what seemed like another endless highway. Anna sat in the back seat of the deputy's patrol car, only half listening to his words and to the faint squawk of the two-way radio.

'I wouldn't've believed it if I hadn't watched the DVD myself,' Sanchez continued. 'Guy put me under, but good.'

Despite what she'd seen tonight, despite all the blood and the drama with Royer and Worthington and little Evan Fairweather – who sat pressed up against her now – there was one thing that clung to Anna's mind. Something Royer had said:

Sideshow psychic.

Anna had seen a few psychics on TV in her time and never given them much thought. But Royer's words tonight had stirred something in her brain.

A revelation of sorts.

Over the years, Anna had forgotten many things about her childhood, but one thing she'd always remember was her mother's belief that there are people out there who possess certain powers. People whose minds are tuned into some cosmic frequency that broadcasts information the rest of us aren't privy to. Events from the past, the present – and even the future.

Anna's education – hell, her common sense – had taught her to doubt such things, but considering what she'd been going through the last few weeks, she had to wonder: could her mother have been right? Do true psychics exist?

She thought of the lullaby she'd sung to Evan, the sadness of the melody, the prophetic words, as if they had been written with an eye towards some predetermined future and a desire for release:

> *Every little star*
> *Way up in the sky*
> *Calls me.*

What had her mother been thinking about when she wrote those words? Did she know about the pain she'd one day have to endure? That she'd be leaving this world sooner than most? Could she see things, predict things, that others couldn't?

And, by extension, what about Anna?

Could these visions she'd been having, these terrible glimpses of carnage, be some kind of ominous portent?

The thought that she might have some other-worldly ability frightened her. But at least it was an explanation. And she desperately needed explanations, because the alternative was even more frightening.

'There it is,' Deputy Sanchez said, pointing towards a distant spot on the horizon. Anna could see bright lights flashing. A lot of them. 'We'll be there in a couple minutes.'

The place was a dump.

Sanchez pulled the squad car to the kerb in front of the lobby doors, which were flanked by large, stone palm trees in serious need of a new paint job. The sign over the doors read, in even more flashing bright lights, DESERT OASIS HOTEL-CASINO.

'Oasis' was being generous.

Gambling had never interested Anna. She'd been to a casino only once before in her life, in better days, when she was still working out of San Francisco. A suspect's trail had led her and her partner to the Thunderhead Resort, a sprawling Native American golf and gambling mecca, about a two-hour drive outside the city, that catered to high rollers and tour buses full of Gold Coast retirees. Although several years old, the hotel and casino were spotless, meticulously maintained, with even a touch of old-world elegance to them.

The Oasis was the exact opposite. The kind of low-rent establishment that stirred up phantom smells the moment it came into view. Smells you just knew would assault you as soon as you stepped through its doors: mould and mildew mixed with several decades worth of cigarette smoke.

Anna glanced down at Evan, who hadn't said a word the entire drive. If only out of necessity, the boy seemed to have bonded with her, and it had been Worthington's suggestion that she shepherd him to the Oasis.

'I've gotta finish processing this crime scene,' he'd said. 'And I have a feeling he'd be more comfortable with you.'

Royer had initially objected, of course, but finally gave in, apparently having decided to wash his hands of anything to do with Special Agent Anna McBride.

Which was fine with her. Anna welcomed the chance to get away from him. Away from the snide remarks, the judgemental stares.

She knew she should have kept her mouth shut earlier, should have played along and been the good little soldier, but she'd been betrayed by her usual impulsiveness. She was a cliché – her own worst enemy – and reassignment to middle-of-nowhere South Dakota was looking more and more like a real possibility.

Assuming, of course, she managed to hang on to her job at all.

'Where are we?' Evan asked, finally breaking his silence. He had pulled away from Anna and was staring out at the flashing lights.

'Disneyland,' Sanchez told him as he killed the engine. 'Disneyland for grown-ups.'

Disneyland for losers, Anna thought.

Maybe she'd fit right in.

Evan shook his head. 'I don't want to go to Disneyland.'

'It's okay,' Anna said. 'We won't be here long. There's someone who wants to meet you. Someone who can help us find Kimberly.'

Evan brightened suddenly, peeking past Anna's shoulder towards the lobby doors. 'Is she here?'

'No. But we'll find her. I promise.'

It was a promise she knew she shouldn't make. If the man who had slaughtered the people in that house had taken Kimberly with him, then little Kimberly's fate was all but sealed.

'You want me to go in with you?' Sanchez asked.

'We'll be fine,' Anna said, then popped her door open and climbed out.

Scooping Evan into her arms, she carried him through the lobby doors, then set him down and took his hand.

She hadn't been wrong about the smell. Especially the cigarette smoke.

Despite the early hour, the place was fairly active and Evan stared wide-eyed at the rows of clanging slot machines and the mix of bleary-eyed tourists who filled the stools in front of them.

A couple of aisles over, a jackpot siren went off and Evan flinched, grabbing Anna's arm.

'It's okay,' she said, although she wasn't quite sure that was true. Bringing the boy to Daniel Pope was not her first – or even last – choice, and parading him through this seedy environment didn't much help. But she took his hand again, found an empty aisle and guided him towards a glowing red sign that read HOTEL REGISTRATION.

They were about halfway to it, moving past a row of mostly empty blackjack tables, when a uniformed security guard stepped into their path.

'Excuse me, ma'am. There are no children allowed in here.'

Anna immediately brought her creds out. 'I'm looking for one of your employees. A man by the name of Daniel Pope.'

The guard's eyebrows raised. 'He in trouble?'

'No. He's expecting us. Where can I find him?'

'He's got a room in the residential section. 408. You'll either find him there or in the poker room.'

'And where's this residential section?'

The guard pointed towards a hallway near the registration desk. 'Through there. Elevator on your left.'

Anna nodded. 'Thank you.'

A few moments later, she and Evan were riding an excruciatingly slow elevator to the fourth floor, Evan squeezing her hand so tightly it was starting to go numb.

'Is this where Kimmie is?' he asked.

'No, dear. I told you, remember? We're here to see Mr Pope.'

'Who's he?'

Before she could answer, the elevator lurched to a

halt and the doors slid open, revealing a man in khaki pants and black polo shirt leaning casually against the hallway wall as if he had been waiting for them.

Daniel Pope.

Apparently the guard had alerted him.

Anna recognized him immediately, although the television footage and the photos in the newspaper hadn't quite done him justice. He was Hollywood handsome, without the slick phoneyness that usually went with it.

But what really struck her was his eyes. Dark and haunted and quietly intelligent.

Despite a calculated immunity to such things, Anna felt a slight lurch inside her chest as his gaze fell upon her – and it had nothing to do with motion of the elevator. He seemed to be looking *into* her, rather than at her.

'Mr Pope?' It was a silly question. She already knew the answer.

'Crimen ut tutela,' he said, then crossed himself in an overly elaborate gesture, as if offering a papal blessing. Then, pushing away from the wall, he gave her a smile and, despite the joke, Anna thought it seemed forced.

Or maybe she was letting her knowledge of the man's history colour her perception. That Pope was able to smile at all was a miracle to Anna.

She produced her credentials again. 'Anna McBride,' she said, guiding Evan into the hallway. 'This is Evan Fairweather.'

Staring at the boy, Pope seemed momentarily lost

in a memory, but recovered quickly and crouched down, offering a hand to shake.

'Hi, Evan. I'm Danny.'

Evan eyed the hand warily, then finally brought his own up and shook it. 'Is Kimmie here?'

'No, son, I'm afraid she's not. But I'm told you might be able to help us find her.'

Evan went silent, shaking his head.

'You thirsty?' Pope asked. 'Do you like soda?'

A nod this time. 'But my mom doesn't like me to drink it.'

'How about a glass of milk, then?'

'. . . Okay.'

'Why don't you and Agent McBride come to my room? We'll order up some drinks and talk for a while. That sound good?'

A shrug now, and a tentative one at best.

'It's a deal then,' Pope said. 'Follow me.'

8

Pope wasn't sure he felt comfortable letting an FBI agent into his room, even if she was the most beautiful FBI agent he'd ever seen.

No, scratch that.

Special Agent McBride was not really beautiful, not in a conventional way. Not like Carmen and Feather or any of the other showgirls he'd brought up to this room. But there was something about her that struck him the moment those elevator doors opened. Something about the wary expression, the slightly untamed hair, the conservative, yet form-fitting clothes.

And then there was the scar.

It ran down the left side of her face, from temple to jaw bone, still new, from the looks of it. She had covered it with make-up, but it was still plainly visible – a thin, pink, slightly puckered reminder of a very close call.

That scar was the kicker. The thing that made her human. Less . . . FBI. A not-so-subtle sign of vulnerability – a vulnerability she tried to hide with a curt, professional demeanour.

But Pope had always been able to see past such barriers, to dig deeper than most, to the real person beneath. It was a gift that had helped him quite a bit in the past.

Although that thought was instantly laughable when you considered how badly he had fucked up with Susan.

But then how could he have known the darkness in her heart?

How could anyone know?

Unlocking his door, he pushed it wide and gestured for McBride and the boy to enter. Shortly after hanging up on Jake, he'd made a quick follow-up call to fill in some of the details, then took a few moments to clean the place up, stashing any incriminating pot paraphernalia, all the while wondering why he had agreed to this meeting in the first place.

The role he had chosen for himself on this planet, post-tragedy, was that of the sufferer, the wronged man who painted on a fake smile twice a night, six nights a week, to sell overpriced cocktails to unsuspecting tourists. Giving in to Jake's request had been uncharacteristic. And even now, despite the presence of Special Agent McBride, he wished he had remained true to himself and told his cousin no.

But then there was Evan, standing there with a quiet solemnity that Pope understood all too well. Knowing intimately what little Evan was going through, what he may have seen and what he might remember with careful and calculated prodding – coupled with the possibility that they might be able to find a missing little girl – was enough to get Pope to immediately reconsider that wish.

Maybe, for the first time in a long, long while, he could actually help someone. Do some good for once.

Gesturing towards the bed, he said, 'Have a seat.'

Evan did as he was told, perching himself on the edge of the mattress, but Agent McBride stayed on her feet, taking in the place with undisguised distaste. Not that he could blame her. A room at Caesar's it wasn't. It didn't even meet the standards of Circus Circus.

But at least the bed was made.

Picking up the phone on his nightstand, Pope called down to Kelly in room service and ordered two Cokes and a glass of milk.

'You hungry, too?' he asked Evan, but the boy shook his head and returned his gaze to the carpet, where it had been fixed ever since Pope had ushered them inside.

Ordering a couple of breakfast muffins anyway, he hung up and noticed that Evan had developed a serious case of the wiggles. Grabbing hold of McBride's hand, the boy tugged on it until she leaned down and let him whisper in her ear.

Before she could ask, Pope gestured to his bath-room doorway. 'In there.'

Evan hesitated, but McBride gently touched his shoulder. 'It's okay. Go ahead.'

The two seemed to have a connection and that was a good thing. Working with children could be tricky, and having someone who was trusted present would help the boy relax.

Glancing warily at Pope, Evan slid off the bed, then went into the bathroom and closed the door behind him.

'Poor kid looks like he was struck by lightning,' Pope said.

'He pretty much was. Did Deputy Worthington give you the details?'

Pope nodded. 'I could say something cute about kids being resilient, but this isn't the kind of thing you bounce back from. Not easily.'

McBride studied him a moment, considering his words, and he knew she was weighing them against what she'd heard or read about him over the last couple of years.

It was a look he'd seen a hundred times on a hundred different faces.

After the usual awkward moment that accompanied even the most innocuous reference to Pope's past, McBride said, 'Just for the record, I'm not a hundred per cent on board with this.'

'If it makes you feel any better, neither am I.'

'Then why do it?'

'Because my cousin's a persuasive man.'

'Cousin?'

'Deputy Worthington.'

Surprise flickered across McBride's face, then she nodded as if this explained something she'd been puzzling over. 'Evan's pretty fragile right now.'

'I'm not interested in compounding his pain. I'll walk him up to the water's edge, but I'm not about to make him jump. The moment we've got anything tangible to work with, I'm bringing him out.'

Apparently satisfied, McBride looked out the window, taking in his morning view. She gestured towards the distant lights, the barbed wire. 'Is that what I think it is?'

'If you're thinking state prison, then yeah. That's exactly what it is.'

She frowned. 'Why would you build a casino so close to a prison?'

'That's one of the questions I ask myself nearly every morning. But I'm not complaining. Whatever the reason, it works out just fine for me.'

'Why's that?'

'That's where they're holding my ex-wife.'

McBride seemed startled by this revelation. 'Is that supposed to be a good thing?'

'I assume you know my history.'

'I think the whole world does. But why on earth would you want to be so close to the woman who . . .' She paused suddenly, looking as if she'd been about to step into something sticky and had just managed to avoid it.

Pope finished the sentence for her. 'Killed my kid? That's another question I ask myself every morning. But the answer isn't complicated. I just want to make sure she stays right where she is.'

'I don't think you have much to worry about.'

'Probably not. But her new lawyers are working

on the appeal as we speak, claiming diminished capacity and ineffective assistance of counsel. They're pushing for a new trial.'

'It'll never happen.'

Pope shrugged. 'I almost hope it does.'

McBride's eyebrows raised. 'Why?'

'Because the moment she shows her face outside those gates,' Pope said, nodding towards the view, 'she's a dead woman.'

9

Anna wasn't sure if what she'd just heard constituted a genuine threat or was simply the muttering of a grieving father. Professionally, her inclination was to take Pope seriously, but what did it matter? The chances of his ex-wife winning an appeal were virtually non-existent.

Still, there was an intensity in those eyes that was hard to ignore. She could imagine Pope standing here every morning, staring out at that prison complex as he quietly plotted, positioning himself in his mind, weapon ready, waiting for those front gates to open . . .

Pure fantasy, she decided. No matter how wronged this man had been, she didn't sense the killer instinct in him. Couldn't see him pulling a trigger.

Of course, she'd made that mistake before, and had a nice little reminder of that fact every time she looked in the mirror.

All she really knew about Pope was what she had seen on CNN and read in the papers. She knew the Bureau had had some involvement in the case, but the investigation had been handled by the Vegas field office and seemed a world away from her life in San Francisco.

Her first memories of it were the photos on Headline News. A fragile-looking freckle-faced kid, smiling for the camera. Benjamin Pope, five years old. He had been missing for two days, victim of a carjacking by a large Hispanic man – or so his mother had said. There were daily press conferences and hourly briefings and wild speculation by often misinformed news media, focusing more and more on the parents, whom police refused to name as possible suspects in the disappearance.

She remembered Pope's pleas for the kidnappers to return his child and the not-so-quiet rumours that had accompanied those pleas. The talk around the San Francisco Field Division water coolers was that the press conference was a sham, cover for a man who had murdered his own kid.

The rumours grew into angry accusations when the burnt-out shell of the family wagon was found in the desert, less than a mile from Ludlow, California.

The charred remains of Benjamin Pope were found inside.

None of the evidence collected pointed to a carjacking, and an autopsy revealed that Ben may well have been dead *before* the fire. Within a day of the discovery, Susan Leah Pope had broken down and confessed to torching the SUV. It turned out that she had been poisoning Ben for months and it had finally caught up with him.

Those less educated about such things believed that Daniel Pope had somehow used hypnosis to force his wife to do the unspeakable. Both CNN and Fox had devoted entire hours to this hare-brained theory, but such accusations were quickly quashed by an FBI psychologist, who patiently explained that hypnosis was not mind control.

If anything, Pope was a casualty. The victim of a severely disturbed woman. Just like his son.

How he had wound up here in this hotel room, or why he had chosen to take to the stage and put himself out there as a target for the crackpots and the rubber-neckers, was a mystery Anna doubted she'd ever be able to solve.

And she couldn't begrudge the man his fantasy, no matter how dark it might be.

There was a knock at the door. Pope crossed to it and pulled it open to reveal a cute but overly perky girl in a hotel uniform holding a tray with two cans of Coke, a small carton of milk and what looked like two apple muffins.

'How's this for service?' the girl asked, smiling the kind of smile that, to Anna's mind, indicated more than friendship. When her gaze fell on Anna, however, the smile momentarily froze, then abruptly vanished – along with her perkiness.

Pope took the tray from her. 'Thanks, Kel, I'll see you later.' Then he closed the door and turned. No goodbyes. No explanations. No apologies.

Anna didn't know what to make of this, but then

it wasn't really any of her business. As Pope carried the tray to the dresser top, she glanced around the room again, surprised to discover that there were no photographs or keepsakes or mementos to be found. Just a generic, rundown hotel room that told the visitor nothing about the man who occupied it.

She was pondering the significance of this when the bathroom door opened and Evan stepped into the room, fumbling with his zipper, having trouble zipping it back up.

He looked so small, framed by the doorway, his face pale and gaunt, reminding Anna, oddly enough, of her mother during those last few days. It was enough to break your heart. And her reluctance to put him through this grew even stronger.

He finally finished zipping, then looked up at her. 'Can we go now?'

Pope was the one who answered. 'We haven't had our drinks yet.'

'I'm not thirsty any more.'

'Okay . . . but I think Agent McBride is.'

He threw Anna a glance and she immediately caught on – although, if pressed, she would have agreed with Evan. She just wanted to leave.

Thinking of the missing girl, however, she said, 'I could definitely go for something cold and wet,' then moved to the dresser and grabbed a can of Coke. 'Can we hang around for just a few more minutes, kiddo?'

Evan looked at her again and shrugged. 'I guess so.'

Pope patted the bed. 'Have a seat. I want to show you something.'

As Evan reluctantly climbed back onto the mattress, Pope crossed to his nightstand, opened the drawer, and took out a black velvet drawstring pouch. The boy's gaze immediately shifted to it and Anna thought she saw a tiny spark of curiosity there.

She was curious herself.

Pope returned and crouched next to Evan, offering him the pouch. He hesitated before taking it.

'Go ahead,' Pope said. 'Open it up.'

Evan did as he was told, loosening the drawstring with his small fingers. Reaching inside, he pulled out a black plastic box, about the size of a Rubik's cube.

Evan stared at it, looking disappointed.

'Turn it over,' Pope said.

Evan turned the box over to reveal a hole cut into the opposite side, the word *Metamorphosis* written in gold paint above it. Inside the hole was what looked like a golf ball made of mirrors – a miniature disco ball – surrounded by several LED light bulbs.

Pope reached over and flicked a switch at the top of the box. The LEDs came on and the ball began to spin, its tiny mirrors reflecting the light across Evan's face.

Evan stared at it, eyes shining, and Anna thought he might be showing just a hint of a smile.

Pope flicked the switch again, turning it off. 'They sell these in the gift shop downstairs,' he said. 'Pretty neat, huh? After we're done here today, you can take it with you.'

'Really?'

'Definitely. But first we're gonna use it for a little experiment. Is that okay with you?'

Evan shrugged. 'I guess.' He paused, working something over in his head. 'Are you a doctor?'

'Not really,' Pope said. 'I'm a hypnotherapist. A hypnotist. Do you know what that is?'

Evan thought about this for a moment. 'You mean like Kaa?'

'Kaa?'

'From *The Jungle Book*. He's a snake.'

'Ahhh, right,' Pope said. 'The one who put Mowgli in a trance and tried to swallow him. My son used to watch that movie. But what you see in cartoons isn't quite the same as real life. There's nothing scary about hypnosis. It doesn't hurt. It's just a way to help you relax, so you don't feel all tight inside. You understand?'

Evan nodded. 'I think so . . .'

'Let me show you,' Pope said, then took the box from the boy's hands and patted the bed again. 'Lie down for a minute.'

Evan hesitated, then did as he was told, but his body looked stiff and uncomfortable.

'That's good,' Pope said, then held the box up.

He hit the switch again and the ball began to rotate, light flickering across Evan's face.

'Now all you have to do is watch and keep watching – don't look away. Pretty easy, huh?'

'Uh-huh.'

Anna watched also, suddenly aware that those

mirrors reminded her of something, but she wasn't sure what.

Something from the crime scene?

'Now just let your body sink into the bed,' Pope said. 'Let your arms and legs get really, really loose. Can you do that?'

'Yes,' Evan said again, keeping his gaze on the spinning ball.

'Good. Now pretend you're sinking deeper and deeper into the mattress, like you're on your own little private elevator and it's taking you down, down, down . . .' He paused. 'Can you feel it?'

'Uh-huh,' Evan said and blinked a couple of times. They were slow, lazy blinks, as if he was having trouble concentrating.

'It's okay to close your eyes if you want to.'

Evan fought his drooping eyelids for a moment, then finally closed them.

'That's good, keep letting your muscles relax. And as the elevator finally stops, its doors open and all you see are beautiful white clouds. You feel your body starting to float now, as they carry you away.' Pope stopped the spinning ball and quietly set it aside. 'Are you floating?'

'Yes,' Evan said, his voice soft. Barely a whisper.

'Attaboy, you're doing great. Keep lying there for a minute, okay? Just let your body float.'

'. . . Okay.'

Pope waited a moment. Then he said, 'I'm gonna count backwards now. And as I do, you'll feel more relaxed than you've ever felt before. Are you ready?'

'Uh-huh.'

'Okay. Five . . think about your feet, let all of the tightness in them drain away. Four . . . now your legs are relaxing, the muscles loosening up, melting into those clouds. Three . . . concentrate on your stomach and arms now, let the tension go. Two . . . loosen your shoulders, your neck, your head. And one . . . just let yourself float away . . .'

Pope gently took hold of Evan's right wrist and raised his arm slightly. 'When I let go, relax your arm and let it float, like it's on its own separate cloud. Okay?'

'Okay.'

To Anna's amazement, when Pope released the arm, it stayed in place. Just seemed to be floating.

Pope waited another moment, then turned to Anna. 'He's under.'

'That quick?'

'Kids are more receptive than adults. Better imaginations. More open-minded.'

'Except for the arm, he looks like he's sleeping.'

'He can hear everything we're saying, right, Evan?'

'Uh-huh,' Evan murmured.

'All we're dealing with here is an altered state of consciousness. If you've ever meditated, you've pretty much put yourself into a hypnotic state.'

'I'm not really a wholegrains and falafel kind of girl,' Anna said.

Pope smiled. 'Okay, how about this? You ever fall asleep watching Leno?'

'Sure.'

'You know that feeling when you first start to drift off? You're still aware of what he's saying, you may even be laughing at his jokes, but you feel removed from the whole thing – like you're detached from the real world?'

Anna stiffened. Pope had just described what had happened to her in Royer's car, and at the crime scene this morning – what had been happening to her with increasing frequency ever since she woke up in the hospital.

Detached from the real world.

Even when those awful images flooded her brain, she was always vaguely aware of what was going on around her, as if she were trapped between duelling realities.

'Did I say something wrong?'

She was suddenly aware that Pope was staring at her with those intense eyes. She might as well have been standing there naked.

She felt flustered. 'No, not at all.'

'You sure? You lost a little colour for a moment there.'

Covering her discomfort with a dismissive flick of the wrist, she said, 'Let's concentrate on Evan.'

Pope nodded and turned back to the boy. 'What do you say, Evan? Shall we concentrate on you?'

Evan kept his eyes closed. 'Okay.'

'Good. Go ahead and let your arm float back down again.'

Evan lowered his arm.

'Now what we're gonna do,' Pope said, 'is help

you remember some stuff. If you start to feel uncomfortable, if your body starts to get tight again, just let me know. And, don't worry, Agent McBride will be here the whole time, okay?'

'Okay.'

'Good,' Pope said, then looked up at Anna as if asking her for permission to continue.

Still slightly flustered, Anna had to wonder: was this really the only way to proceed? Was putting Evan in a trance, and risking further trauma, truly worth it? Or was it one of those choices you look back on with regret?

None of these questions could be answered, of course. Not by her. Not with her history. Not in the shape she was in.

Detached from the real world.

The way things were going, she figured she was probably one vision away from basket case.

Yet, despite her reluctance, she quietly nodded.

10

'So you like cartoons, huh?'

'Uh-huh.'

'My cousin Jake and I used to watch a show called *Mr Peabody and Sherman*. You heard of it?'

'It's on Cartoon Network. Me and Kimmie watch it every time.'

'Then you know about Mr Peabody's wayback machine.'

'Uh-huh.'

'Well, what I want you to do now is pretend that *you've* got a wayback machine. But instead of a big one like Mr Peabody's, yours looks just like a TV remote and you're holding it in your hand. Okay?'

'Okay.'

'Take a look at it and pay close attention to the buttons. The red one takes you back a hundred years, the green one goes back about ten, but the big blue one is the one that takes you back to yesterday. You see it?'

'Uh-huh.'

'Go ahead and give the blue button a push.'

'Okay.'

'Now the room is starting to spin – spinning around and around and making your stomach tickle – but in a good way, like the merry-go-round at the playground. Can you feel it?'

A laugh. 'It feels funny.'

'I'll bet it does. But don't worry, it's not going to spin very long, because you don't have far to go. And now it's slowing down, and when it stops completely, you'll be back at home, yesterday afternoon, right after school, and you'll feel relaxed and comfortable.' A pause. 'Has it stopped yet?'

'Uh-huh.'

'And where are you now?'

'In the kitchen. Mommy made frosted grams.'

'Is your mom there with you?'

'Un-unh. She's getting ready for work. She told me to put some on a plate and get glasses of milk for me and Kimmie and Tammy. We're playing Donkey Kong Barrel Blast.'

'I know Kimmie's your sister, but who's Tammy?'

'She watches us while Mommy's at work. She's in high school.'

'I see. Is it just the four of you in the house? Or is anyone else there?'

'Just me and Kimmie and Tammy.'

'Okay. What time does your mom usually go to work?'

'Right before *Batman and Friends*. But we're not gonna watch, cuz Tammy wants to play Donkey Kong instead.'

'Then let's go forward a little. Look down at your remote again and find the yellow button. The yellow one takes you forward in time, but not too far, just a little skip. You see it?'

'Uh-huh.'

'Go ahead and press it once.'

'Okay.'

'Now after a quick spin, just a few hours have passed and *Batman and Friends* has been over for a while. It's around dinner time and your mom is at work. Where are you now?'

A pause. 'In my room.'

'And what are you doing there?'

'Talking to Tammy.'

'What about?'

'She says she's got a secret she doesn't want Kimmie to hear.'

'What kind of secret?'

'I dunno. She won't tell me. She says it's a surprise. But she's gonna have to break the rules and she doesn't want Kimmie to cry.'

'What rules?'

'When Mommy's at work, we're not supposed to leave the house. But Tammy says we have to.'

'Why? Where does she want to go?'

'To the rec centre. She says there's somebody there she wants us to meet.'

'Who?'

'I dunno. But we're not supposed to leave and Kimmie's gonna cry, so Tammy says we have to pretend we're gonna meet Mommy. We're not supposed to lie, either, but Tammy says it's okay if it's for something good.'

'How far away is the rec centre?'

'Far. It's over by Kmart. But Tammy's gonna drive us. She's got her licence and everything.'

'Okay. You're doing great, Evan. Now I want you to look down at your remote again, give the yellow button a press and take another little jump forward until you're at the rec centre. Can you do that for me?'

'Uh-huh.'

'Good. So where are you now?'

'In the gym, watching the big kids play basketball. Tammy bought us Slurpees.'

'Is she there?'

'No. She went to find her friend. She says he's late.'

'Do you know her friend's name?'

'She called him Rick.'

'Is he one of the high-school boys?'

'No. Tammy say he's older.'

'Older, huh? How much older?'

'I dunno. But I wish they'd hurry up, because Kimmie's almost finished with her Slurpee and she wants to know where Mommy is.'

'Okay, let's go forward again. Push the yellow button and jump ahead a little.'

'Okay.'

'Where are you now?'

'At McDonald's. Rick took us there in his Mustang.'

'He drives a Mustang, huh? What colour is it?'

'Black. With an orange flame on the side. It's really cool.'

'Are you inside McDonald's or out in the car?'

'In the car.'

'Are Kimmie and Tammy there, too?'

'No, they went to get burgers and fries.'

'So it's just you and Rick, then, huh? What does he look like?'

'Tall. Really tall. With black hair and a ring in his eyebrow and a tattoo of a dragon on his neck. Him and Tammy were holding hands and kissing and stuff, but he looks like he should be her uncle or something.'

'Is he Tammy's boyfriend?'

'I dunno, I guess so.'

'Okay. So what are you and Rick doing right now?'

'Talking.'

'What about?'

'All kinds of stuff. Baseball, video games . . .'

'Anything else?'

'He says he's been wanting to see me and Kimmie for a really long time.'

'Oh? Has he told you why?'

'Yeah, but I think he might be playing a joke or something. Like April Fools.'

'Why do you think that?'

'I dunno. I just do.'

'You must have a reason.'

A pause.

'It's okay, Evan. Just stay relaxed. Nobody's going to hurt you.'

'If it was true, he'd be kissing Mommy, not Tammy.'

'If *what* was true? What did Rick tell you?'

A longer pause.

'Evan?'

'He says he's . . . He says . . .'

Another pause.

'Evan?'

It came on without warning.

Evan uttered a small cry of distress, then his entire body went rigid.

'Oh, shit!' Pope said.

Then the boy began to convulse, bucking violently on the bed, chest heaving, legs kicking.

McBride moved towards them, face full of alarm. 'What's happening?'

'Grand mal seizure. He must be epileptic.'

His breathing uneven and laboured, Evan sucked in air, then stopped breathing altogether as foam began to gather at the corners of his mouth, his face darkening.

Pope reached down and grabbed the boy's jeans, working to unfasten the button, loosening the waistband as Evan continued to buck and kick, making the task more difficult than it should have been.

'He's turning blue,' McBride said.

'He'll be fine. We just have to let it run its course.'

'What about his tongue? Shouldn't we stick something in his—'

'No. That's TV bullshit. Just let him be.'

Evan let out a loud, shaky breath – some of his colour returning – then suddenly sucked in another, uttering short animal-like grunts as his body continued to convulse.

'We have to *do* something.'

'There's nothing *to* do,' Pope said. 'Trust me, my grandfather was epileptic, I've seen this a hundred times.'

Eyes still shut, mouth foaming, Evan bucked and kicked, his small body shaking the bed violently, reminding Pope of Linda Blair in full possession mode—

– then, finally, thankfully, the convulsions began to subside until the boy was still.

Pope quickly turned Evan on his side, letting the fluids drain from his mouth onto the bedspread. Sweat had formed on his forehead and McBride crouched next to him and carefully wiped it away with her hand, smoothing his hair back.

He opened his eyes then and blinked up at them, his voice high and thin and shaky.

'I want my mommy,' he said, and burst into tears.

11

'Evan had a seizure. Looks like epilepsy.'

'Oh, Jesus,' Worthington muttered. His voice sounded as if it were coming through a wire stretched between two tin cans.

Anna hated cellphones.

She had considered calling Royer, had known it was proper protocol, but hadn't felt like dealing with the inevitable headache. She figured she was sparing *him* one as well.

Instead, she'd dug out the business card Worthington had slipped her just as she and Evan were climbing into the cruiser, and had called him directly.

'I'm sure glad we had that medic take a look at him,' Worthington said sourly.

'It's not like he was wearing a sign. But Pope told me if he'd known, he never would've put him under.'

'I wouldn't think so. Is Evan all right?'

'I'm sure he's been better. The hotel doctor is checking him over.'

'Hotel doctor? At the Oasis?'

'I have a feeling it's one of Pope's poker buddies.'

'Figures,' Worthington said. 'What about the session? You have any luck?'

'Not much, but it may be enough. Turns out the babysitter broke the house rules and took the kids on a surprise field trip. Introduced them to a guy Evan thinks was her boyfriend – only he's probably twice her age.'

'That sounds promising. You get a description?'

'Adult male, first name Rick. Dark hair, eyebrow ring, dragon tattoo on his neck. Drives a black Ford Mustang with a flame on the side.'

'Should be easy enough to track. I'll put out an alert and we'll check with Tammy's friends, but it doesn't sound like anyone from around here.'

Judging by the neighbours who had stood gawking in the street, Anna wasn't surprised. Ludlow was more Travis Tritt than Tommy Lee.

Then she remembered the photo on the Fairweathers' camera and a thought struck her.

'Didn't you say the carnival's still in town?'

There was a pause on the line, Worthington's silence filled by an annoying digital static. Then he said, 'A carny. I should've thought of that. Those lowlifes are always hitting on the high-school girls. They've got an encampment on a vacant lot next to the campus. If he's still around, ten to one that's where we'll find him.'

'Whatever you do,' Anna said, 'approach with caution. If he's our guy and he's got Kimberly with him . . .'

'Don't worry, we'll do a little reconnaissance before we strike. You want to be part of this?'

Anna felt a sudden rush of adrenaline. 'Definitely.'

'Then you'd better get back here ASAP. We'll need time to organize, but I don't want to drag this thing out. Not if there's a chance the girl's still alive.'

'What about Evan?'

'Sounds like he needs to stay put for a while. Leave him with Danny.'

Anna looked around the hotel corridor, noting the stained carpet and faded wallpaper. This was no place for a seven-year-old boy.

'I'm not sure that's a good idea.'

'He'll be fine,' Worthington said. 'I'll make some calls and get someone from social services out there as soon as possible.'

'And if Pope objects?'

'He won't.'

'He didn't seem too thrilled about this whole proposition in the first place. And to be honest, I'm not sure he's entirely stable.'

Worthington laughed, but it was a dry one, with little humour attached. 'I've known Danny Pope for nearly forty years. Considering what he's been through, he's about as stable as they come.'

Anna thought about this, and despite her initial misgivings concerning the entire enterprise, decided Worthington was right. Evan had fallen asleep shortly after his seizure, and social services would probably be out here before he even woke up. It didn't make much sense to sit around and stare at him.

There was Kimmie to think about.

A killer to catch.

And . . . something more.

Call it fate, a feeling, just a sliver of intuition, but Anna suddenly felt as if what had happened out here in the desert was somehow related to her visions.

Was that even possible?

The onslaught of images that had assaulted her back at the crime scene seemed to have been triggered by the photo of Rita Fairweather and her kids. The Ferris wheel in the background. The house of mirrors. And although she knew, instinctively, that the little girl plaguing that dark corner of her mind was not Kimmie – not even close – there was something synchronistic about those images. About this case.

Something about it all that just . . . fit.

She wasn't sure how – wouldn't even try to guess why – but she knew that she was meant to be here. Meant to be part of this.

Thoughts of sideshow psychics once again rose from the back of her brain. Maybe she *was* one after all.

Or just plain nuts.

When she returned to Pope's room, the so-called hotel doctor was finishing up his exam. He was an old guy, with rheumy eyes, who smelled faintly of Preparation H and carried the distinct air of a man who, at one time in his career, would have been perfectly comfortable performing back-room abortions.

'Vital signs are all stable,' he said, rising from the side of the bed. 'He'll be fine in an hour or two. Best thing now is to let him sleep.'

Stuffing a stethoscope into his black bag, the doctor nodded to Anna and Pope, then headed back to the casino or wherever it was he'd come from. When the door closed behind him, Anna turned and told Pope about the phone call with Worthington, immediately broaching the subject of babysitting.

Pope baulked. Big time.

'Do I look like I'm equipped to take care of a kid?' He gestured to their surroundings.

'Worthington said you wouldn't mind.'

'Nice of him to consult me first. But that's Jake for you. Always trying to keep me engaged. He hasn't quite accepted the fact that I'm a lost cause.'

'A lost cause with a flair for the dramatic,' Anna said.

Pope frowned. 'That's why I do a show six nights a week. You want tickets?'

'What I want is for you to keep an eye on Evan.'

Pope shook his head. 'I promised Jake two hours. No more, no less.'

'Then you still have some time left. It's only until social services gets here. I wouldn't leave him, but—'

'Then don't.'

'Look,' Anna said, studying him intently. 'I don't know if you're enjoying this woe-is-me act, or if you just can't help yourself, but I saw the way you interacted with Evan, and I know *you* know exactly what he's going through right now.'

Pope faltered a bit. Seemed thrown by her assessment of him. 'So what's your point?'

'Just do the right thing, okay? Watch him until

someone comes to pick him up, so I can go help Worthington snag the son of a bitch who did this to him.'

Pope stared at her a moment, then shifted his gaze to the sleeping figure on the bed. Evan looked smaller and more fragile than ever.

Then Pope went away for a while, and Anna knew he was lost in a memory. Something bittersweet. Painful.

When clarity returned, he looked at her again. He'd made his decision.

'All right,' he said. 'Go.'

'Thank you.'

Pope shook his head and stared out his window at those ever-present prison lights.

'Just do us all a favour and catch the mother-fucker.'

12

They used the tried-and-true dog-walker ploy.

They waited in two unmarked vans, parked about a block and a half from the strike zone, Anna cramped in the back with Royer, who still had the remnants of an angry scowl on his face.

Despite their close proximity, he had managed to avoid saying a word to her since she'd returned from the Oasis. It occurred to her that they wouldn't even be here if she hadn't spotted Evan in the first place, but doubted that this meant much to Royer. Their partnership, such as it was, was over.

Anna shifted uncomfortably. The air in this god-forsaken town had not gotten any cooler, and she figured the temperature inside the van was a good two degrees hotter than it was outside. Sweat trickled down her back and along her armpits and, judging by the smell, she wasn't the only one feeling the heat.

Even the Oasis would be better than this.

Although he was ignoring *her*, Royer had made it clear to Worthington that he thought this operation was a mistake. Back at the Fairweather house, he'd urged the deputy to wait for him to call in a Bureau strike team, a suggestion that hadn't sat well with anyone present.

'What exactly are you trying to tell us?' Worthington had asked, to which Royer had no reply. Next to these rugged, sun-baked deputies, he looked like a prissy prep-school kid, and as they all silently piled into the vans, it was *Royer* who was the appendage, the excess baggage. And though she tried to resist, the thought of this had made Anna smile.

The carny encampment was little more than a collection of tents, trailers, old motor homes and beat-up cars, parked haphazardly on a dusty vacant lot next to the high-school campus. Several big rig trucks emblazoned with the words O'FARRELL AMUSEMENTS were lined up against the kerb across the street.

Just beyond the encampment stood the dark silhouettes of the trucks' contents – the arcade stands and rickety metal rides that dominated the school's football field.

Under the fading moonlight it looked to Anna like an extension of the junk yard behind the Fairweather home. There was, she thought, a sad, almost pathetic poetry to it all. Travelling carnivals were quickly becoming a thing of the past, and this one looked as if it had overshot retirement by several, hard-worn years.

The dog walker, a lean female deputy dressed in civilian clothes and sporting an iPod, was walking her German Shepherd along the encampment's side of the street. A typical local out for a pre-dawn stroll.

She paused a moment to let the dog sniff at the

base of a lamp post, then raised a hand to her left ear to adjust an earbud.

The van's radio crackled. 'Looks like I've struck gold here, Jake.'

Worthington, who sat up front with Sanchez, raised his mic. 'What've you got?'

'Black Ford Mustang with a flame on the side. Parked between two motor homes.'

'That's our guy,' Worthington said. 'You see any movement inside the trailers?'

'Not a thing. What do you want me to do?'

'Get back to the van. We're going in.'

They went in fast and hard, in two teams of four, each of the deputies moving with a speed and agility that put the lie to Royer's unspoken assumption that they weren't skilled enough to handle such an operation.

Each team took one of the motor homes parked near the Mustang, two covering the windows as the other two made swift entry through flimsy aluminium doors, weapons and flashlights raised.

Sanchez accompanied Worthington into the second motor home as Anna and Royer circled it outside. Screams and shouts filled the air and, seconds later, lights began coming to life all over the yard. Doors and canvas flaps flew open as alarmed carnies poked their heads out of their motor homes and tents to find out what the hell was going on.

The two motor homes in question were quickly flushed out, a couple of dazed and confused occupants emerging from each, only half-dressed and blinking. A male and female from one, two females from the other, all looking disoriented.

And not a Tommy Lee wannabe among them.

Or bearded lady, for that matter. Just four frightened people, wondering what they'd done wrong.

Royer and two deputies pointed weapons at them, Royer shouting, 'Get down! Down on your knees, hands locked behind your head.'

The four did as they were told, one of the women starting to cry. Anna heard a banging sound from inside the motor home near her, then Worthington emerged, and he didn't look happy.

'Shit!' he said, spitting the word out as if it had assaulted his tongue. He shone his light into the Mustang, then moved to the two women he and Sanchez had just chased outside.

'Where's the man who owns this car?'

One of the women, the one who was crying, stammered, 'H–He's not here.'

'Where *is* he?'

'I–I'm not sure – he went out after we dropped the awnings.'

'After you what?'

'After we closed for the night.'

'Son of a bitch,' Worthington said, looking as if he wanted to put a fist into the side of the motor home.

But then his gaze shifted abruptly, levelling on a spot past Anna's shoulder, his eyes widening just enough to tell her that something was up.

She turned and saw a tall man in white boxer

shorts scrambling out of a tent several yards away, and even from this distance she could see the dark patch of a tattoo on his neck.

Tommy Lee, a.k.a. Rick.

And he didn't stop to wish them all a good morning.

Raising her weapon, Anna shouted, 'Freeze!' and wasn't surprised when he ignored her.

A split second later her feet were moving and she was running after him as he tore around the side of the tent.

Picking up speed, she followed, but then the pain in her tweaked ankle returned, her gait faltering as the suspect rounded a corner and disappeared behind another motor home.

'Stop!' she shouted, but knew it was a wasted effort.

Pushing past the pain, she flew around the motor home, emerged onto a clearing and spotted Rick about halfway across it, his long, muscular legs propelling him like a gazelle towards a dark cluster of trees at the edge of the property.

There were houses beyond the trees, and Anna knew that if he managed to reach them, he might be impossible to find again – not to mention the potential threat he posed to the occupants.

She had to catch him, but her ankle hurt and her breath was starting to come up short and she wasn't sure she could.

No sooner had she thought this than someone blew past her. It was – to her surprise – Royer, moving

like a blur through the darkness towards Rick, effort-
lessly closing the gap between them.

If Rick was the gazelle, Royer was definitely the
cheetah, and just before Rick reached the trees, Royer
took a flying leap and tackled him, dust billowing as
the two hit the ground hard and rolled.

Royer came up first, slamming a fist into Rick's
face – twice in rapid succession – then flopped him
over and cuffed his hands behind his back.

Then he was on his feet, SIG Sauer in hand,
pointing it at the back of Rick's head. 'Where's the
girl, you son of a bitch!'

Rick spit dirt, his mouth bleeding. 'Fuck you!'

'Where is she?' Royer punctuated the question
with a kick to the ribs.

Rick howled, rolling into the pain, his body involuntarily curling into the fetal position.

Royer pressed his SIG against Rick's temple, making it clear what his intentions were. 'Last chance,
asshole.'

'All right, all right,' Rick gasped. 'She's in the tent.
Back in the tent.'

Without a word, Anna did a 180, saw Worthington
and another deputy coming up fast and signalled for
them to turn around.

'In the tent,' she shouted. 'She's in the tent!'

Still huffing for breath, she picked up her heels
and ran, following them back to the encampment.

By the time they got there, one of the deputies was
already emerging from Rick's battered tent, a young

girl in bra and panties squirming in his grip, tears in her eyes.

'Please,' she begged. 'Please don't tell my mom . . .'

'What's this?' Worthington asked. 'Where's the kid?'

'This is all I got,' the deputy told him.

The girl, a high schooler wearing too much make-up, was sobbing now, mascara running down her cheeks. 'Please . . . You can't tell her about this, she'll *kill* me . . .'

Ignoring the plea, Worthington pushed in close. 'What's your name?'

The girl hitched a breath, blinking blackened tears at him. 'Are you gonna call my mom?'

'Your *name*,' Worthington snapped.

The girl flinched, taking a moment to find her voice again. 'Wendy. Wendy Johanson.'

'How long have you been with this guy, Wendy?'

'Are you gonna—'

'Just answer the goddamn question.'

Fresh tears filled her eyes and she lowered her gaze. 'I met him at the arcade last night. He runs the coin toss.'

Worthington grabbed her chin, forcing her to look at him. 'That isn't what I asked you. How *long* have you been with him? All night?'

She shook her head. 'No. He had to work. We hooked up around two.'

'Did he have a little girl with him?'

Her face went blank. 'What?'

'A girl. A four-year-old girl.'

'Why? Is he married or something? He said he wasn't—'

'Answer me.'

'No,' she said, shaking her head. 'He was alone. I don't know anything about a little girl.'

'You're sure about that?'

'I'm not stupid. I think I would've noticed if he was dragging a kid around with him. Why are you asking me this? What did he do?'

Worthington just stared at her for a long moment, and Anna thought he was weighing the girl's words, trying to decide if she was telling the truth. But Anna herself had no doubts. This kid was clueless. Just another of a string of restless teenagers Mr Rock-and-Roll had talked into sharing his sleeping bag.

'Shit!' Worthington said finally, then looked at the deputy. 'Put her in the van and call her mom.'

'No!' the girl cried. 'She'll *kill* me!'

'Maybe next time you'll think twice about fucking around with a guy old enough to be your father.' He turned again to the deputy. 'And while you're at it, radio Marcus, tell him to round up some volunteers. We're gonna tear this place apart.'

The deputy glanced around at the gathering crowd of angry carnies. 'You sure that's a good idea?'

'We don't have a choice,' Worthington said, then turned, looking off in the direction they'd come from. 'Where the hell is my suspect?'

As if on cue, Royer emerged from behind a motor home, pushing Rick in front of him.

'Right here,' he said.

They were both covered with dirt and Rick's face looked as if it had been worked over a bit more. Either that or those two punches had done a helluva lot of damage.

Worthington nodded, his gaze locking on Rick's.

'Put him in the tent,' he said.

13

Pope was dozing in his chair by the window when his cellphone chirped for the third time that morning.

Groaning, he snatched it off the table next to him and stared bleary-eyed at the screen.

Sharkey again.

Shit.

Glancing at the bed, he noted that Evan hadn't stirred. The only sign of life was the gentle rise and fall of the boy's small chest. Pope marvelled at his ability to sleep despite the mountain of crap that had fallen on him in the last handful of hours.

Pope himself had never been one for sleep. Not even when he was Evan's age. He used to drive his parents nuts, never clocking out for more than four or five hours a night. And lately, despite all the pot he consumed, he'd managed to pare that down to two or three. It wasn't enough, he knew, but he continued to function in his own pathetic way.

His phone chirped again.

Reluctantly scraping a thumb across the keypad, he clicked it on.

'What's up, Sharkey?'

'Me, unfortunately. Any guesses why?'

'I'm a hypnotist, not a mind reader.'

'He wants to see you. Again.'

Pope let out another groan. 'You're kidding, right?'

'If I were, I'd still be in bed. Get your ass upstairs. I don't wanna have to come get you.'

'What's this about?'

'I don't know and I didn't ask, but we'll find out soon enough.'

Pope glanced at Evan. 'It'll have to wait. I've got company.'

'She'll keep.'

Pope checked the clock near his bed. Just past five. Outside, the sky was beginning to show just a hint of light.

Where the hell was that social worker?

'It's not that easy,' he said. 'Give me an hour or so and—'

'*Now*,' Sharkey told him. And the tone was not friendly.

Fuck.

Pope was about to suggest that Sharkey and his boss go straight to hell, but knew that wouldn't be wise. Over the last couple of years, thanks to a woefully bad string of luck, Pope had managed to dig himself into a 200,000-dollar hole with Anderson Troy. A debt that had more or less turned Pope into an indentured slave.

With a resigned sigh he said, 'I'll be right up.'

'That's a good boy.'

Sharkey clicked off.

Pope looked at Evan again, wondering if he should call Jake, see if social services were making any progress. He figured there wasn't much chance of the boy waking up while he was gone, but didn't really want to leave him alone.

Before he could stop himself, he was thinking about Ben again. About the good times, when he and Susan would stand over their son's crib, watching him sleep, thinking they were the luckiest couple in the world, having a child so perfect. So beautiful.

And later, when Ben was five – a young genius, Pope was sure – all those trips to the hospital, no longer the perfect son, but prone to a myriad of ailments that the doctors had trouble diagnosing.

Little did anyone know that it was *Susan* they should have been examining. Susan who had been causing Ben pain. A classic case of Munchausen by proxy. A mental illness that had led directly to their son's death.

It was an accident, Susan later told investigators in a teary-eyed confession – a confession Pope wouldn't have believed she'd made, if he hadn't seen the tape himself. After years of systematically abusing their son, of turning him into a sick little boy in a twisted attempt to gain sympathy and attention, she had finally gone too far. Setting the wagon on fire, then claiming she'd been carjacked had been a desperate attempt to cover up the crime.

An attempt that had almost worked.

Pope supposed he should have sympathy for Susan, but he didn't. Just the opposite, in fact. Hating her somehow made it easier to cope. Made him feel less guilty that he hadn't seen the signs, hadn't realized the truth before it was too late.

Pope's gut burned. At times like this, he would normally distract himself with a game or a beautiful woman or a bowl of dope, but none of those was an option right now. For the first time in what seemed like an eternity, he was responsible for someone, and he cursed Jake for making that happen.

There was no telling what Troy wanted or how long it would take. The only option was to find a substitute babysitter. Someone he could trust. Or, at least, rely on.

Moving to the phone by his bed, he punched in a two-digit code. A moment later a familiar voice answered the call.

'Room service.'

'Hey, Kel, it's me, Danny.'

Pope had been expecting another face-to-face with Troy, but it was more than that. Much more.

Troy had gone a bit overboard with the hired muscle – mostly because he had no real friends – but Pope rarely saw them all assembled in the same room at the same time.

Sharkey was here, looking sleepy and miffed, along with Arturo, and the so-called twin defenders, Joshua and Jonah, whom Pope always thought of as a single entity. He'd never seen them apart.

Then there was the strange creature who sat in a corner of the room, observing them all from a distance as if close contact might somehow contaminate him.

The Ghost.

He always wore dark suits and orange tinted glasses – something about light-sensitive eyes – and reminded Pope of an undertaker.

Pope wasn't sure what the guy did, exactly, or why they called him that, but he could make a pretty good guess, and his presence here did not bring on thoughts of happiness and light.

It was at times like this that Pope wondered how the hell he had ever allowed himself to fall in with this sorry lot.

But who was he kidding? He knew all too well how it had happened. The debt he owed Troy had not been accumulated over a single night, and was not the result of a single bad hand, but rather a string of *horrendous* hands that stretched the entire two-year span of time that Pope had been haunting the Oasis. He was hopelessly addicted to poker in all its forms and was notoriously bad at playing the game.

It would be years before he worked off his debt. Most of his take from *Metamorphosis* – a show that had been all Troy's idea, in lieu of an actual cash payback – went straight to the man himself, including interest. The rest went to room and board. And whether he liked it or not, Pope was locked into a payment plan that wouldn't be changing any time soon.

Or would it?

The way everyone was staring at him, he couldn't be sure. He glanced down at the carpet just to make sure he wasn't standing on plastic, and made a mental note to keep Arturo within his line of sight.

'So,' he said to Troy, who was once again sprawled on the sofa. 'Still having problems with Nigel Fromme?'

'I think we've gotten beyond poor Nigel, don't you?'

Pope had no idea what that meant and told him so.

'Come on, Daniel. Don't play dumb.'

'I'm not playing,' Pope said. 'I am dumb. Dumb as rocks. I think I've proven that more than a few times. So why don't you pretend I just got off the short bus and tell me what the hell you want.'

He hadn't meant to sound so hostile, but fear does that to you. It's not easy to stay calm when you've got half a dozen pairs of eyes staring you down, especially when you have no idea why.

Troy, however, didn't seem to notice his tone – which wasn't unusual for a guy who was so self-absorbed.

'I like to think that I've been a good friend to you, Daniel. I've given you a place to live, an opportunity to display your talents, and a relatively painless way to relieve yourself of your financial burden.'

Pope said nothing.

'When you came here, you were a broken man. But by inviting you into this little family of mine, I think I've been instrumental in changing that fact. Helped you glue some of the pieces back together, so to speak.' He paused. 'Am I wrong about that?'

Again Pope said nothing. He knew Troy wasn't really expecting an answer. Certainly not the one Pope was likely to provide.

'I don't think I am,' Troy said. 'What I am, is surprised. Surprised that you would accept my generosity, then turn around and stab me in the back.'

Say what?

Pope responded this time. Didn't hide his confusion. 'I'm not sure I follow.'

'You've been smoking a little too much weed, my friend. I might have to cut you off.' He paused. 'You had a visitor this morning. Why don't you tell me about her?'

'What's to tell?'

Troy frowned. 'For starters, do the initials FBI mean anything to you?'

Ohhhhhh, crap, Pope thought.

He truly *was* as dumb as rocks. He should have known this is what Troy was on about.

The presence of Special Agent Anna McBride at the Oasis was quite a threat to a man like Anderson Troy. It didn't matter that she knew nothing of Troy's illegal activities and probably couldn't care less. *Troy* didn't know this. And Troy's concern was understandable.

Pope put on his best, reassuring smile. 'You've got it all wrong,' he said.

'Of course I do.'

'No, seriously. It's not what you . . .'

Before he could finish his sentence, the twin defenders flanked him, each grabbing an arm and holding him in place. Pope instinctively stiffened, starting to resist, but their grip tightened just enough to hurt.

He glanced at Sharkey, but Sharkey's face was cold and impassive.

Troy rose from the sofa. 'How much do they know about me?'

'They?'

Troy sighed. 'The FBI, my friend. Pay attention.'

Pope shook his head. 'Not a thing. She wasn't here about—'

The blow was so sudden and so painful that Pope seemed momentarily to leave his body. Unfortunately, not quite fast enough to avoid the burst of fire that had engulfed his left kidney. Somehow Arturo had managed to get behind him to deliver the punch.

So much for keeping the little bastard within his line of sight.

Pope's knees buckled, but the twin defenders stood him back up, Arturo circling.

Troy seemed unfazed by the tears of pain gathering in Pope's eyes.

'How much do they know?' he repeated.

'Will you let me finish a sentence, for Christ's sake?'

The second blow was to the solar plexus, again coming so swiftly that Pope had no time to prepare – as if that would have made a difference.

ROBERT GREGORY BROWNE

With a gasp, he doubled over, then tried to distract himself from the pain by biting down hard on his lower lip – which didn't work, of course. Now his gut *and* his lip hurt.

There were many times over the last two years when Pope believed he had bottomed out. Had gotten as low as a man could get. But at this moment, standing in this room as these men beat him – knowing he had allowed himself, through his own stupidity, his own careless actions, to be here – he had to congratulate himself. He had reached a brand-new low.

And this time he might not come up for air.

'Listen to me,' he gasped. 'I'm trying to tell you, you've got nothing to worry about. She doesn't know a thing about you. Doesn't even know you exist.'

'Are you telling me she's just another one of your recreational fucks?'

'No, it isn't like that. She came to me for help on a case. Like the old days. My cousin Jake sent her.'

'That's the cop, right?'

'Yes.'

Troy turned to his crew. 'You see, that just goes to show what a generous guy I am. Despite Daniel's direct relationship to an officer of the law, I let him into our little circle here with open arms.'

'I didn't ask to be included,' Pope said.

The next blow came to his ribcage, and if something didn't crack, it surely bent, as pain blossomed along his right side.

'The point is,' Troy told him, 'I trusted you. Offered you a helping hand when you needed it most.

And even if you're telling the truth, and this FBI agent knows nothing about my extracurricular activities, what assurances do I have that that won't change in the near future?'

'Only my word,' Pope croaked. 'She got what she wanted and left. I don't expect to see her again.'

'And what about the kid? She won't come back for him?'

Pope stiffened. He shouldn't have been surprised that Troy knew about Evan, but he was. And for some reason that frightened him more than anything else.

'No,' he said. 'They're sending someone out to pick him up.'

'Another cop?'

'Social worker.'

'And why did she bring him here in the first place?'

'It's a long story. It's got nothing to do with you.'

'You should know by now that everything that goes on in this hotel has to do with me. Just give me the highlights.'

So Pope did, explaining about the murders, and the hope that they might be able to get information out of Evan under hypnosis.

When he was done, Troy stared at him for a long moment, then finally smiled. 'Thank you for clearing that up. I'm sorry we had to be so rough on you. But I don't like surprises. You should have warned me she was coming.'

Pope knew he was right, but said nothing.

'You see,' Troy continued, 'considering the nature of my business, when it comes to matters of security and stability, my comfort level is relatively low. And I'm sure you can understand that having a federal agent get curious about me is something I'd like to avoid.'

'Sure,' Pope said. Although at this point, he was in too much pain to really give a damn. 'But like I told you, she doesn't even know you exist.'

'How can you really be sure of that?' Troy asked. 'As far as any of us knows, she could be using that so-called case she's working on as a ruse to get to you. And, by extension, to me.'

Pope looked at him. This was getting ridiculous. 'So what are you saying? The boy's part of it? Some kind of junior agent?' He tried, and failed, to keep the sarcasm out of his voice and barely suppressed a laugh. 'For Christ's sake, Troy, quit letting your ego cloud your judgement.'

He knew the moment the words were out of his mouth that he'd made yet another reckless mistake and couldn't fathom why he'd said them in the first place. But they were out there now and he couldn't pull them back. And any hope he had that Troy would ignore them died the moment he looked into the man's eyes.

Troy's next utterance didn't help much, either.

'You . . . insolent . . . little . . . fuck.'

Pope knew he had just crossed a line he shouldn't even have approached. Considering Troy's history, he was likely to react like a toddler who's just been smacked in the face by a cold, unloving parent.

And, true to form, Troy gestured to his crew and

said with barely controlled fury, 'I've had it with this moron. He's more trouble than he's worth. Take him out to the desert and do that thing you do so well.'

'Wait a minute,' Pope said, feeling panic rise. 'What the hell are you doing? I saved your *life* for Chrissa—'

Another quick blow, straight to the gut. Pope doubled over.

Goddamn, that hurt.

'I knew you'd bring that up,' Troy said. 'And I believe I've repaid that debt several times over. But you've failed me twice in one morning, Daniel. And that's more chances than most people get.'

He gestured with two fingers and the twin defenders started dragging Pope towards the doors.

'Hold on, boss. Are you sure this is a good idea?'

Sharkey speaking now.

Sharkey coming to the rescue.

'He's a liability,' Troy said. 'Knows more than I ever should have allowed him to know. And if he's careless enough to invite a federal agent into this hotel, he deserves whatever he gets.'

'But if he's got the FBI sniffing around him, won't it be a little suspicious, he suddenly goes missing?'

Troy took a moment to consider this.

'Maybe. But the man has a history of self-destructive behaviour.' He paused, the wheels still turning. 'Make it look like suicide.'

14

'What do you people want from me?' Rick shouted. 'I didn't do a goddamn thing!'

'Then why the hell did you run?'

The interior of the tent was an oven. There was enough sweat in the room to drown a small rodent. Even Royer had done the unthinkable and taken his jacket off. But he seemed to be enjoying himself.

Anna thought if he were interrogating a prisoner at Guantanamo, he'd be the first to suggest they try something with a little more *oomph*. Something to ratchet up the stakes.

She could hear the echo of angry voices outside, the sound of barking dogs, more deputies and volunteers arriving, gearing up to go through the encampment from tent to trailer, looking for the missing girl.

Mr Rock-and-Roll was kneeling at the centre of the tent, hands still cuffed behind his back.

'I'm tellin' you,' he said, 'I didn't *touch* the bitch. It's her word against mine.'

Royer stood over him in gladiator pose, fists

clenched. 'I don't give a damn about some high-school pop tart.'

'Then what's this about?'

'The girl,' Royer said. 'Where's the girl? Where's Kimberly?'

Rick frowned at him, looking confused. 'Kimmie? What do you want with her?'

'We found the boy, numb-nuts. He puts all four of you in the car together.'

Rick swivelled his head towards Anna and Worthington. 'Will one of you assholes please tell me what the hell is going on here?'

'Eyes front,' Royer said, snapping his fingers.

'Fuck you!'

Without even a moment of reflection, Royer swung a fist into Rick's face, knocking him to the ground. The attack was abrupt and brutal, Royer grunting like a Neanderthal.

It was a classic case of overkill. Royer trying to prove he had as much testosterone as Worthington and his deputies. This show was more about ego than finding a missing girl.

Anna hated macho posturing almost as much as she'd come to despise Royer, and she didn't believe in this hands-on approach to interrogation.

Fortunately Worthington didn't seem to like it much either, and as Royer reached again for the suspect, the deputy threw his hands up.

'All right, that's enough.'

Royer turned. 'Do you want the girl or don't you?'

'Putting him in a coma won't help us find her. Now back off.'

Royer eyed him defiantly, then finally stepped away. 'Fine,' he said. 'He's all yours.'

Worthington crouched down and helped Rick sit upright. His mouth was bleeding, a nasty purple bruise forming on his left cheekbone – a nice complement to Royer's earlier tune job.

'One chance,' Worthington said. 'That's all you get. You understand?'

Rick stared at him. 'You people are certifiable.'

'Just tell us what you did with Kimmie.'

'I didn't do shit with her. Why do you keep asking me that? What happened? Is she okay?'

'Cut the crap,' Worthington said. 'Agent Royer wasn't lying. We know those kids were in your Mustang. So if you don't want me to sic him on you again, you'd better goddamn well explain.'

'Explain what? I took them for a ride, got some burgers. What's the big fuckin' deal?'

'I think you know.'

'That's the thing, man, I *don't*. What are you gettin' on me for? Is this about the restraining order? Cuz if it is, you got one helluva way of enforcing it.'

Worthington frowned. 'What restraining order?'

'The bitch went to court on me. I'm not supposed to get within a hundred yards of her house.'

'Which bitch are we talking about now?'

'Who the fuck you think? Rita. She thinks she's too goddamn good for me.'

'Is that why you killed her?'

The words stopped Rick cold. He looked as if he'd just been struck by another one of Royer's blows. And in that instant, his whole demeanour changed.

'Wait a minute, wait a minute,' he said, then paused a moment, as if he were having trouble translating something spoken in a foreign tongue. 'What exactly are you telling me here? Rita's dead?'

'That's the long and the short of it,' Worthington said.

Rick just stared at him, dumbstruck, his eyes getting moist. He blinked a couple of times, forcing the tears back, and with sudden clarity Anna knew they had the wrong man. She'd seen a lot of suspects lie in her time, but nobody was this good an actor.

He didn't know about the murders.

He didn't know anything.

'Oh, for Chrissake,' Royer said, his face twisting in disgust. 'Let me at this guy.'

Worthington held up a hand, looking intently at Rick. 'Let's start this from the beginning. How do you know Rita Fairweather?'

Rick took a moment, then said, 'We used to hook up when I came to town. Until about three, four years ago.'

'What happened then?'

'She went psycho on me. Tells me she wants me to quit the show and move in with her. Maybe get married, give them all a stable home. I told her she was nuts, so she cut me off.'

'Why the restraining order?'

'I kept trying to get with her. Called her up a lot,

even went out to that dump she calls a house. She got so pissed she went straight to court on me.' He paused. 'That was a couple years ago.'

'So she was afraid of you.'

Rick shook his head. 'She wasn't afraid of shit. She's a bitch with a capital B. She'd already stuck the knife in, she just wanted to twist it a little.'

'Interesting choice of words,' Worthington said. 'But none of this explains why you took Evan and Kimberly on a field trip last night.'

'That's what I'm trying to tell you. She wouldn't let me near them. Kept me in the dark so goddamn long, that when she finally dropped the bomb, I just wanted to meet them. Evan at least. He's the only one she was sure of.' He shrugged. 'So I sweet-talked the babysitter into bringing him to me.'

'This is such bullshit,' Royer said. 'Why would you give a damn about Rita Fairweather's son? Unless you wanted to diddle the little bastard.'

Both Rick and Worthington looked at him as if they thought this was one of the dumbest questions they'd ever heard, and Anna had to agree.

The answer was obvious.

'What do you think, Einstein? I'm his fuckin' father.'

It had all been a waste of time. Dragging Evan out to the Oasis, the raid, interrogating Mr Rock-and-Roll. Maybe if Evan hadn't had a seizure they would have learned something useful, but it was too late now. They couldn't risk putting him under again.

Stepping outside the tent and taking in the drama around the encampment – carnies shouting angrily as deputies threw open door after door, probing trailers and tents with their flashlights – Anna thought back to that moment just before Evan's seizure, remembering his words:

He's been wanting to meet me for a really long time. He says he's . . . He says . . .

He's my dad, Anna thought.

And that's all last night had been for Rick. A guy trying to make contact with his son.

True, the neighbours had told Worthington's team that the father was dead, but Anna thought Evan and Kimmie might well have had many fathers over the last several years. A parade of men that Rita Fairweather had taken up with.

She also knew that Rick being Evan's biological father didn't rule him out as a killer and kidnapper. It might even bolster a case against him. But she wasn't buying. She knew they'd gotten it wrong.

And out there somewhere was the real killer.

Did he still have Kimmie with him? Or was it too late?

Anna looked up at the sky, wishing she had a god's-eye view of the world, or maybe some sort of missing persons GPS device that would allow her to home in on Kimberly and her kidnapper, wherever they might be.

Just follow the two little dots, apprehend and arrest.

If only it were that easy.

Hearing a shout, she snapped her head around and levelled her gaze on a commotion near the centre of the encampment. Two deputies were trying to fend off a burly, overweight carny swinging a baseball bat.

'You got no right!' he shouted, going for a line drive to a deputy's forehead.

The deputy ducked, grabbed a handful of dirt and threw it into the fat man's face as the other deputy tackled him, taking him down. The baseball bat flew, clattering against the motor home behind them, before bouncing harmlessly to the ground.

'You got no right!' the carny shouted again as one of the deputies cuffed his hands behind his back. 'This is my *home*!'

Anna felt ashamed. Here they were, disrupting the lives of these poor, working people – and for what? There was nothing to look for here. Nothing to find. And she couldn't help feeling that some, if not all, of this was her fault.

She could hear Worthington continuing to question the suspect and knew it was only a matter of time before he reached the same conclusion she had. Royer, however, would be tougher to convince. He was a bulldog, plain and simple – and not a very smart one at that.

Like so many agents she'd met in her time with the Bureau, he lived in a black and white world, good guys and bad guys, with nothing in between. And while he might think his motives were pure, and that the end justified the means, his stubbornness, his inability to see the many different colours in the world, his willingness to compromise basic human ethics for the 'greater good' made him – in Anna's estimation – one of the bad guys.

Unfortunately, there wasn't much she could do about . . .

A sudden chill swept through her. An odd sense that she was being watched.

She looked out at the growing crowd of carnies, standing in their nightshirts and underwear, watching the fat man continue to struggle with the deputies, but no one seemed to be paying her the slightest attention.

Yet the feeling persisted.

Turning, she looked towards the edge of the encampment where it met the carnival grounds – a hundred yards or so away. A row of canvas arcade tents formed the border between them.

Nothing there.

She was about to turn away when she saw movement in the shadows beneath one of the canopies. A dark figure, hard to see in the early morning light, but the shape was unmistakably a man.

Was he watching her?

She couldn't be sure.

He stood there a moment, facing her direction, then suddenly turned and started walking away, moving deeper into the carnival grounds.

And as he stepped out of the shadows, dread flooded through Anna, a dread so deep that it took everything she had to remain standing, an image from one of her visions blossoming in her mind.

And the feeling she'd had earlier, the one she'd

felt so strongly while standing in the hotel hallway – that this was all somehow connected to her visions – came back to her with undeniable force.

This wasn't just any man. She was sure of it.

He was wearing a baseball cap.

A red baseball cap.

15

They were in the elevator, somewhere between the first and second floors, when Pope made his move.

The twins had gone ahead to get the car, leaving Sharkey and Arturo to escort Pope out of the building, Sharkey ragging on him the entire ride down from the fourteenth floor.

'You gotta be the biggest fuckin' fool I ever met. How long you been hanging around this dump, you don't know what kind of hair-trigger the boss has?'

'Long enough,' Pope said.

'Damn straight. And bringing some FBI snatch into the building? That's just plain stupid.'

Pope didn't disagree.

But his stupidity wasn't the issue at the moment. What mattered right now was extricating himself from this situation as quickly as possible – a feat not easily accomplished when the two men flanking you are skilled professionals.

Not that Pope himself was any slouch. There was a time when he had regularly tortured the speed bag and popped a few curls before heading into the office every morning. Always something of a natural athlete, he'd even taken the Las Vegas Metropolitan Police Department up on its offer for self-defence training. And while nearly two years of debauchery had undoubtedly softened him, he felt confident that he still had some skills of his own.

Of course, none of this had taught him how to handle two thugs in an elevator, especially when your gut and left kidney felt as if they'd been assaulted by a jackhammer. But in the end, it was the elevator itself that saved him.

As Sharkey blathered on, Pope stood watching the numbers light up on the panel above the door – 8, 7, 6, 5, 4, 3 – wondering when, and if, he should make his move. Then the elevator made it for him by suddenly jerking to a halt, stalling just before it reached the first floor.

That jerk was enough to throw all three of them off-balance. Taking advantage of the moment, Pope brought his elbow up quickly, cracking Arturo's nose with an audible *snap*.

The move was so uncharacteristic and unexpected that Arturo hadn't seen it coming. He shrieked and grabbed for the damage, blood spurting between his fingers as Pope spun towards Sharkey and brought a knee up hard into his crotch.

Sharkey grunted and doubled over, sinking to his knees on the elevator's well-worn carpet.

While all of this was happening, the car lurched into motion again, continuing its descent, and a moment later the door slid open at the ground floor, inviting Pope to flee.

Hands grabbed at him before he was able to clear the threshold. He jerked an elbow back again, half-expecting to feel the heat of Arturo's knife sinking into his ribs. But the hands had a fairly good grip on him now and spun him around until he was face-to-face with Sharkey, who was still struggling to breathe.

As Pope tried to pull away, Sharkey slammed him back against the door's rubber bumper and pinned him there, wheezily sucking air.

'Don't . . . even . . . try,' he said between breaths, then reached round and jabbed the emergency stop button.

Pope stopped struggling, resigned to the fact that he had pretty much shot his wad. So much for all that time in the gym. It was only then that he glanced down at the floor and saw Arturo lying in a heap, out cold, blood pooling around his now-broken nose.

Pope knew he'd caused some damage, but this?

'Jesus. Did I do that?'

'Hardly,' Sharkey said. 'I wanted some alone time.'

Apparently past the worst of his pain now, Sharkey released Pope, who considered bolting, but didn't figure he'd get far.

'I should shoot you just for the knee to the nads,' Sharkey continued, 'but I've never killed a civilian, and I don't intend to start now. Especially one as pathetic as you.'

Pope looked at him. Civilian?

'Am I missing something here?'

'I could fill a warehouse with the things you miss.'

'So what exactly is going on?'

'What do you think?' Sharkey said. 'I'm letting you go.'

Pope was flabbergasted. 'Why the hell would you do that?'

'Does it look like we have time for a detailed conversation? Rumpelstiltskin here isn't gonna sleep forever, and he damn sure won't be happy when he wakes up. Let's just say I'm not who you think I am.'

Pope ran that little morsel of information through his head for a moment, completely stymied.

Then it him. 'Holy shit. You're a *cop*?'

It was the only thing that made any sense.

'Just know *this*,' Sharkey said. 'Our mutual bene-factor is gonna be pissed when he finds out you're on the loose. So you need to get low and stay low, because I can damn well guarantee he'll be sending us after you. And God save you if he unleashes The Ghost.'

'What about you? Will you be okay?'

'I'll tell him you hypnotized me.'

Pope smiled. 'How do you know I didn't?'

'Ha ha,' Sharkey said. 'Now get out of here, and don't say a goddamn word to your FBI friend. I don't want two and a half years of hard work blown because of some second-rate lounge performer.'

Pope patted his shoulder. 'Thanks, Shark. Sorry about the balls.'

He was about to head down the hallway towards

the rear exit when he suddenly realized he'd forgotten something. Turning, he went for the stairwell instead.

Sharkey said, 'Are you outta your mind? What are you doing? I said get out of here.'

'The kid,' Pope told him. 'I almost forgot the kid.'

Less than a minute later he was pushing open his hotel-room door. Evan was still fast asleep on the bed, but Kelly was curled up in the armchair, Pope's pipe and lighter in hand, glazed eyes staring at the miniature *Metamorphosis* disco ball that sat spinning on the table next to her.

'These things really trip me out,' she said, then looked up at Pope, offering him the pipe and lighter. 'You want a hit?'

Pope immediately crossed the room and snatched them away from her. 'What the hell is wrong with you? There's a kid in the room.'

'He's asleep and I was bored,' she said. 'You ever heard of cable? Books maybe? Magazines?'

She was twenty-four years old and all woman, but sometimes acted as if she were still sixteen. She'd never made a secret of the fact that she was attracted to Pope, but he hadn't been able to bring himself to close the deal. It just didn't feel right.

'First,' he told her, 'a kid's a kid, asleep or otherwise. Second, you shouldn't be rummaging around in my personal stuff. And third, I need to borrow your car.'

The last one threw her for a loop. 'What?'

'Your car. Right now.'

'You're kidding, right? You haven't left this place in – what? Like a year?'

'Things change. And I'm in a hurry.'

'What about *your* car?'

'I signed it over to Troy, remember?'

She rolled her eyes. 'You're an idiot.'

'Hey, what can I tell you? I like breathing.'

Speaking of which, time was wasting. In his mind's eye, Pope could see Arturo coming awake on that elevator floor. He needed to get the hell out of here.

Moving to the bed, he lifted Evan into his arms. The boy stirred, but didn't awaken, instead laying his head on Pope's shoulder, snoring softly against his neck. The move was so familiar and natural that Pope was immediately flooded by memories. He felt the heat of emotion rise, settling in his chest and behind his eyes.

Fighting to turn it off, he said to Kelly, 'I really do need that car.'

She eyed him coyly. 'And what do *I* get out of it?'

'How about a year's worth of cable and a subscription to your favourite magazine?'

'Really?'

Pope sighed. 'The key, Kelly. Give me the goddamn key.'

It was a fourteen-year-old Toyota Tercel with faded paint that had once been cherry-red. She kept it parked in the employee section at the far end of the south lot. Getting to it was tricky, especially with the sky growing lighter and a kid in his arms, but Pope managed to make it without running into Sharkey and crew.

That could change, of course.

Glancing around, he popped open the passenger door, tossed a backpack onto the rear seat and carefully strapped Evan in. The boy stirred again, murmuring something Pope didn't catch, then settled against the seat and fell quiet.

Pope closed him in, then moved around the car and climbed into the driver's seat, which he quickly adjusted for his longer legs. It was an odd sensation, sitting behind the wheel after so long. Especially in a car he wasn't used to.

He was about to turn the key in the ignition when he saw headlights in the distance.

A Lincoln Town Car. About fifty yards away.

It could be anyone, but Pope knew the twins drove a Lincoln and wouldn't be surprised if the alert had gone out and they were cruising the lot, aisle by aisle, in the hope of catching a glimpse of him.

He reached over, adjusting Evan's seat back to full reclining position, then followed with his own. A moment later the Town Car approached, moving slowly.

Did they know this was Kelly's car? Had someone gone to the room and confronted her?

He'd find out soon enough.

Pope held his breath, listening to the low rumble of the Town Car's engine as it came close, then, thankfully, rolled past. He was tempted to take a peek, see if it really was the twins, but he'd been foolish

enough for one morning and saw no point in compounding his troubles.

Once it was gone, he waited a full minute before
putting his seat upright again. Glancing around, he
saw no sign of the Town Car. They must've headed
over to the North lot. Quickly starting the engine,
Pope shifted into Drive and pulled away.

He was nearing the parking-lot exit when Evan
stirred again.

'. . . watching her,' he murmured.

Pope looked at him. The boy's eyes were closed.

Talking in his sleep?

'. . . watching . . .' Evan said.

Could he be dreaming about Kimberly? Was he
remembering what happened? Pope reached over and
gently stroked the boy's forehead.

'What was that, kiddo?'

Evan said nothing for a long moment and Pope
returned his attention to the road.

Then the boy spoke. More clearly this time.

'He's watching her . . . been watching her all
morning.'

'Who's he watching?' Pope asked. 'Kimmie?'

Evan's brow furrowed, but his eyes remained
closed. 'No . . .' he murmured. 'Anna . . .'

Pope had no earthly idea who Anna was.

Another sister?

No. Wait a minute.

Wasn't that Special Agent McBride's name?

They were approaching the freeway now. Pope
took the westbound on-ramp, heading towards Ludlow.

If he floored it, he could be there in less than twenty minutes.

'*Who's* watching her, Evan? Who's watching Anna?'

'The man,' Evan said.

'What man?'

Evan didn't respond, his brow continuing to furrow as if he were battling some unseen force that was trying to prevent him from talking.

Then he said, 'The man in the red hat.'

16

By the time she reached the arcade tents, he was nowhere in sight.

Pausing near the patch of ground where he had been standing, Anna noted two crushed cigarette butts in the dirt. If they were his, it meant he'd been standing there for quite a while.

Had he been waiting for her?

Continuing on, she moved between two tents and emerged at the far end of the football field. More tents, about half a dozen of them, were lined up along the right side of the field with a wide aisle between them, flaps closed and tied down for the night.

Anna had been to enough carnivals to know exactly what was behind those flaps. Ring toss, balloon darts, shooting galleries, milk bottles – games all designed to take your money and give you nothing in return.

When she was a teenager, one of her boyfriends had known how to beat them all and she'd had a room full of cheap stuffed animals to prove it.

Moving down the aisle, she searched the grounds,

but saw no sign of the man in the red baseball cap, wondering now if she had only imagined him. At the rate she was going, that certainly wasn't beyond the realm of possibility.

But assuming he *wasn't* a figment of her imagination, who, then, was he? Could he be the same man from her visions? The one who was terrorizing the little girl?

And, if so, how was he connected to this case?

Down the centre of the field were the food booths. Smaller canvas tents and gaudily painted trailers that promised caramel apples, snow cones, hot dogs and cotton candy. A few of the tents were sponsored by local businesses and the PTA.

As a young child, Anna had spent a weekend working in a carnival food booth, alongside her mother, who had been the leader of Anna's Blue Bird troop. They'd worn matching blue and yellow uniforms, selling hamburgers and chilli fries to Anna's classmates and their families.

Two years later, her mother was dead.

Turning now, Anna moved into the adjacent aisle, searching the shadows for any sign of movement.

The left side of the field held the carnival rides, all eerily dormant in the early morning darkness. Ferris wheel, carousel, Tilt-A-Whirl, miniature roller coaster, and a couple of newer rides she'd never seen before. All were painted in vibrant reds and yellows and oranges – although some of that paint had faded over time and no one had bothered to slap on a new coat.

Once again feeling the sensation that she was being

watched, Anna swivelled her head towards the carousel, about fifteen yards away. All she could see were the painted ponies, half-hidden in darkness.

Yet the feeling persisted.

Stopping in her tracks, she kept her gaze steady, waiting. The world seemed to have gotten very quiet. The commotion behind her, the carny encampment under siege, was little more than a faint murmur now.

Then, after a long moment, something inside the carousel moved. A subtle shift in the waning darkness.

Was he in there?

Reaching to her side, Anna pulled her Glock free from its holster and raised it, pointing it towards the shadows. 'You,' she said. 'Lock your hands on top of your head and come out.'

No response. No movement. Nothing.

'FBI. Lock your hands on top of your head and come out. *Now.*'

Still nothing.

Anna inched closer, about to chalk all of this up to her overworked imagination, when she spotted something in the dirt just three yards away. A small object, made of plastic.

Checking the carousel shadows for movement again – and seeing nothing – she holstered her Glock and stepped over to the object, crouching down to take it in her hands.

A pink My Little Pony.

Just like the ones on Kimberly's bedspread.

Anna knew it could have been dropped by almost

anyone over the last several days, but she didn't think so – and a renewed sense of dread washed through her as she thought about the significance of the toy.

Had it been placed here for her to discover?

Was the man in the red baseball cap telling her that he had—

'Chavi?'

The voice rose from the shadows behind her.

Startled, Anna jumped to her feet and spun, ripping her Glock from its holster again, pointing it towards a patch of darkness near one of the food booths.

Was he in there?

'FBI,' she said, trying to keep her voice steady. 'Come out. Slowly. Hands raised.'

'Is it you, Chavi?'

The voice had a vaguely European lilt. English was not his first language.

'I'm not gonna ask again,' Anna told him. 'You're interfering with a federal investigation. Show yourself.'

No response. Not even a hint of movement.

Then, from off to her right: 'I've made mistakes, Chavi. Many mistakes. More than I can count.'

Anna jerked towards the sound of the voice, pointing her weapon at the Tilt-A-Whirl. It seemed to be coming from one of the cars now.

'But in the end, I always find you. I always will.'

Suddenly feeling very vulnerable, she stepped backwards, retreating into the shadows near the carousel. 'Who are you?'

'You don't know me? You don't remember?'

'Cut the bullshit. Where's Kimmie? What did you do with her?'

'Ahhh,' the voice said. 'She was another mistake. And after all the trouble I went through to find her. All the blood I shed. That poor mother fought quite hard to protect her child.'

Anna stepped forward again, straining to see him, her finger brushing the trigger.

'But not to worry. Each mistake I make brings me closer to the one I seek.' A pause. 'Am I closer now?'

'Just tell me what you did with Kimmie, you freak. Where *is* she?'

'Where they all are, of course. With the angels.'

The voice came from the left this time, near the Ferris wheel. Disoriented, Anna turned again, trying to pin him down. 'What are you telling me? You killed her, too?'

'Freed her,' he said. 'I freed them all.' Another pause. 'But what about you, Chavi? Are you a mistake?'

'Why do you keep calling me that? Who's Chavi?'

There was a long moment of silence. Then:

'The girl who stole my soul.'

The voice was directly behind her now. Something touched the left side of Anna's ribcage and a jolt of pain ripped through her. Losing her grip on the Glock, she fell to the ground, her body spasming violently.

Stun gun. She'd been hit by a stun gun.

The man in the red baseball cap stepped out of the shadows and stood over her, his face obscured by the bill of the cap.

Crouching beside her, he reached out and touched her head. Smoothed her hair.

His breath stank of cigarettes.

'Is it really you, Chavi? Have I found you again?'

And all Anna could see was his crooked yellow smile.

17

They were nearing the Ludlow off-ramp when Evan had another seizure.

Except for the occasional murmur about red hats, he'd slept quietly for most of the ride. Pope had spent their short time on the road wondering if the boy's mutterings had come from something more than a simple nightmare.

But at the moment, it didn't much matter. Pope had more pressing things to think about.

Like staying alive.

He checked his rear-view mirror for what must have been the hundredth time in the last few minutes. He half-expected to see Arturo and crew blasting towards him on the highway, but the road looked empty. No sign of headlights except for the big rig and the motor home he'd passed a few moments ago.

Pope figured his best bet was to get Evan back to Jake, who could make sure that he was properly taken care of. Hanging out with a fugitive from the fuck-up factory was probably not the best place for a kid to be.

Pope still wasn't quite sure why he had agreed to watch him in the first place.

Or was he?

No matter how much he tried to deny it, there was something about Evan that brought out Pope's paternal instincts. Instincts he thought had died along with Ben.

They were about a mile out of Ludlow when Evan twisted in his seat and started murmuring again.

'. . . Chavi . . .' he said.

Pope glanced at him, saw that he was still asleep, his brow furrowed as if he were concentrating heavily.

'. . . Is it you, Chavi?'

Pope frowned. What the hell was going on in this kid's head?

Evan was quiet for another long moment. Spotting the Ludlow off-ramp ahead, Pope pointed the nose of the Tercel towards it and accelerated, wondering what his next step would be.

Should he ignore Sharkey's request and tell Jake what had happened? Or was it possible that Jake already knew about Troy and Sharkey?

No, if Sharkey was involved in a long-term under-cover operation, Pope doubted some dirt-water sheriff's deputy would be in the loop. And maybe it was best to leave it that way. Whatever Sharkey was up to, it wouldn't be good for Troy – and that was just fine with Pope. Multi-millionaire or not, the guy was almost certainly a psychopath and Pope didn't relish being on his hit list.

They were nearing the off-ramp when Evan let out

a small cry of pain. Pope spun his head towards him and saw his body stiffen, knowing immediately what was coming next.

Then Evan started convulsing, his eyes flying open, rolling back in his head until only the whites were visible.

Holy shit.

Pope jerked the wheel and hit the brakes, skidding to a halt in the gravel beside the road. Reaching over, he quickly unfastened Evan's seatbelt as the boy bucked and kicked, his head rolling from side to side.

'Easy,' Pope told him, trying to calm himself as much as Evan, knowing he was probably speaking to deaf ears. 'You'll be fine, son. You'll be fine in just a minute.'

Pope was reminded of the first time he'd witnessed an epileptic fit. His Grandpa Joe – a Vegas real-estate broker – convulsing by the pool on a hot Sunday afternoon as Grandma M stood over him, a glass of iced tea in hand, telling everyone with a tight, embarrassed smile, 'Don't worry. He'll be just fine.'

But Pope *was* worried now. There was something different about Evan's seizure this time. It was more than your typical grand mal. He was sure of it. The convulsions seemed twice as violent as before, and Evan continued to cry out in pain, hands clutching his chest as if he were having a heart attack.

A hospital. Pope had to get him to a hospital.

Putting the Toyota in gear, he was about to dig out, when all at once Evan was still, the attack over. Done.

Gripping the wheel as he tried to calm himself, Pope stared at the boy, saw that his eyes were closed, sweat beading on his brow. His breathing was uneven, but was gradually getting steadier.

Heaving a shaky sigh of relief, Pope shoved the gear-shift back into Park and just sat there a moment, memories of Ben once again forcing their way out of the lock box he tried so hard to keep them in. But this time he let them come, let the sadness envelop him.

And before he knew it, tears flooded his eyes.

What had he been doing to himself these last two years? Why had he allowed his grief to control him? Allowed himself to fall prey to the cards, the pot, the women – when all he had to do was cry? To release the pain. The toxins. Purge them from his soul.

What he had become did not honour the memory of his son. If Ben could see him now, he'd be ashamed. Mortified, in fact.

Pope blinked away his tears and looked at Evan again. He was about to reach over to wipe the sweat from the boy's forehead, when Evan suddenly bolted upright, showing only the whites of his eyes.

'He's hurting her. You have to stop him. He's hurting her!'

Pope just stared at him. 'What?'

'The man in the red hat. He's hurting her. He's hurting my Anna.'

A chill ran through Pope. One so strong that his teeth nearly chattered. Despite his admitted indifference to the idea of unexplained phenomena like ghosts and UFOs and psychic healers and, yes, past lives – looking at Evan, he knew one thing for certain:

This was no fucking nightmare.

'Help her!' Evan cried. 'Don't let him take her away.'

Pope grabbed him by the shoulders. 'Where, Evan? Where is he taking her?'

'The house of mirrors. Dr Demon's House of Mirrors. Do something. *Now*.'

Pope didn't need much more of a kick in the ass than that. Quickly pulling Evan's seat upright, he strapped him in again, jammed the Tercel into Drive and hit the accelerator, shooting back onto the off-ramp.

He wasn't sure what Evan was babbling about, but the bit about the house of mirrors had triggered something in his mind:

The carnival.

The carnival was in town.

Pope had spent part of every summer of his childhood haunting the grounds of Ludlow High, flirting with girls, riding rides and navigating the maze inside Dr Demon's House of a Thousand Mirrors.

Middle of July meant carnival season, and whatever was going down there did not bode well for Special Agent Anna McBride.

Pointing the Tercel in the direction of the school, he fumbled for his cellphone and hit speed-dial.

Two rings later, Jake was on the line.

18

He had her by the collar and was dragging her through the carnival grounds as if she were nothing more than a sack full of old bones.

Every time Anna tried to resist, he hit her with the stun gun again, sending a spark of electricity straight into her central nervous system, dazing her, her heart pounding uncontrollably. Every shock seemed to drive her deeper into her own mind. She felt as if she were floating in and out of darkness, only half-conscious of the world around her.

Then, as she came into the light again, she tried to twist away, grabbing at his hand, feeling the coarse flesh and the hardened bones beneath it – the hand of a working man, a farmer, a peasant—

– a carny?

He was dragging her towards the dark doorway of one of the carnival sideshows – the one from the photograph in Evan and Kimberly's room—

– Dr Demon's House of a Thousand Mirrors.

And as she tried to pry his fingers loose, he brought the stun gun down again, jabbing its probes against her neck for what must have been the fourth or fifth time, sending another jolt through her.

This one drove her so deep into the darkness that she felt as if she were tumbling through a long black tunnel, only to emerge into light on the other side, shadows flickering in it, moving across a surface of some kind.

But what was it?

As her eyes cleared, Anna realized that she was now staring up at the tattered ceiling of a moving car, tree shadows flitting across it as its old engine rumbled and the road bumped beneath her.

But how had she gotten here? Had she lost consciousness long enough for him to hoist her into a car and drive away?

No, something was wrong. Very wrong.

Anna remembered those shadows. Remembered them from one of her visions of the little girl. Had the trauma of what was happening to her brought on another episode?

If so, the experience was no longer the detached, observational view she was accustomed to. No glimpses of mayhem and carnage that faded from the mind almost as quickly as they came.

This time it was happening to *her*.

She was the little girl.

Anna had somehow inhabited the girl's mind and body, experiencing every pain, every thought, every fear as if it were her own.

The pungent smell of cigarette smoke filled her nostrils. Something constricted her mouth and she realized it was taped shut. Glancing down, she found that her wrists and ankles were bound – the wrists and ankles of a ten-year-old – duct tape wrapped around them, making it nearly impossible to move.

She was lying on the back seat of the car, and for some reason she kept thinking about someone named Stinky.

Mr Stinky, to be more precise, who had been hit by a bus.

Confusion crowded Anna's brain. Her thoughts seemed to be intermingled with those of her host and she had trouble discerning whose thoughts were whose.

Looking out her window through the little girl's eyes, she saw that they were driving through a dark forest, thick green trees growing black in the waning twilight.

Turning slightly, she strained to see the car's driver, but all she saw was the red baseball cap sitting atop a closely cropped head of dark hair. Just above his collar line was a tattoo – another goddamn neck tattoo – but instead of a dragon, this one looked like a wheel, a wagon wheel, with at least a dozen spokes, a couple of them missing:

It was symbol of some kind, but of what?

Shifting her gaze, Anna caught a glimpse of the

driver's face in his rear-view mirror: a single dark, brooding eye, obscured by a cloud of cigarette smoke.

An ornate locket dangled from a chain on the rear-view mirror, clacking against the windshield as they bumped along.

And all at once, Anna knew she was about to die.

Brakes squeaked as the car came to a sudden halt. The driver pushed his door open and got out, moving stiffly, as if some sort of physical handicap was slowing him down. A moment later the trunk was unlatched, the car bouncing slightly as the man pulled something out of it.

Then Anna's own door flew open and, for the first time, she got a full view of his face.

The sight made her shudder.

It was a study in God's plan gone wrong. The entire left side looked as if it had been squeezed by forceps at the moment of birth – a misshapen, lopsided mess.

Anna flinched, the little girl in her instinctively squeezing her eyes shut as revulsion welled up. She couldn't bear to look at him.

Then hands grabbed her, those same coarse working man's hands, pulling her out of the back seat, dropping her roughly to the ground. She let out a yelp of pain, her breath hot against the tape, as the man took her by the collar and dragged her through fallen leaves, her bound wrists and ankles making it impossible for her to resist.

He dragged her into the middle of a forest clearing, struggling to carry a small, battered suitcase in his free hand. Dumping her to one side, he crouched down, laid the suitcase on the ground and opened it, taking a moment to make his choice. Then he brought out a narrow-bladed knife. Suitable for boning.

It was covered with dried blood.

The wind was high, bending the trees above them, leaves swirling around Anna as she began to cry uncontrollably, desperately wriggling her wrists, trying to loosen the tape. But it was no use. She wouldn't be going anywhere until the man in the red baseball cap sent her there.

Grabbing her left hand, he closed it into a fist, then pried the index finger loose and extended it, staring down at her out of his one good eye, a crooked yellow smile forming on that hideous face.

'I've come for what is mine, Chavi. I've come to make it right.'

Chavi. The same name he'd called her back on the carnival grounds. Back in the real world.

The girl who stole my soul.

Is that what he was here for now?

Was he the Devil incarnate? Some kind of demon who cuts the life force out of his victims only to leave them to wither away and die?

'Don't cry, my darling. The pain you feel will be mine for eternity.'

Then, wiping the blade on his sweater – a ratty blue pullover – he brought the knife down to her finger and—

—a voice shouted out from the distance—

'Hold it! Stop right there!'

Suddenly, the wind and leaves and the bending

trees disappeared and Anna opened her eyes to discover that she was back on the carnival grounds, only feet from the entrance to the house of mirrors, the man in the baseball cap still clutching her collar as—

—Deputies Worthington and Sanchez ran the length of the football field towards them, moving past the carousel, Worthington bringing his weapon up to fire—

'Stop! Let her go!'

—and Anna grabbed hold of his arm, twisting away from him, anticipating another shock—

—but he didn't resist this time, didn't bring the stunner down, because his attention was on the deputies. Instead, he turned, diving sideways towards the black doorway of the house of mirrors as—

—Anna grabbed for his ankle, managing only to get hold of his shoe. It came off in her hands as he disappeared into the darkness.

Tossing it aside, she scrambled to her feet, but the repeated shocks to her system had rendered her too weak to stand and her body betrayed her, legs buckling. She went down hard on her knees, pain shooting through them—

—but before she hit the ground, Worthington and Sanchez were there, grabbing her, carefully sitting her down.

'Are you okay?' Worthington asked.

Anna pointed towards the black doorway. 'In there. He's in there.'

'I know, I saw him.'

'There must be a back way out.'

Worthington rose and turned to Sanchez. 'You cover the front.'

But Sanchez wasn't listening to him, his attention now drawn to something off to the side of the house of mirrors:

A small, lifeless form in the dirt.

It looked to Anna like an oversized rag doll.

A bloody rag doll.

Sanchez quickly stepped over to it, his face churning in anguish as he approached.

'Sweet Jesus,' he said, then crossed himself.

'What? What is it?' Worthington was still trying to keep his attention centred on that black doorway, as if he expected the man in the baseball cap to come bursting out of it at any moment.

Sanchez said nothing, turning instead and moving away. He paused, then leaned forward and vomited into the dirt.

That was all the answer they needed.

And as Worthington finally turned, looking at the figure on the ground, Anna knew from the horror spreading across his face—

—that they had just found Kimberly Fairweather.

19

'Consider yourself toast, McBride.'

Royer stood at the rear doorway of the ambulance, a smug, self-satisfied smile on his face. Anna sat on a gurney inside, a paramedic applying ointment to the half-dozen burn marks on her neck.

They hurt like hell.

On the carnival grounds, sheriff's deputies and citizen volunteers were in the midst of an expanded search. This time for the man in the red baseball cap.

'I just got off the phone with the brass,' Royer said. 'They're recommending beach time, and possible termination.'

'What the hell for?'

'What the hell do you think? You haven't changed, McBride. Once a fuck-up, always a fuck-up.'

'You're blaming this on *me*?'

'You had the perpetrator in your hands and you let him get away.'

Anna gestured to the burn marks. 'In case you didn't notice, I wasn't exactly in control of the situation.'

'Maybe if you'd followed proper procedure you would've been. Face it, McBride, even your daddy won't get you out of this one.'

Anna stared at him. She was weak and tired and depressed and just wanted to cry. But she refused to show it. 'Does that make you feel good, telling me that?'

'You'd better believe it.'

'Then enjoy yourself while you can. Because when Internal Affairs comes calling, I'm sure they'll want to know why you were beating the crap out of an innocent man while your partner was up to her elbows in shit.'

Royer's smile faltered.

'Not to mention that there was a little girl being butchered less than two hundred yards away.'

Then it disappeared altogether.

'That's right, Teddy. There are a lot of different ways to spin this thing and, the way I see it, I'm not the only one on the hook here.' Now *Anna* smiled. 'Better pack your thermals. I hear the winters in South Dakota are brutal.'

Royer went through a round of face roulette before finally settling on a glare. Unable to come up with a clever retort, he resorted to an uninspired 'Bitch', then turned and walked away.

The paramedic, a fortyish blonde with world-weary eyes, said, 'I think you just lost him a few nights' sleep.'

'It won't last,' Anna told her. 'Third or fourth time he looks in a mirror, he'll be back to normal.'

The paramedic chuckled, then, finishing her work, gestured to the burn marks. 'You'll be in pain for a few hours, but I think you'll live.'

Happy day, Anna thought. She'd gladly accept a less promising prognosis if it meant Kimberly Fairweather was still alive.

Missing is always better than dead.

When her mother first passed away, Anna made up little scenarios in her head that she'd really been kidnapped by faeries, or had gone to Hollywood to be a movie star. It was okay for her mom to be gone, but not dead. Anything but dead.

And this morning Anna had almost joined her.

She couldn't believe how stupid she'd been, letting that freak get control of her so easily. She had to keep reminding herself that Kimberly had already been butchered by then. There was nothing she could have done to prevent what had happened to the poor girl.

But for some reason that thought didn't comfort Anna. This night, this morning, had gone from bad to truly devastating in a few short hours.

Watching the scene on the carnival grounds, she wondered if the man in the red baseball cap was watching, too. The house of mirrors had already been thoroughly searched, but there'd been no sign of him, not even a hint that he'd ever been inside. And what was most puzzling was that there had been no back doors, no escape routes.

So where the hell had he gone?

Anna couldn't tell you why, but she sensed he was still around. Out there somewhere. Waiting.

I've come for what is mine, Chavi.

I've come to make it right.

The image of Kimmie's body wouldn't leave her.

She was a mistake, he'd said. But what exactly did that mean? Was he feeling guilty? Remorseful?

Not a chance. Kimberly's murder was number four for the night. This asshole didn't make mistakes and he didn't feel a thing except blood lust. And just as he'd had no trouble bringing that stun gun down time after time, Anna knew he wouldn't hesitate to kill again.

She thought about her vision, the strongest one so far. Red Cap dragging her through the leaves into the centre of that clearing, bringing out that knife, crusted with dried blood.

She thought of the tattoo on the back of his neck: a wheel with missing spokes. Its significance was beyond her at the moment, but at least it was something. Some small clue they could cling to, to help them identify the sick fuck. She hadn't bothered to tell Worthington that she'd only seen it in her vision. That was one small detail he didn't need to know.

There was no doubt in Anna's mind now that she was meant to be here. The things she'd seen – no, *experienced* – so closely echoed what had happened to Kimberly that there could be no mistake that this was where she belonged.

But even if what she'd experienced was a premonition of some kind, an intimate preview of Red Cap's next victim, Anna wasn't sure she *wanted* to be here. The visions had begun to take their toll and every time she had one now, she felt just a little less stable, a little less in control. And how can you stop a mad man if you don't have control?

Anna felt the urge to cry again. *Let it all out*, her mother used to tell her.

After Mr Stinky was hit by that bus, she had cried and cried for . . .

Anna paused, her rapid-fire thought process screaming to a halt.

Mr Stinky?

'So, how are you holding up?'

Anna snapped out of her reverie and realized she'd been staring intently at her left hand.

It was trembling.

Looking up, she was surprised to find Daniel Pope standing in the same spot Royer had stood just a moment ago.

'What are you doing here?' she asked.

'Long story.'

'Where's Evan? Did social services come get him?'

She glanced around the grounds, hoping to hell the boy wasn't out there somewhere, where he might catch a glimpse of his sister in a body bag.

'There was a slight change of plans,' Pope said. 'But don't worry, he's fine. I took him to Jake's house.'

'Why there?'

'His wife Ronnie's a nurse. She's watching him until they get the whole social services thing worked out. We figured for the time being he's better off with a real family anyway.'

'I assume you know about Kimberly?'

Pope nodded.

'And Evan?'

'I haven't told him, but I have a feeling he already knows.'

'He seems like a pretty intuitive kid.'

'More than intuitive.'

There was weight to the statement and Anna frowned. 'What do you mean?'

Pope said nothing for a moment. He seemed to be searching for the proper approach.

'Neither of us was here when this all went down,' he said, 'but we might as well have been. I got the whole play by play from Evan. And this may be hard to believe, but I think he saved your life.'

Anna's frown deepened. 'I don't understand.'

'Why don't we go get some coffee.'

They went to the Hungry Spoon, a coffee shop in a strip mall about a block away from the school. The mall itself was relatively new, but the Spoon had been standing for decades, and looked it.

It was the high-school hangout, but at this time of the morning there were only a few local businessmen in attendance, drinking coffee and reading the paper before heading out to the office.

Pope had worked here as a busboy when he was a teenager. Except for the wait staff and the yellowing linoleum, the place hadn't changed. He remembered working Friday nights when Jake and their buddies were out getting high and chasing girls.

And then there was the shy school girl who regularly came in for a glass of milk and a slice of French apple pie. She always sat in the back booth, a pile of books around her, scribbling furiously in a notebook between bites.

He and Susan didn't get together until years later, but after they were married, she always joked that she had been stalking him, even back then.

The thought of that made him shudder.

But in his own way, wasn't he now stalking *her*?

He and McBride found a table away from the counter. They ordered coffee, and as McBride spoke to the waitress, Pope looked again at the scar on her face. The concealer she'd used had fallen victim to sweat and exertion, and the scar stood out in bas-relief, a thin pink blemish on otherwise flawless skin.

McBride, however, didn't seem at all self-conscious about it. Didn't seem to even realize it was there. But Pope wondered whose blade had cut her and, for reasons he couldn't explain, felt the sudden urge to punish the bastard.

'So,' McBride said, after the waitress had gone away. 'How exactly did Evan save my life?'

'He's the reason Jake and Sanchez were there. The reason they found you.'

'You'll have to explain that one.'

'Let me back up a little. I'm getting ahead of myself.' He wasn't quite sure how to start. He thought about it a moment, then said, 'I had a little trouble at the Oasis.'

'What kind of trouble?'

'Let's just say I had problems with some of the personnel, and leave it at that. The point is, I needed to get out of there, but the social worker hadn't shown up yet and I didn't want to leave Evan alone.'

'So you brought him here.'

He nodded. 'Evan was still out when I left, but when I got him to my car, he started talking in his sleep. He kept saying your name.'

She looked surprised. '*My* name?'

'It's Anna, right?'

She nodded. 'I know he likes me, but I didn't think I'd made *that* much of an impression.'

'Don't sell yourself short,' Pope said. 'But the thing is, I don't think he was dreaming.'

'What do you mean?'

'Keep in mind this was all happening while I was trying to get the hell out of there, and at first I thought he was having a nightmare, but in light of what's happened since, I'd say it was anything but. More of a hypnotic trance, actually. I was able to engage him in conversation.'

'And what did he say?'

Pope paused, wanting to get this right. '"He's watching her. He's watching Anna." And when I asked him who, he said, "The man in the red hat."'

McBride stiffened. 'Is this supposed to be funny?'

'Not particularly, no.'

She leaned towards him. 'You talked to Worthington. You know what happened.'

'Yes, but—'

'He told you about the man who attacked me.'

'Yes,' Pope said. 'But this is straight from Evan's mouth. *Before* the attack.'

155

She shook her head. Pope noticed she had lost some colour. 'All this really means is that it's coming back to him. This freak killed his family and he's remembering.'

'That's what I thought at first. But why would *you* be part of that memory? It doesn't make much sense.'

'He's confused, is all. Mixing things up.'

'I don't think so,' Pope said. 'And neither will you, once I'm finished.' He paused. 'You look a little pale. Are you okay?'

'I'm fine,' she said, but he sensed it was a lie. There seemed to be a quiet pulse of fear in her voice. She was conflicted and afraid, and hiding it about as well as she hid her scar.

The waitress came over with their coffee. McBride dumped cream and sugar into her cup, which surprised Pope. She didn't seem the cream and sugar type. And the way her hands were trembling, he thought she might want to forgo the caffeine altogether.

'Are you sure you're okay?'

She sighed then, leaning back. 'You caught me. I'm not even close to okay. I'm tired, I'm cranky, and I'm still trying to regain control of my body. And once we're done here, I may have to find a bed somewhere and lie down.' She took a sip of her coffee, grimaced. 'So go on. Let's get this over with.'

It was a nice little speech, but Pope thought she'd left a whole lot out. He sipped his own coffee, which was just as awful as he remembered. Then he said, 'When we got close to Ludlow, Evan had another seizure.'

McBride's eyes widened. 'What?'

'He's fine now. But here's the thing: it didn't seem like your typical grand mal.'

'Then what was it?'

'I'm not sure. But as soon as he came out of it, he started shouting. About you again: "He's hurting her. You have to stop him. He's hurting my Anna."'

McBride frowned. '*My* Anna?'

Pope nodded. 'He was pretty much on another planet when he said it, but those were his words. Then he told me that the man in the red hat was taking you to the house of mirrors.'

She stared at him a moment, then started to rise. 'Okay, that's it. I think I've about reached my bullshit quota for the day.'

Her protest seemed hollow, however, as if the believer was battling the sceptic inside her, and the believer was definitely winning.

She moved out from behind the table and stood, but Pope grabbed her wrist. Her tremors were more violent now.

'I know it sounds crazy,' he said, 'but I think the kid is psychic.'

'Let go of me.'

'That's how he knew where you were. When I called Jake and told him, he didn't believe a word of it, but he went looking for you anyway.'

'Let *go*,' she said, wrenching her arm free. He could see that her fear had compounded. Despite the air conditioner blasting down on them, she was starting to sweat.

'Look,' he said, 'I'm not trying to give you a hard time. I heard what I heard.'

'And maybe you're as confused as he is. I really don't need to be getting into this right now. I've had a pretty fucked-up night.'

'Just answer one question.'

'What?' She was sweating profusely now and seemed on the verge of a panic attack. Something was going on here that went well beyond the possibility of a psychic kid.

'Have you ever heard of someone called Chavi?'

McBride's face fell. '*What?*'

'He seemed to be talking to this person. "Chavi . . . Is it you, Chavi?"'

If she'd lost a little colour before, McBride lost it all now, saying, 'I have to get out of here. I have to go.'

And then she was across the room and out the door, Pope rising, fumbling for his wallet as he watched her. He dropped a few bills on the table and followed.

In just the short time they'd been in the Spoon, the heat outside – heat Pope had spent a lifetime in but had never gotten used to – had grown unbearable. McBride was working her way unsteadily across the strip mall's parking lot, headed back towards the high school.

He caught up to her, touching her shoulder, and she spun on him, wobbling slightly, her eyes filled with tears.

'Leave me alone.'

'What's going on?' Pope said. 'What's wrong?'

'I can't do this any more. It has to stop. I can't . . .'

And then she fainted. Dead away.

Part Two

OUT OF THE PAST

20

There were stars on the ceiling.

Anna saw them the moment she opened her eyes. The shades had been drawn and the room, while not quite dark, was dim enough for the stars to shine. They had been carefully painted in Day-Glo yellow against a dark-blue sky and were surrounded by multi-coloured planets.

Anna turned her head and took in the rest of the room. Posters on the wall: Kobe Bryant executing a perfect three-point toss, Homer Simpson munching on a doughnut.

The dresser held a TV/DVD combo unit with a stack of Disney movies next it. A gaming console. Glove and baseball. A collection of tiny action figures, lined up for battle.

Obviously a boy's room. But whose?

As soon as she sat up, Anna knew. On the night-stand next to the bed was a double-hinged picture frame, one side showing a photo of a freckle-faced boy on his dad's lap – Pope and his son, Benjamin.

The other side was blank.

Was she in Vegas? That didn't seem likely. The last thing she remembered was Pope getting in her face outside the coffee shop, the sun beating down on her so hard she thought she was going to pass out.

And she'd been crying. The events of the night, the visions, thoughts of her mother, the man in the red cap, the burns on her neck, Pope's insistence that Evan was psychic, her belief that *she* herself might be psychic – hell, the last few weeks of her sad, sorry life – had all been too much for her to bear. An enormous pile-up of physical and emotional freight that had caused a cave-in.

Overwhelmed was as good a word as any.

But the chances of Pope driving her forty miles to sin city were fairly remote, and this definitely wasn't a suite at the Oasis.

So, she was still in Ludlow. But where?

Hearing voices from another room, Anna got to her feet and discovered she wasn't wearing shoes. She found them at the foot of the bed, quickly slipped them on, then moved to the door and opened it a crack, peeking out.

Across a narrow hallway was a kitchen, bright sunlight streaming in through its windows. An attractive woman in her mid-thirties was framed by the kitchen doorway, talking to someone out of sight.

'Look at you,' she said. 'When's the last time you had a full night's sleep and a decent meal?'

'Don't start,' a voice told her.

Pope.

'We've been worried about you, Danny. Especially

162

Jake. You're so isolated out there. And living so close to the prison – that's just creepy.'

'Turns out I've been evicted,' Pope said. 'I won't be going back any time soon.'

'Good. We've got plenty of room here.'

'That might not be a good idea.'

'Why?'

'Take my word for it,' he told her.

'Because of your friend? Invite her to stay a while, too.'

A small laugh. 'We aren't exactly friends. I barely know her.'

'You wouldn't have gone to all the trouble of bringing her here if she didn't mean something to you. She could just as easily be lying in the back of an EMT wagon.'

'Somebody collapses in your arms, you tend to feel responsible for them.'

The woman smiled. 'Of course it doesn't hurt she looks like a supermodel.'

'Really? I hadn't noticed.'

'Oh, please. Just tell me this isn't another one of your conquests.'

'You don't think much of me, do you?'

'What's to think about?' the woman said. 'Back in high school, you would've come after *me* if Jake hadn't put a stop to it.'

'Good old Jake,' Pope said. 'Ruined it for everyone.'

They laughed. And while the laughter seemed a bit forced, even melancholy, there was a warm camaraderie between them that Anna envied. She had few friends and less family and spent most of her time on the job. She'd never been close to her father. After her mother died, she'd been cared for by a succession of nannies, some good, some bad, but none worth remembering.

She hadn't known Pope for more than a couple of hours, yet she knew he was a man who kept his pain private. But at least he had the option of sharing it with people who cared about him. Like this woman.

Anna didn't have that option.

She did, however, know where she was now.

Worthington's house.

Why they had a special room for Benjamin Pope wasn't quite clear.

As the woman and Pope continued to laugh, the woman's gaze shifted slightly. 'You still hungry, hon? You want another bowl of cereal?'

'No, thank you.'

Evan. Subdued yet polite.

'You want to go lie down again? I can put the TV on. Find some cartoons.'

'Is Kimmie coming here?'

The woman's smile froze on her face as Anna's gut tightened. They hadn't told him yet.

Why hadn't they told him?

Turning, she moved to the TV set on the dresser and quickly searched through the pile of movies. When she found the one she wanted, she stepped into the hall and a moment later was standing in the kitchen doorway.

'Hey, kiddo, look what I found.'

She held up a copy of *The Jungle Book*.

Three pairs of surprised eyes turned to her. Evan, who sat at a small dining table next to Pope, flew across the room, wrapping his arms around her waist – a move that both startled and pleased Anna.

She tousled his hair. 'Easy, hon, I'm a little banged up.'

'Did you find Kimmie?'

'We're gonna have to talk about that. But why don't we give good old Mowgli a spin first?'

Evan nodded. 'Okay. Will you watch with me?'

Anna exchanged looks with Pope and the woman, whom she could only assume was Worthington's wife. She gave Evan a squeeze.

'I wouldn't miss it for the world,' she said.

Most people in law enforcement would agree that the best way to break bad news to a family member is to simply come out and say it. But it's never easy. Never tidy. And reactions may vary, but they're never good.

Evan's was no exception.

They were sitting in the Worthingtons' living room, halfway through the movie, Evan's interest in Mowgli and the bare necessities waning, when she finally told him.

'Kimmie won't be coming home,' she said.

Evan looked up at her. 'Why not?'

'She's with your mommy.' Red Cap's words tumbled through her head. 'She's with the angels now.'

'No,' Evan said. 'I want her back. They have to come back.'

165

But he knew that wouldn't happen and he burst into tears, throwing himself against Anna, pressing his head into her chest. And she did her best to comfort him for the second time in the last several hours, murmuring softly that he'd be okay, that everything would be okay.

But it wouldn't be.

All these years later, Anna still lived with her pain. And while the worst of it had passed, a dull, persistent ache continued to plague her and she knew it always would.

She supposed the fact that Evan's father was still in the picture was some small consolation for the boy, but she didn't imagine Mr Rock-and-Roll's involvement in his life would ever amount to much.

Something she could relate to.

A couple of orphans was what they were. And as she glanced at Pope, who sat in an armchair across from them, she saw the face of yet another orphan.

What a sorry bunch they were.

What a sorry bunch indeed.

21

'I'll share my secrets, if you share yours,' Pope said.

Evan was asleep again, curled up next to Anna on the sofa. Worthington's wife – Ronnie – had run to the market despite Pope's insistence that they wouldn't be staying.

It may have been Anna's imagination, or simple intuition, but Pope seemed uneasy. The way he kept glancing out the front window, she wondered what kind of trouble he'd gotten himself into back at the Oasis.

'Secrets, huh?'

'Share and share alike,' Pope said.

'Then you won't mind telling me who you're running from.'

He raised his eyebrows. 'Am I that obvious?'

Anna shrugged. 'To trained eyes, I suppose.'

'Then let's just say I got on the wrong side of a wannabe bad boy with some very nasty friends.'

'Let me guess,' Anna said. 'Gambling debts?'

'Among other things. But the cops are already on to him and I made a promise that I wouldn't talk to anyone about it. Especially the FBI.'

'If it means anything to you, I'm about to be retired.'

'A promise is a promise,' Pope said.

'Just tell me this: are you expecting one of those friends to show up here?'

'That would be pretty stupid of them, but the sooner I get out of here, the better I'll feel.'

'So what's stopping you?'

Pope hesitated. 'Evan, for one. He's just lost everyone he has and I don't want him to feel abandoned.' He paused. 'Besides, it's not every day you stumble across a psychic kid.'

'You're still on that kick?'

Pope looked at her. 'I don't think you're as sceptical as you pretend to be. The way you reacted to the news, I've got a feeling there's a whole lot going on inside that brain that you'd just as soon not talk about. So maybe I'm not the only one who's on the run.'

Touché, Anna thought. And it struck her that perhaps Pope wasn't just some peripheral player in this drama. That he was as much a part of this thing – this cosmic plan – as she was.

But to what end?

'Do you believe in fate?' she asked.

Pope took a moment to answer. 'I guess certain things happen for a reason, but I also think we make our own fate. The universe gives us guidelines, and it's up to us to either follow them or discard them.'

'You've thought about this.'

'When your wife poisons your kid, then fries him in the family car, you tend to think about a lot of things.'

His bluntness caught her off-guard. 'Your son's name was Benjamin, right?'

Pope nodded.

'And that room you put me in. That was his?'

Another nod. 'Thanks to Susan, Ben spent a lot of his time in and out of hospitals. First in Vegas, then here in Ludlow. Jake and Ronnie wanted him to have a place to stay where he felt comfortable.'

'That's very generous of them.'

'They're generous people,' Pope said. 'But enough about that. It's your turn now.'

'For what?'

'We're sharing secrets, remember?'

Anna felt the internal wall go up, about to tell him that she hadn't agreed to anything.

Why was she so reluctant to talk about what was happening to her? Was she afraid he'd laugh? Call the loon patrol? Or was it simply a matter of conditioning? Maybe she'd spent too many years alone inside her own head, never sharing more than superficial thoughts and feelings, even with the handful of men who had flitted in and out of her life.

Pope was staring at her now, waiting. She'd never seen eyes so . . . unnerving. A gaze that was trying to reach beneath the surface.

But there was something about him. Something familiar. And maybe it would be in her best interest to trust him.

'Be careful what you ask for,' she said.

'I wouldn't ask if I didn't want to know.'

Feeling as if she were about to paddle straight for

the rapids on an increasingly dangerous river, Anna took a deep breath and said, 'I don't think Evan is the only one who's psychic.'

Pope listened intently as McBride laid it all out for him, everything she'd been going through these last few weeks. It came out of her in a rush, as if she were purging the data banks, her voice trembling sometimes, just as her hands had.

She spoke of strange visions, and a little girl in danger, and tattoos, and doubts about her sanity, and the growing belief that fate had brought her here to Ludlow, that what she was seeing in her mind, what she had experienced out on that football field, could well be a preview of things to come.

Pope tried to listen without judgement, the rational part of his brain wanting to dismiss it all, but he knew that this stuff was real. What he'd seen happen to Evan was neither illusion nor coincidence.

And maybe McBride was right. Maybe fate *did* have a hand in this. Maybe the universe was working in its own mysterious way to bring them all together. McBride, Pope, Evan, Jake and – yes – the man in the red hat.

When she finished, McBride looked both embarrassed and anxious. 'I don't suppose you believe a word I've just said.'

'Am I that hard to read?'

She paused, uncertainty in her eyes. 'Then you do believe me?'

'What can I say? I'm a big fan of the Twilight

Zone.' He smiled. 'The truth is, I've always straddled the fence when it comes to this kind of stuff, but fifteen minutes in the car with Evan was enough to convince me there's something to it.'

'Then maybe I'm *not* crazy.'

'Either that or we both are. But I'm willing to gamble. So tell me about the girl.'

'That's the thing,' McBride said. 'There's not much to tell. Until this morning, all I got were glimpses of her, and those always faded away so quickly I sometimes had to wonder if I'd seen them at all.'

'But this morning was different.'

She nodded. 'It was like *I* was there, this time. Inside her head. *I* was the girl.'

'And you didn't feel that way before?'

'No,' she said, then paused. 'I mean, I don't think so. I've never really remembered enough to know. Just enough to turn me into a flaming fruitcake.'

A sudden thought came to Pope. He looked at her scar, gestured to it. 'How long ago did that happen?'

McBride touched the side of her face. 'Why?'

'Indulge me.'

He could see that he'd provoked a memory she'd just as soon not dwell on. 'A little over a month ago.'

'How?'

'Is this really necessary?'

'I won't know until you tell me,' Pope said.

McBride sighed, then took a moment to gather her thoughts. 'I was attacked. My partner and I were working undercover in conjunction with the DEA, posing as buyers, in contact with a local narcotics distributor who was said to have ties with cartel out of Hong Kong.'

'This was in Victorville?'

She shook her head. 'Up in San Francisco. We spent months developing those contacts, and I stupidly came to trust someone I shouldn't have.'

'The story of my life,' Pope said.

'I was the lead agent on the case and was pretty full of myself, thought I could do no wrong. But when the bust came down, the person I'd trusted turned on me, and I didn't pull the trigger when I should have.'

'You considered him a friend.'

'Whatever that means,' she said. There was a bitter tinge to the words. 'But that's no excuse. Thanks to me, the perps escaped, my partner wound up with a bullet lodged in his spine and I got a three-day stint in the hospital.' She gestured to her face. 'And this.'

'I'm sorry,' Pope said.

'So am I. I fucked up and people got hurt.'

Pope shrugged. 'You're human. You made a mistake. Show me someone who hasn't.'

McBride looked at him, smiled. It was a weak one, but it looked good on her. 'You sound like a man who might be ready to move on.'

The notion surprised Pope, but maybe she was right. Could it be that all he really needed was a purpose?

'Let's get back to you,' he said. 'Besides the cut, how badly were you hurt?'

'A few bruises, and a pretty nasty concussion.'

'Were you out for any length of time?'

She nodded. 'Several hours.'

'And these visions. When did they start? Before or after the incident?'

'After. One of them woke me up in the hospital.'

Pope thought about this. 'I'm no expert,' he said, 'but I've heard that sometimes when people are victims of severe head trauma, certain doors can be opened.'

'Doors?'

'Doors that normally stay closed.'

'You think the concussion somehow linked me psychically to this little girl?'

'Based on what you've told me, the link may have been there already. All the concussion did was trigger the memories.'

McBride frowned. 'Memories?'

'You aren't psychic,' Pope said. 'What you're seeing is not something that's *about* to happen. It's something that already has.'

The frown deepened. 'What exactly are you telling me?'

'That the little girl in your visions is you.'

22

To Pope's surprise, the idea angered McBride.

'Are you saying that what I've been experiencing is some sort of repressed memory?'

'More or less,' he told her.

'That's absurd.'

'This whole subject is absurd, but we both know that something's going on here that defies rational thinking.'

'Then why do you seem to be looking for a rational explanation? I think I would've remembered if some fruitcake had kidnapped me. And not in bits and pieces.'

Pope held his hands up. 'Before you go getting a snake up your butt, calm down a minute and let me finish.'

'If this is the kind of bullshit you're shovelling, I'm not sure I want you to.'

Pope shook his head. 'You haven't even *heard* the bullshit yet.'

'Meaning?'

Pope sighed. This topic was fine for late-night poker games with psychopathic computer nerds, but this woman was truly hurting. She needed an explanation for what was happening to her and the one he was about to provide would undoubtedly provoke more questions than it answered.

But he ploughed ahead anyway. 'Have you ever heard of something called PLR?'

She thought about it a moment. 'Not that I remember. But maybe I've been blocking that out, too.'

He ignored the sarcasm. 'PLR stands for Past Life Regression. It's a form of hypnotherapy that explores memories of our previous lives.'

She flinched slightly, as if she'd just been pinched. '*Reincarnation*? That's what you're selling?'

'Look,' he said, 'I know how it sounds.'

'I'm not sure you do.'

'A couple minutes ago you were asking me about fate and telling me you think you might be psychic. Is the idea that our souls have been around for a few thousand years really that much of a stretch?'

She took another moment to think about that, allowing herself to calm down. Then she said, 'Maybe you have a point. But like I told you, I'm not a falafel and wholegrains kind of girl.'

'This isn't restricted to New Age whack jobs,' Pope said. 'Eastern religions teach it. I have colleagues who believe in reincarnation as fervently as some people believe Christ rose from the dead. There are highly educated psychiatrists who think past-life trauma may have a direct causal relationship to nightmares and anxiety attacks.'

'None of which tells me what *you* think.'

Pope saw no reason to lie to her. 'I've done a bit of past-life therapy in my time, but nothing that really swayed me one way or another.'

'So why push it now?'

'Because, based on what you've told me, it seems to fit. What you've described sounds more like memories than psychic visions.'

McBride shook her head. 'There's a flaw in your theory.'

'What?'

'If I'm tuning in on memories from some past life, how could the perp be the same guy? One creep in a red baseball cap is bad enough. But two? I don't think so.'

'How old are you?' Pope asked.

The question threw her. 'Twenty-eight. Why?'

'Twenty-eight years isn't all that long. Maybe you were born the moment that little girl died.'

McBride seemed stunned by this possibility, but remained unconvinced. 'So this guy kills me once, then tries again nearly three decades later?'

'Crazier things have happened.'

'But why?' she asked. 'Unless this is the mother of all coincidences, how would he even know who I am?'

'I don't know. But he called you Chavi, remember? "Is it you, Chavi?"'

'He was hallucinating.'

'That may well be, but it sounds to me like this Chavi person is the key to this little mystery. You and your attacker are somehow connected to her.' He nodded to the sleeping boy. 'Maybe Evan, too.'

McBride looked as if a long, dark shadow had just fallen across her grave.

'This is insane.'

'Maybe. But for whatever reason, he seems fixated on you. And unless we can stop him, I wouldn't be surprised if he tried . . .'

Pope paused, his gaze shifting to the view outside the living-room window.

Ronnie had just pulled up in the Worthington Suburban and was unloading a couple of plastic bags full of groceries. Beyond the truck, another car pulled up across the street.

A Lincoln Town Car.

Two large figures in the front seat.

The twin defenders.

'Shit!' Pope said, getting to his feet.

'What? What's wrong?'

'I underestimated the stupidity of those morons.'

McBride turned, saw the Town Car. 'Your friends from the Oasis?'

'The B-Team,' Pope said. 'Help Ronnie with those groceries, then get Evan, get to the truck and have her get you the hell out of here. And make it look natural. No need to tip our hand.'

'And what hand is that? Look, I'm a federal agent. I think I can—'

'You're in no condition to be playing tag with these assholes. Take care of Evan.'

'And what do you plan to do?'

'I don't know, but I don't want anybody else in the line of fire. So, hurry up.'

McBride glanced at Evan, weighing a decision, then quickly nodded and headed towards the door.

Jake's office was down the hallway. Pope went inside and moved around the desk to the painting that hung above the credenza. A Robert Knudson reproduction. *Sunrise at Zuni Mission.*

Pope took the painting off the wall and quickly dialled the combination to Jake's safe, hoping he hadn't changed it in the last couple of years.

It clicked open and he reached inside, pulling out the Glock 9 that Jake always kept there.

If you were raised in Ludlow, chances were pretty good that you knew your way around firearms. Pope's father, who had died of emphysema when Pope was barely out of his teens, was a former Army Staff Sergeant who had trained him well.

Pope checked the magazine, saw that it was full. When he got back to the living room, McBride, Evan, Ronnie and the truck were gone, leaving only the Town Car.

The twin defenders were watching the house. Waiting.

Pope kept out of sight. He needed to talk to them, but he knew they weren't here for conversation.

Cursing Anderson Troy – and himself for ever picking up a deck of cards – he headed towards the rear of the house.

*

He approached them from the rear driver's side, keeping the Glock raised in case he was spotted in the side mirror.

Before they knew what hit them, he threw open the rear passenger door, slid onto the seat and touched the muzzle of Jake's Glock to the back of Jonah's head.

'Easy now, I come in peace.'

Both Jonah and Joshua froze.

'Sure as hell don't feel that way,' Jonah said. 'Come on, Danny. Put the weapon down.'

'Unless you're here on a diplomatic mission, I don't think so. Get your hands on your head.'

They both did as they were told.

'What are you doing?' Joshua said. 'You ain't no Rambo.'

'You're right. I'm just a guy who wants to be left alone. Especially when I'm with family and friends. So tell Troy that he's got nothing to worry about. Half of what I know about him is forgotten and the rest is locked away forever.'

'We don't tell him what to do,' Jonah said.

'I'm not asking you to. Just pass along the message. Think you can manage that?'

'Won't do you a lick of good,' Joshua said. 'The man makes up his mind, it takes an act of Congress to change it.'

'Fine,' Pope told him, then gestured with the Glock. 'Give me your phone.'

'What for?'

'Just reach into your pocket – slowly – and hand it across.'

Joshua sighed, took his phone out and gave it to Pope. 'Sharkey's right. You *do* have a screw loose.'

'What's Troy's direct line?'

'Hit three.'

Pope smiled. 'Not one? He finds out, he won't be happy.'

'Fuck you,' Joshua said.

Pope thumbed the third keypad. The line rang twice in his ear, then clicked on.

'Is it done?'

Troy. Up close and personal. Pope wished he could reach through the phone and wring his neck.

'Sorry to disappoint you, Andy, but the boys and I have been having a discussion about how stubborn you are, and they thought I should give you a call.'

Troy was silent a moment and Pope knew he was seething. 'We're beyond disappointment, Daniel. I'm about ready to kill you myself.'

'You might want to reconsider,' Pope said. 'Because if you or any of your lackeys come near me again, I may have to remember all these things I've forgotten about you. And I'll be sure to do it in the presence of law enforcement.'

'You think I'm afraid of that redneck cousin of yours?'

'A couple hours ago, you were about to piss your pants over the FBI. You don't call these guys off, you'll be wearing a diaper twenty-four/seven.'

Troy chuckled, but there was no humour in it. 'This is a new side of you, Daniel.'

'No,' Pope said. 'Just the old one paying a visit. So are we clear about this? Or do I have to—'

The hand came out of nowhere, moving at hyper-speed. Joshua slammed a palm against Pope's face and sent the phone flying, a jolt of intense pain shooting through his skull.

Reaching across the seat, Joshua ripped the Glock out of Pope's hand, then jerked him around and pulled him into a choke hold, the massive arm squeezing against Pope's neck, cutting off his air.

'Uuhhhh,' Pope said, arms flailing, hammering against the offending chunk of ham as everything around him started to grow hazy. He couldn't believe how quickly the tables had turned. Jonah was right, he wasn't any Rambo, he was the goddamn comedy relief – only what was happening to him wasn't the least bit funny.

His blows were about as lethal as gnat bites and there was nothing he could do to stop the vice from tightening. The interior of the car grew dimmer and all he wanted to do was breathe, but that wasn't pos-sible right now and might never be again.

He twisted and turned anyway, trying desperately to shake himself loose, his heart pounding violently as darkness closed in on him.

Then suddenly, just as he thought he was going to pass out, the arm went slack and Pope felt Joshua's entire body go stiff.

'That's right,' a sharp voice said. 'Let him go.'

It was McBride. Anna McBride – the most beautiful

goddamn federal agent in the world. And Pope knew by the way that Joshua had stopped moving that she had a weapon pointed at him.

'I won't ask again. Let him go. And keep your hands where I can see them.'

Joshua hesitated, then did as he was told, and Pope collapsed to the floor between the seats, sucking in precious air, his throat on fire, his neck feeling like a deflated inner tube.

'You, over there,' McBride said. 'Put yours on the wheel, where I can see them.'

Pope heard movement up front and could only assume that Jonah had complied. Then a door opened.

'Okay now. Step outside, one at a time, then turn and face the car. You boys just bought yourselves a ticket to the Ludlow County jail.'

Thank God for small miracles, Pope thought.

And stubborn women.

23

Deputy Sanchez did the honours.

Anna watched as he guided the two handcuffed hulks into the back seat of his cruiser. They were barely able to squeeze in.

He and Worthington had showed up shortly after she'd ordered the two out of their car – a call from Ronnie, no doubt – and she had welcomed the back-up.

Ronnie, who had taken Evan down to a neighbour's house, was back now, trying her best to tend to Pope, who sat on a nearby kerb, holding a bag of ice to his neck.

He looked shaken, but thankful to be alive.

He caught Anna watching him and gave her a small nod. His eyes seemed darker and more intense than ever, and she thought she saw a hint of embarrassment there. But he wasn't trying to hide it, like most men would. Macho pride did not seem to be part of Daniel Pope's lexicon.

Which, of course, endeared him to her. Attracted her.

Jesus, she thought. Get a grip, Anna.

Everything that's happened in the last few hours and you're thinking about how appealing this guy is?

The human mind's ability to compartmentalize was nothing short of amazing. Nothing short of a *miracle*, in her case.

As Sanchez's squad car drove the two perps away, Worthington approached her. 'Looks like my sorry sack of a cousin owes you his life.'

'I guess that makes us even. If he hadn't called you this morning, I probably wouldn't be standing here.'

'Yeah, I'm still trying to figure that one out. I'm sure as hell not buying this whole psychic kid thing.'

'That's not the half of it,' Anna said.

'Oh? What else is he trying to sell you?'

'I'll let you know when I've finished processing it.'

'Fair enough,' Worthington said. 'He tell you what this new ruckus was all about?'

Anna shook her head. 'Some vague story about cops and crooks and gambling debts. It's all connected to the Oasis.'

Worthington rolled his eyes. 'Why am I not surprised? Knowing Danny, it'll probably take a loaded bong and crowbar to get the full story out of him.' He looked over at Pope and sighed. 'I just wish he'd quit pretending to be a fuck-up and get back into the real world.'

'I'm the last person to be judging anyone. But speaking of fuck-ups, is Royer still around?'

Worthington grinned, returning his gaze to her. 'I

told him the request for his help was rescinded. He seemed a little out of sorts when he left.'

'Does this mean you want me out of your hair, too?'

'The request was rescinded for *his* help, not yours.'

'Thanks,' Anna said. 'But just so you're up to speed, I'm about to be suspended.'

'Then I guess we'll just have to deputize you.'

Anna smiled. There was certainly something special about the Pope/Worthington DNA. 'Any progress on our perp?'

Worthington shook his head. 'He's a phantom as far as I can tell. The head carny says he's not one of theirs, and I don't think they're covering for the guy. I had them take that goddamn house of mirrors apart, piece by piece, and there's just no way he could've gotten out of there.'

'What about the shoe?'

'I've got a forensics guy looking at it, and those cigarette butts you told us about. They look like they could be a foreign brand. At some point I'd like to sit you down with a sketch artist, but I'm not feeling too hopeful right now.'

'Any luck with the tattoo?'

'That's the good news,' Worthington said.

'Oh? What did you find?'

He gestured to Pope, who was on his feet now. 'Let's get our wannabe fuck-up back inside, grab some lunch, then head into my office. I'm gonna need a computer for this.'

Anna nodded. 'Sounds like a plan.'

*

It was the best tuna-salad sandwich she'd ever tasted. Whipped up by Worthington and Pope, no less. A throwback to their stoner days.

'The secret is the capers and the red onion,' Worthington said. 'They give it bite.'

The two men worked together with an effortless rhythm that spoke of their affection for each other.

For the first time since she'd met the man, Anna saw a Pope from another era. And despite a lingering reticence, he seemed a bit more at ease now. At home. He was still fighting it, but it was a fight Anna didn't think he'd win.

She hadn't realized how hungry she was until she took that first bite. She quickly devoured one sandwich and asked for another and Worthington gladly obliged.

They allowed themselves only small talk as they ate, Worthington telling stories of their childhood in Ludlow. Pope's broken collarbone, caused by a skateboarding accident. The dime-store shoplifting incident that landed them both in jail until Worthington's father, the Ludlow County Sheriff, bailed them out. The secret field trip to Vegas when they were seventeen, complete with home-made IDs.

Somewhere in the middle of this, Ronnie, who had gone back to the neighbour's to fetch Evan, returned with the boy in tow.

Pope rose at the sight of him, his voice slightly hoarse. 'Hey, kiddo, I've got something for you in my backpack. Almost forgot about it.'

He disappeared for a moment, then came back

carrying the little black box with the miniature disco ball. He flipped the switch on top and the ball began to spin as he held the box out to Evan.

'I promised to give it to you, remember?'

Evan stared, but didn't reach for it. His eyes didn't light up. No hint of a smile. And Anna knew that a part of him had shut down and wouldn't start back up again for a long time. A very long time.

Apparently reaching the same conclusion, Pope hit the switch, bringing the ball to a stop, then set the box on the kitchen counter and tousled Evan's hair.

'It's here when you're ready for it, okay?'

'Okay,' Evan said.

A few minutes later, Anna, Pope and Worthington were gathered in the back office, Anna and Pope watching as Worthington returned his Glock to the safe, then flicked a switch on his computer monitor.

'When you told me about the tattoo,' he said to Anna, 'I was pretty sure I'd seen it somewhere before.' He dropped into his desk chair as the screen came to life, then opened up an Internet browser, typed in a URL. 'So I did a quick Google on my cruiser laptop and found this.'

A moment later a web page blossomed onscreen and at its centre was a familiar-looking graphic:

Anna's heart skipped.

'This is it,' she said. 'Except his tattoo was missing a couple of spokes.'

'So what is it?' Pope asked.

'The Roma chakra,' Worthington said.

'The what?'

'The symbol of the Romani people. They adopted it in the early seventies, but it's been around for decades. Based on an earlier Hindu version.'

'Pardon my ignorance, but who are the Romani people?'

'Gypsies,' Anna told him. 'Only I'm pretty sure they consider that a derogatory term.'

'That they do,' Worthington said. 'I found that out the hard way a few years ago when I busted a drifter for shoplifting. I made the mistake of calling her a gypsy and she almost bit off my nose. She was part of a Roma caravan camped just outside of town.' He nodded to the screen. 'And she had one of those tattooed on her forearm.'

Anna's heart skipped another beat.

'So then our guy's a gypsy?' Pope said.

'Based on Anna's description, it sure as hell sounds like it. We don't have any caravans on the radar right now, but I've got a call out to the Barstow and Vegas PDs to see if they've encountered any.'

'So what exactly does this thing signify?' Pope asked.

'It's a wagon wheel. Gypsies are nomads. Used to travel from town to town in wagons.' He paused. 'But it also represents the Roma soul.'

Anna's heart seemed to stop altogether now. 'The soul?'

He nodded to the screen. 'That's what it says.'

'How oddly appropriate,' Pope muttered.

Worthington looked at him. 'Meaning what?'

'Just a theory I've been working on. Agent McBride here can tell you all about it.'

But Anna was barely listening to them. Her mind had locked onto that one word, that single syllable that was like an icy wind rattling inside her chest.

Soul.

The girl who stole my soul.

Was that why there were spokes missing from Red Cap's tattoo? Did it represent a missing or broken soul?

Worthington seemed to be waiting for Anna to say something, but she wasn't quite ready to revisit Pope's claims of past lives and concussions and reawakened memories. What little sense any of this made to her at the moment did not fill her with warmth.

'I'm not sure it matters what this stands for,' she said. 'And right now I'm not feeling too optimistic about finding this guy.'

'Maybe you should be,' Pope said.

Anna turned. 'Why?'

'Because we both know he's killed before. And that simple fact could help us quite a bit.'

Worthington frowned at him. 'Do you two know something about this clown that I don't?'

Pope ignored the question, his gaze on Anna. 'We

189

can stop him. Before he comes after you again. And I think he will.'

'You don't know that,' she said.

'I'd put money on it. All we have to do is take a look at the previous killing. Dive in, get some details, then go from there.'

'And how do you plan on doing that?' she asked.

'I think you know,' Pope said, then raised a hand, giving her a Svengali-like finger-wave.

And there was no doubt in Anna's mind what he meant by this.

He wanted to hypnotize her.

24

'Would one of you mind telling me what the hell you're talking about?'

Pope turned to Jake, offering him a weak smile. 'Maybe you don't want to know.'

'Spill it, Danny. What kind of nonsense are you spewing *now*?'

The choice of words didn't surprise Pope. While he himself had always tried to keep an open mind, Jake was a rationalist and sceptic who believed only in what could be seen or experienced or explained. And if he *had* no explanation, he'd look for one based on evidence, not what he called voodoo speculation.

When they were kids, Jake had been the first to question the existence of the Easter Bunny and Santa Claus, just as he had later proclaimed – during a pot-fuelled soliloquy – that the story of Christ's crucifixion and resurrection was a long-standing and commonly told myth. A myth that had travelled from religion to religion, culture to culture, for centuries before Jesus was supposed to have been born.

'The only evidence that he ever existed is the

Bible,' Jake had said. 'And that's neither historical nor accurate, and was never really meant to be.'

'What about faith?' Pope had made the mistake of asking.

'Faith is nothing more than wishful thinking, based on conditioning, fear and the desire for a reward. Ask any kid if he believes in the Easter Bunny, he'll tell you with the greatest conviction that he does. It's the same for those who believe in religious deities. Or ghosts and goblins, for that matter.'

'I hope you realize,' Pope said, 'that you just insulted about ninety per cent of the world's population.'

Jake, who had just taken another hit of weed, exhaled a plume of smoke. 'So sue me. The truth isn't always pretty.'

Except for the switch from a pipe to a deputy's badge, Jake hadn't changed much since those days. To tell him now about McBride's visions and the theory that she'd been murdered in a previous life – by the same perpetrator no less – made about as much sense as telling him that Dorothy's adventures in Oz were based on true events. Especially after Pope had already sprung the Evan's-a-psychic story on the poor guy.

But the popcorn was already out of the box and Pope felt he had no choice but to offer him a full confession. So he laid it out for Jake, sparing him nothing, as Special Agent Anna McBride remained uncharacteristically mute.

When Pope was finished, Jake leaned back in his

chair and laughed. It was a smug, I-know-better-than-you laugh that set Pope's teeth on edge.

'What's so funny?'

'You remember when we were about fourteen and you were convinced that the old abandoned Smoke-house was haunted?'

'Of course I do.'

'You got a bunch of us together to spend the night there. Me, Tommy Walsh, Billy Kruger, Joey Shepherd. And while all you wimps were shitting your britches over some rustling noises, I took a closer look and found a family of cats living inside one of the walls.'

'This is different,' Pope said.

'Is it? The problem with you, Danny, is that you're always a little too quick to believe the unbelievable.'

'That's not true.'

'I know you've convinced yourself that you're a straight thinker, open to any possibility. But that's never really been the case, has it?'

Pope wondered if Jake was right. Had the fence he'd been straddling all these years been leaning slightly to one side? Even if that were true, did it really matter at this point?

'Are you telling me you have a rational explanation for any of what I've just told you?'

'No,' Jake said. 'But that doesn't mean there isn't one.'

'Well, until you find it—'

'What? We toss reason to the wind and waste time on some ridiculous fantasy?'

'You know what happened with Evan,' Pope said. 'You don't want to believe it, but everything he told me turned out to be true.'

'Pure coincidence, Cuz, and the sooner you see that the better off you'll—'

'Shut up, both of you.'

They turned, staring at McBride as she rose from her chair. Her face was pale again. She looked frightened, yet filled with a new sense of resolve.

'This is happening to *me*,' she said. 'Not you. So all that really matters is what *I* think. And even if this past-life regression thing is a complete bust, it's all we've got right now.'

She looked at Jake as if she was daring him to contradict her. When he said nothing, she turned to Pope. 'So now that that's settled, where do you want to do this thing?'

They adjourned to the living room.

The Worthingtons had a soft, leather recliner in there and Pope said he thought it would be the best place for Anna to relax.

She settled in, feeling a small nervous knot in her stomach. Even though she'd seen him at work and knew it was harmless, she felt as if she'd just climbed into the dentist's chair.

Deputy Worthington sank onto the sofa to observe, promising not to interfere, but making sure to let them both know that he'd be 'watching for the cats'.

I'm sure you will, Anna thought.

Bending down next to her, Pope pulled the lever on the side of the recliner, pushing her back until she was nearly lying down.

She waited silently, hearing the faint sound of a television – Evan and Ronnie watching cartoons in the den – as Pope went around the room, closing the blinds to dim the light.

He carried himself with the subtle authority of a man who was completely within his element, like a practised and confident lover, so skilled in the art of seduction that the moves were second nature to him.

As he slid a footstool over and sat next to her, Anna couldn't help feeling that attraction again. And despite her better judgement, all she could think was that she wanted him to touch her. She didn't care how. She just wanted to feel his hands against her flesh.

A moment later she got her wish. It was a simple gesture, his fingertips touching the back of her forearm as he said softly, 'Okay. All I'm going to do is help you to relax.'

The warmth emanating from those fingertips, the electricity they generated, did something to Anna that was difficult to describe. She couldn't tell you why, but she felt immediately and completely under his power. It was as if that touch – dare she say it?—

—was the touch of a soulmate.

And in that moment, any trepidation she'd felt, any uncertainty, immediately dissolved.

She knew she was being silly. This man was almost a complete stranger to her and this was neither the time nor the place to be thinking such things, but Anna couldn't help herself. If Pope were to lean forward at this very moment and tell her to remove her clothes, she knew that despite Worthington's presence and the sound of that television in another room, she'd gladly oblige.

Fortunately, Pope had other ideas.

'Close your eyes,' he said softly.

There was a quality to his voice now that she hadn't noticed before. The hoarseness was gone, replaced by a kind of amorphous sensuality. And as he spoke, he seemed to be both *inside* and outside of her head.

Anna closed her eyes as Pope continued to speak, letting the words caress her, envelop her.

'Take a deep breath,' he said. 'Fill your lungs, then let the air out slowly.'

She did as she was told, letting her body relax as she exhaled.

'I'm going to count backwards from ten,' Pope continued. 'And as I do, you'll feel yourself falling, very slowly, into a state of complete relaxation.'

He began to count, pausing after each number.

'Ten . . . nine . . . eight . . .'

Anna felt as if her chair was dissolving beneath her. Then she was falling – floating really – a leisurely descent into the darkness of a long, black corridor, as Pope's voice continued its caress.

'Seven . . . six . . .'

He had told her earlier that, under hypnosis, the subject is always aware of her surroundings, is still conscious to some degree, but Anna couldn't be sure that this was true. With each number he spoke, she felt as if she were floating further and further away from the real world.

'Five . . . four . . . three . . .'

When he finished counting, the words he said were little more than vague abstractions, formless murmurs that surrounded her in the darkness. She *sensed* more than she actually heard, as if his words, his voice, were part of her own consciousness.

A part of her being.

Then the darkness itself began to envelop her, seeping into her skin until she was little more than vapour, and she felt as if she were floating backwards in time, drifting deeper into her memories as fleeting images of the past filled her head:

Her arrival in Victorville, the fiasco in San Francisco, her graduation at Quantico, a college love affair, the boarding schools, her mother's funeral, her mother's goodnight kiss . . .

Her entire life played on her own private movie screen, the memories vivid. Alive.

All along the way she sensed that Pope's voice was guiding her, asking her questions. And while she was aware that she was responding, wanting somehow to please him, she couldn't quite tell you what her answers were.

And before she knew it, she was in a small dark place, the sound of a beating heart in her ears. A liquid sound, a warm, comforting thrum that seemed in perfect synchronization with her own heartbeat.

Then she felt herself fading away, only faint tendrils of the vapour remaining. The vapour that was once Anna McBride.

And in the dark distance came another sound. The sound of a ringing bell.

A school bell?

Anna felt herself being pulled towards that sound.

And a moment later, she was gone.

25

When the bell rang, Jillian Carpenter's stomach went sour. She didn't want to go home.

She never wanted to go home these days.

'I hate him,' she'd told Suzie during recess.

'Why?' Suzie asked. 'You said he's nice to you. What's the big deal?'

'He's always hogging the TV. Last night, I wanted to watch *Gimme a Break!*, but my mom let him watch *The Fall Guy* instead. She says we have to share now.'

'*Gimme a Break!* was a rerun.'

'So?' Jillian said. 'It's our TV, not his.'

But that wasn't quite true. It *was* his TV now. Craig Winterbaum was part of their family, whether Jillian liked it or not.

And she definitely did not.

Mom had met Craig at a garden show down in Fullerton last year, and before Jillian knew it, they were dating full-time. Then, about a month ago, he'd asked Mom to marry him and, to Jillian's everlasting dismay, she'd said yes.

The wedding came less than two weeks later. They had decided to jump right in, Mom had told her, and got married at the courthouse, in front of a judge. Jillian had watched the whole sickening thing, her stomach feeling more sour than ever as Craig slipped a gold band onto Mom's finger.

The thing was, she and Mom were a team. That's what Mom had always said. Ever since her dad left, when Jillian was six, it had been just the two of them. And even though she missed her dad sometimes, the last four years had been just fine with her.

Until Craig came along.

Jillian had stayed with her Aunt Maggie while he and Mom went on a honeymoon in Las Vegas. Now they were all back home, their first official week as a new family, and Mom and Craig kept getting all kissy-face on the sofa while Jillian tried to watch TV.

Ugh.

'Jillian?'

Jillian snapped out of her daydream. Mrs Gann was standing over by the blackboard, staring at her.

'Yes, ma'am?'

'The bell rang, dear. Did you need something?'

Jillian looked around the room and felt her face get hot. All the other kids were gone.

She did that sometimes. Got so caught up in her own thoughts that she didn't know what was going on around her.

'No,' she said, then quickly gathered up her books

and papers, stuffed them into her desk cubby and shuffled out of the room. 'Bye, Mrs Gann.'

'See you tomorrow, dear.'

Suzie had saved her a spot in the bus line. Jillian and Suzie had been best friends ever since kindergarten, when Suzie's family moved in next door to Jillian's. That was back before the divorce, when she and her mom and dad were living on Randall Street.

When they sold the house, Jillian had been afraid she'd have to move too far away and go to another school, but they got lucky and found an apartment close by. Jillian was relieved, because she couldn't imagine having to go to another school and make new friends and all that. And she couldn't imagine being without Suzie.

Suzie said, 'So did you ask?'

'Ask what?'

'About Big Mountain, dumbo.'

Big Mountain was the new amusement park that had opened up over in Allenwood, which was about a half-hour drive away. Right before they got married, Mom and Craig had taken her and Suzie to opening day, and Suzie couldn't stop talking about it.

'I forgot,' Jillian said.

'Forgot? How could you forget? Your birthday's only two weeks from Saturday.'

Suzie was dying to celebrate Jillian's eleventh birthday with another trip to Big Mountain, but the truth was, Jillian wasn't all that excited about the idea.

She'd had fun, sure, but not *that* much fun, and there was something about the place that had given her the creeps.

First off, Big Mountain wasn't all that big. Northgate shopping mall was bigger and even had a McDonald's. Second, it was supposed to be brand-new and everything, but Craig told them that all Big Mountain had really done was buy a bunch of old rides and stuff from a park that closed up in Oregon somewhere, then slap some new paint on them and add a big plaster mountain with a tunnel in it, so that sky cars could go through.

And Craig should know, because he worked for the company that owned Big Mountain.

'Are you sure it's safe?' Jillian's mom had asked.

'We're not looking for a lawsuit,' Craig said. 'They test those rides like crazy before they let anyone get on them.'

And that was the other reason Jillian wasn't so thrilled about Big Mountain. If Craig Winterbaum worked for the company that owned the place, how good could it really be?

'Promise me you'll ask tonight,' Suzie said.

Jillian didn't want to, but she didn't want to disappoint Suzie either, who was not only her best friend but practically her *only* friend – and vice versa. So she nodded reluctantly. She was about to say 'Promise' when the whistle blew and all the kids started piling onto the buses.

It was almost their turn when Jillian had a sudden inspiration. Anything to keep from going straight home. Craig had taken a day off from work and he and Mom were probably on the sofa right now, going at it.

'You wanna walk today?'

'Huh?' Suzie said.

'I got car-sick yesterday. I feel like walking.'

Suzie looked around, then shrugged. 'Okay.'

They quickly got out of line.

The bus ride home usually took about ten minutes, but walking was a different story. Carl's Liquor Store was on the corner of Crestwood and Mill, and whenever they walked, Jillian and Suzie usually stopped there for Pixy Stix.

Jillian's favourite flavour was lime, but they were out today and she had to settle for grape. It didn't hit the spot like lime did, but it was better than nothing.

They were coming out of the store, Suzie still blathering on about Big Mountain, when Jillian noticed the car.

It was an old thing, kinda funky-looking, and she was sure it was the same car she'd seen parked outside of school a couple of times.

And on her street the other night.

She had been getting ready for bed when she noticed it. Just happened to look out her bathroom window and saw it parked below. There was someone sitting inside, but it was too dark to make him out, and all she could see was an arm dangling out of the driver's window, cigarette in hand.

For a moment Jillian had thought it might be her dad, because he had always smoked cigarettes, but then that didn't make much sense. Dad had moved to Idaho with his new girlfriend four years ago and didn't seem all that interested in staying in contact with her. So why would he be parked outside her apartment building?

But whoever it was, Jillian got the sense that he was watching her. And she didn't like it. It made her feel kinda crawly, like she had spiders inside her blood.

So she made sure that both the window and her curtains were shut, even used a clothes pin to seal the gap between the curtains, then promptly tossed off her school uniform and climbed into the shower.

She knew she should have told her mom about the car, but she hadn't. Every time she thought about it, Craig had been there. Craig was always there.

Now here the car was again. Parked outside Carl's Liquor Store.

But why? Did the driver live in the neighbourhood?

'That's it,' she said to Suzie. 'That's the car I told you about.'

Suzie looked at it. 'The Rambler?'

'Is that what it's called?'

Suzie nodded. 'My uncle has one just like it. He collects old cars.'

'Does he live around here?'

'He lives in New Jersey, dumbo. You know that.'

'I thought maybe he moved or something,' Jillian said. 'Who do you think it belongs to?'

'Probably some hobo. Come on, let's go.'

But Jillian wasn't ready to go yet. Curious, she started towards the car.

'What are you doing?' Suzie asked, sounding a little nervous.

'I wanna look inside.'

'What?' She sounded alarmed now.

'Just a quick look,' Jillian said. 'I'm not gonna get in or anything.'

'What if somebody catches you?'

'I'll tell him we thought it was your uncle's car.'

Moving up to the driver's window, she took a look inside. The seats had rips in them and the ashtray was hanging open, overflowing with funny-looking cigarette butts. Jillian had never seen yellow cigarettes before.

Then she noticed a crumpled pack lying on the passenger's seat. It had some kind of foreign language written on it.

There was a locket dangling from the rear-view mirror. It looked like it was open, but the reflection from the window made it kinda hard to see, so Jillian bent down a little to get a different angle.

Inside was a photograph. A really old one, from the looks of it. A faded black and white. Jillian had seen pictures like it in her history book, from back when cameras were first invented and everybody stared into them like they were possessed by the Devil or something.

The girl in the photograph looked that way, too. Was probably about fifteen or sixteen with curly black hair and really big dark eyes. Her skin looked brown, like she'd spent a lot of time in the sun, and she had a shawl on her head.

She was probably one of the most beautiful girls Jillian had ever seen. And there was something *familiar* about her. Like maybe she was somebody Jillian had known once.

The girl looked like a gypsy. At least the gypsies Jillian had seen in the movies. And Jillian wondered if she was the driver's great-grandma or some other relative, long dead, because if she was still alive, she was bound to be as wrinkly as a sun-dried fig.

Jillian squinted at the photo a moment longer, then stood upright and moved to the rear passenger window. Nothing in the back seat or on the floor except for a crumpled McDonald's bag, which looked like it had been there for weeks. Jillian was about to move on when her attention was drawn to a familiar sight in the back windshield.

That was weird.

Down in the bottom right corner was a Big Mountain parking sticker. One that said: EMPLOYEE.

Craig had one on his car, too. So whoever was driving this old heap worked for the same company that Craig did.

Jillian suddenly got an oogy feeling. Could the driver of the car be Craig himself? She'd never seen him with a cigarette, but that didn't mean he wasn't a smoker.

But why would he be driving this old hunk of junk? And how could he have been in the car sitting outside her bathroom window when she knew very well that he'd been in the living room with Mom?

No, somebody else drove this car, somebody that worked with Craig.

And then a sudden thought occurred to Jillian.

Could Craig have hired someone to follow her? To watch her? To maybe even . . .

No, that was crazy.

Or was it?

What if Craig wanted Mom all to himself, wanted *them* to be a team, so he could spend night after night on the sofa with her, watching *The Fall Guy* or whatever crummy TV show he felt like watching. Wouldn't it be nice not to have Jillian around to make a stink about it?

She *knew* there was a reason not to like the guy. Him with his happy smiles and free passes to Big Mountain. Maybe that's why the place had made her feel so creepy. Maybe whoever he'd hired had been watching her even then.

She tried to think back to the night they'd gone there, trying to remember when she'd first gotten that feeling. Mom and the TV hog were off doing their own thing, while Jillian and Suzie rode the Log Jammer and the Big Mountain Express and just about any other ride they could get on. Craig had given them VIP passes, so they were always able to go to the front of the line without having to have a wheelchair or a cane.

By the time they'd gotten off their fifth or sixth ride, they had decided to get some cotton candy and sit down for while. They found a bench across from the Miner's Magic Mirror Maze, and that, she realized, was when she'd gotten the feeling. The creepy feeling that someone was watching her. Someone inside.

Could it have been the guy from the Rambler?

'Come on, Jillian, let's *go*,' Suzie said. 'Somebody's gonna come.'

Suddenly feeling creepier than she'd ever felt before, Jillian decided that her friend was right. It was time to go, and they'd better go right now. She turned and headed back towards Suzie, grabbing Suzie's hand when she reached her.

She wanted to tell Mom about Craig and the Rambler, and about how she thought he might be trying to kill her. And the sooner she did, the better she'd feel.

'Race you home,' she said to Suzie, then they broke away from each other and ran.

26

'This is ridiculous,' Jake said.

Pope turned sharply. 'You promised not to interrupt.'

'Come on, Danny, are you really falling for this nonsense?'

Pope looked at McBride, but she hadn't stirred. Although she had been responding to his questions clearly and without hesitation, there seemed to be a part of her that wasn't even aware he was asking them. In fact, she was so deep into her trance, so immersed in the world of this little girl, that he thought it might be tough to bring her out again.

'I just told her partner to take a hike,' Jake continued. 'Maybe it's time I suggest she do the same thing. You hear me, McBride?'

'Knock it off, Jake.'

'Who does she think she's kidding? A mysterious car? A gypsy girl? Another goddamn house of mirrors? She's making this stuff up as she goes—'

'Stop,' Pope said.

And to his surprise, Jake did.

They sat in silence a moment. And in that moment Pope realized that Jake looked a little rattled. Maybe the rock-solid foundation he'd been standing on all of his life was starting to show a few hairline cracks.

'I've been doing this a long time,' Pope said, 'and I've seen my share of phoneys. Believe me, she's not faking it.'

'And you know that how?'

'Instinct and experience.'

Jake shook his head. 'You may be good at what you do, Danny, but you've always been too quick to trust people.'

He was right, of course. One of the people Pope had trusted was sitting in jail right now. But that didn't mean McBride was some kind of con artist. Pope knew, without even the slightest hint of uncertainty, that what she had described to them was no fantasy.

They were beyond recall and imagination now. Way beyond. And despite his cousin's yearly subscription to Naysayers R Us, Pope was pretty sure Jake knew it, too.

'You're fighting this too much. Like you're afraid Santa Claus might exist after all.'

'Ho, ho, ho,' Jake said, rising from the sofa. And Pope could see that he wasn't about to give up without a fight. 'Your new girlfriend is either seriously screwed up, or she's playing with our heads something fierce.'

'You don't believe that,' Pope said.

'No? I can sure put it to the test.'

'How?'

'While you kids continue your little charade, I'm going to my office to do some real police work. Feed Jillian Carpenter into the system, see if I get any hits.' He started for the hallway. 'Ten to one, I come up empty.'

'I'll take that bet.'

When Jake was gone, Pope returned his attention to McBride. The interruption hadn't fazed her. Not in the slightest. And he wondered how much deeper she might go.

Touching her arm, he said, 'Talk to me, Jillian. Tell me where you are.'

They ran out of steam near Mercer Street, laughing and out of breath. With each block they'd run, Jillian had started to feel a little better about things, thinking she may have gotten all worked up over nothing.

It wasn't like Craig was a bad guy. Not really. At least not bad enough to want to kill her. All he was interested in doing was hanging around with Mom – and who could blame him? She was pretty cool.

And who cared if that old car was parked outside Carl's? Who cared if it had a sticker from Big Mountain? There were probably a lot of Big Mountain people who lived in the area. They had to live somewhere. And just because she'd seen the car more than once didn't mean anybody was following her.

Did it?

She and Suzie took their usual shortcut through

the alley behind the Mercer Street Laundromat. They were halfway through it when Jillian said, 'Do you think Craig would ever try to hurt me?'

Suzie spun around, walking backwards in front of Jillian. She was working on another Pixy Stick. Cherry. 'I dunno. I don't think so. Why?'

Jillian shook her head. 'I'm just being stupid.'

'Has he ever tried?'

'No. He's always nice. Too nice.'

Suzie tilted the Pixy Stick, tapped cherry powder into her mouth, then swallowed. 'Then I don't know what you're getting all freaked out about. Besides, anybody who can get us free tickets to Big Mountain can't be all . . .'

Suzie stopped in her tracks, looking past Jillian's shoulder, her eyes going wide.

'What?' Jillian said and turned.

Her stomach dropped as she looked towards the mouth of the alley.

The Rambler was turning in, moving towards them. Slowly. The reflection of the sun on the windshield made it impossible to see the driver's face, but Jillian could tell that he was wearing a baseball cap. A red baseball cap.

And she knew, instinctively, that this was no accident. He was here for her.

Turning, she grabbed Suzie's arm. 'Run,' she said, and the two took off, hauling it towards the end of the alley.

The car's engine revved behind them – he was

picking up speed – and Jillian poured it on herself, trying to keep hold of Suzie's arm.

'Come on!' she shouted. 'Don't slow down!'

But Suzie was breathing really hard now, sobbing, and Jillian could feel her starting to fall behind.

The car's engine grew louder and Jillian wanted to turn and look, to see how close he was, but she didn't dare, because she knew that would only slow her down.

Then she lost her grip on Suzie's arm and had no choice but to look. The car was directly behind them now, Suzie stumbling in front of it, tears streaming down her face.

'Help me,' she shouted. 'Help me!'

But it was too late, the car revved and picked up speed, its bumper hitting Suzie, knocking her back and over the hood of the car and into a row of metal garbage cans—

—and suddenly Mr Stinky and his encounter with the bus came to Jillian's mind—

—but Jillian didn't have time to be thinking about such things, because the car was bearing down on her now. And just as it reached her, she grunted and dove to her left, straight into a pile of discarded cardboard boxes—

—as the car roared past her and squealed around the corner.

The boxes went flying as Jillian ploughed through them, landing hard on the ground beneath them, the impact knocking the wind out of her – what little wind she had left.

She lay there for a moment, trying to breathe, trying to figure out what had just happened, when she heard a soft moan coming from the trash cans behind her.

Suzie.

Dragging herself to her feet, Jillian saw that most of the cans were lying out in the middle of the alley now, but Suzie was crumpled up against a wall.

Jillian staggered over to her, knelt beside her. She was alive, but her nose was bloody and one of her legs was twisted funny.

'It hurts,' Suzie said.

'I have to go get help.'

'No. Don't leave me here. He might come back.'

'I have to. You can't walk like this.'

'It's all your fault. You shouldn't've been looking in his car.'

'I'm sorry,' Jillian said. 'I'm sorry.'

But she knew that looking in that car had nothing to do with the attack. She had been right all along. Maybe not the part about Craig – that was just stupid – but she knew that the man in the baseball cap had been following her. Watching her. Ever since they sat outside that house of mirrors.

What she didn't know was *why*.

And for some reason the photo from the locket came into her head. The gypsy girl with her big brown eyes.

Who was she? What made her special to him?

Suzie's face was streaked with blood and tears. 'How am I gonna go to Big Mountain like this?'

'Will you shut up about Big Mountain already?'

'You don't have to yell.'

'I *hate* that place,' Jillian said. 'I hope they close it down and burn it to the ground. I don't care if I never go there a—'

Suzie's eyes went wide again and Jillian froze.

Someone was behind her.

Suddenly an arm wrapped around her – that same arm she'd seen dangling from the Rambler's window – as a hand came up to her face carrying a damp, greasy rag. It covered her mouth and nose, and before Jillian even had a chance to resist, she sucked in a deep, frightened breath—

—and everything went black.

27

'Jillian?'

McBride didn't stir. Was so still, in fact, that Pope wondered if she was breathing.

He touched her wrist, feeling for a pulse.

The beat was there, but erratic. Should he bring her out?

'Jillian, talk to me. Tell me what's happening.'

Still no response.

'Jillian, can you hear me?'

Nothing.

What was going on inside there? Why wouldn't she respond? He'd never seen anything like this before.

'Anna, it's Pope. Listen to me. I'm going to start counting again. And when I get to ten, I want you to open your eyes and—'

McBride's eyes flew open. 'He has me in his car.'

She was trembling. Frightened.

Pope thought she might have spontaneously emerged from her trance, but quickly realized that she was still under. He waved a hand in front of her face, but she didn't react, blind to the real world.

'I'm in his car,' she repeated.

'Where, Jillian? Where is he taking you?'

'I–I don't know, I . . . He put tape on me. On my mouth and my hands and feet. He's going to hurt me. I know he's going to hurt me.'

'Don't worry, I won't let him. Look around. Tell me what you see.'

McBride's head turned, her eyes searching blankly.

'The shadows. Tree shadows. He's taking me into the . . . no, wait. I've seen this place before. I've been here. It's a park. We used to bring Mr Stinky here.'

'Who?'

'My dog. He died when I was . . .' She stiffened. 'Oh, God, he's stopping the car.'

'It's all right,' Pope said. 'Tell me what you see. Tell me everything you see.'

'I want my mom. Please call my mom.'

'Easy, Jillian, it's okay.'

'He's opening my door now. Please. You have to make him stop.'

Pope got to his feet and stood over her. He'd let this go on too long.

'Anna, listen to me carefully. It's time to let Jillian go.'

'You have to stop him! Somebody has to stop him.'

'Anna, I need you to listen to me.'

But McBride was oblivious to him. 'He's pulling me out of the car, he's got the shovel now!' She started thrashing in the chair, as if fighting off an invisible force. 'Help me! You have to help me!'

Pope took her by the shoulders. 'Anna, it's me, it's Pope. You need to let her go. Let her go now. I'm going to start counting from one to—'

'He's dragging me into the middle of the park!' Anna shouted. 'He's got a suitcase with him. He's pulling something . . . Mommy! Mommy, help me! He has a knife! He's going to—'

'*What are you doing to her?*'

The voice was shrill, angry.

Startled, Pope spun around, surprised to see Evan standing stiffly at the mouth of the hallway. He was staring straight at them, but only the whites of his eyes were showing.

'*What are you doing to my Anna?*'

But the voice coming out of him was not his. It was older. More mature.

A woman?

'He's hurting me!' Anna shouted. 'He's got his knife out and he's cutting me! He's cutting my finger!'

Evan moved towards them. 'Don't you see what you've done, you fool? You've opened a door. You have to bring her back. Bring her back now!'

Pope looked from one to the other, feeling as if his mind were about to astral-project straight out of his body. This had to be the most surreal moment he had ever experienced in his thirty-eight years of life.

'Wake her up,' Evan shouted. 'Before it's too late!'

There was noise from the back of the house and Ronnie came running, followed by Jake, both of them exchanging looks with Pope, their faces stretched in alarm.

Worthington stared at Evan in utter disbelief. 'What the hell is going on?'

'Anna, wake up!' Evan shouted. 'You have to come back!'

But Anna kept thrashing, crying out in pain. 'He's hurting me. Make him stop!'

And suddenly Evan was at her side, his blank white eyes staring at her as he grabbed her hand, trying to calm her. 'It's me, darling. It's Mama. Listen to me carefully. You have to come back to me now. Let go of the past and come back.'

But Anna didn't respond. Was still thrashing uncontrollably. She began to grunt as if she were being struck by blows.

Knife blows?

She continued to thrash, crying out in pain. And then, to Pope's horror, she fell still in the chair and the light in her eyes began to grow dim.

Oh, good Christ, he thought, she's dying.

But how could that be? This was nothing more than a hypnotic trance. People don't *die* under hypnosis.

Evan kept talking to her. Almost cooing, now. 'Come back, Anna. Come back to Mommy.'

But she didn't respond.

'Anna, let the little girl go and come back to me. You need to come back.'

When she failed to respond again, Evan did something so unexpected that Pope had to wonder if this was simply a bizarre, twisted dream.

He began to sing, in a low, sweet voice:

> *Every little star*
> *Way up in the sky*
> *Calls me*

And to Pope's surprise, Anna stirred. She could hear him.

> *Heaven in my heart*
> *Wishing I could fly*
> *Away*

Anna jerked her head in Evan's direction. 'Momma?'

> *Drift off to sleep*
> *Into a dream*

'Momma, is it you?'

> *My soul to keep*
> *I do believe . . .*

And then, suddenly, Anna blinked and her eyes came into focus, staring at Evan as if he were a long-lost friend. Tears began to flow as she pulled him into her arms, hugging him furiously.

She was back. A little worse for wear, but present in the room.

'Oh, God,' she said. 'I've missed you so much.'

She released him and Evan smiled, squeezing her hand, stroking her cheek. 'I know, sweetheart. I've missed you, too. And I love you, darling. You'll always be my little star. Always.'

Then he collapsed to the floor.

28

Ed 'Sharkey' O'Donnell was worried.

Two years of his life. Two years spent working deep undercover on a case that involved racketeering, gambling fraud, murder and a string of bribes that stretched all the way to his own department – and some dip-shit hypnotist was about to bring it all crashing down.

The first time Sharkey saw Pope outside of a TV screen was downstairs in the VIP poker room. Pope had a short stack, a bad hand and seemed wilfully determined to lose everything he owned.

But thanks to an impromptu bit of heroism on Pope's part that night – performing the Heimlich manoeuvre when Troy started choking on his personal pizza – Troy had taken a liking to the guy. So much so that he'd fronted Pope just enough cash to keep him from signing over the house he'd closed up and left for dead.

Not only was Troy grateful that he could continue his life of crime, but he felt sorry for Pope, or so he claimed. But Sharkey suspected his attraction to the guy had more to do with Pope's celebrity than any-thing else.

Earlier in the year the 'Little Ben' kidnapping case (as the reporters had dubbed it) had dominated the media for weeks. When Troy wasn't cruising the Inter-net or downstairs playing poker, his attention was fixed on the sixty-inch plasma in his game room, where news of the snatch, the murder and the subsequent trial played endlessly.

If you were good with a remote and timed it just right, you'd get wall-to-wall coverage. The police, the pundits, the overly serious talk-show hosts, all dining on the Pope family corpse.

Sharkey, like most in law enforcement, assumed the kid was dead long before they found him. And after watching a clip of the mother begging for the big bad Mexican car-jacker to bring her son back, Sharkey was convinced that she was the perp. She was as nutty as a fucking fruitcake. A woman who had seen some bad times in her life and had never quite recovered.

But that wasn't his concern at the time. He was smack in the middle of an investigation that had required him to give up his own life as he'd known it. A mole hunt that was so sensitive and so far off the radar that nobody but his handler knew what he was up to.

So when Pope first appeared in that VIP poker room, Sharkey had been curious about him for about three seconds. Troy, however, had decided to adopt the poor son of a bitch, and after months of loaning Pope money and watching him lose it, had cut a deal with him to repay his debt by launching that ridiculous hypnosis show.

'We need a headliner,' Troy had said. 'And Ricky and His Red Hot Horns aren't cutting it any more.'

'I'm not a performer,' Pope had told him.

Troy responded with a statement that made it clear that he wasn't about to take no for an answer. 'Then I guess you'd better learn.'

Within a month, Ricky and the Horns were history. Sharkey had to admit that, despite Pope's reluctance, he handled himself pretty good onstage. As ridiculous as it was – drunken morons jumping around like they were possessed by bigger, louder, drunker morons – the show managed to bring in a good-sized crowd and nearly doubled casino traffic, thus solidifying Troy's belief that he was some kind of genius.

But like anything Troy involved himself in – outside of his criminal pursuits, his big-screen TV and his computer – his enchantment with the show, and with Pope himself, began to fade as the novelty wore off and the crowds grew thinner.

And that was when Troy's paranoia set in. In the past few weeks he'd become more and more concerned about allowing Pope into the inner circle, and Sharkey knew it was only a matter of time before the order came down to have him disappeared.

Pope didn't help things much by being such a smart-ass.

And because Sharkey had let him go, his own investigation could well be compromised. But he'd had no choice. Pope wasn't a mobster, he wasn't a crook of any kind. And Sharkey would be damned if he'd let an innocent man get snuffed on *his* watch.

But after Troy got that phone call from Pope, and the extended silence of the twin defenders, Sharkey knew that Troy was about to go into burn-and-purge mode. Which meant that any chance of uncovering the mole in Sharkey's department just went from difficult to nearly impossible.

It took twenty minutes for his handler, a veteran cop named Billingsly, to return his call. Before his promotion to captain, Billingsly had been Sharkey's squad commander. He had approached Sharkey about the undercover assignment after an informant had told him of a possible connection between Troy's syndicate and the Las Vegas Metropolitan Police Department.

There were a few others in the loop – some high-ranking officials from the mayor's office – but because of the sensitivity of the operation, Billingsly had kept Sharkey's identity on a need-to-know basis. And as far as Billingsly was concerned, nobody needed to know.

'We've got problems,' Sharkey said, then told him what was happening.

Billingsly sounded unconcerned. 'It may not matter. I think I've found our mole.'

Sharkey almost choked on the raisin snail he was munching. 'What?'

'Most of those bank numbers you sent me were dummy accounts, but I finally connected with one. You wouldn't believe how much money Troy's been funnelling into this guy's pockets. He could buy his own private island, for Chrissakes.'

'Who'd you trace it to?'

'He's got a gold shield, I can tell you that much. We'll get into it later. In the meantime, hold tight, and I'll see if I can find out what's going on in Ludlow. I'll try to defuse the situation before your colleagues decide to get talkative. We don't need the Feebs trying to nose in on this.'

Sharkey smiled now. All that worry for nothing. 'Un-fucking-believable,' he said. 'Are you sure you've got the right guy?'

'We're this close to solid, O'Donnell. You've done a helluva job. It's almost time for you to come home.'

Yes, indeed, Sharkey thought. Yes, indeed.

Arturo's nose was broken.

He was standing near the doors to Troy's suite when Sharkey got off the elevator. The nose looked like a small, bruised eggplant and both of his eyes were black.

'I still want to know how I wound up on that elevator floor,' he said.

'I guess you'll have to ask Pope.'

'I'm asking you.'

'Don't get your boxers in a bunch,' Sharkey told him. 'What possible reason could I have for fucking you up?'

'I don't know. But I'm watching you, my friend.'

'Oooh, you're scaring the shit right outta me.' He deposited his shoes, then gestured for Arturo to open the doors and Arturo did, ushering him inside. Sharkey could feel the guy's gaze on him the entire time and had to admit that it didn't feel good. He didn't know how Troy had hooked up with Arturo, but there was no question he was an asset to the organization. If you needed someone killed, that is. Quickly and unimaginatively.

Then there was The Ghost. Get a threat from that spooky bastard and Sharkey really *would* be shitting his pants. But The Ghost was nowhere in sight this afternoon, and that was just fine with Sharkey.

'Nice of you to show up,' Troy said when Sharkey walked into the room. 'Where've you been?'

'Contrary to popular belief, I like to eat sometimes. I was grabbing some lunch.'

'You don't have time for food. You need to be concentrating on Pope. I'm holding you personally responsible for letting him get away.'

'Me? What about the garden gnome?' Sharkey gestured to Arturo, who was lurking just inside the doorway. 'He was there, too.'

'Arturo has some concerns about you.'

Oh, Christ, Sharkey thought. Arturo sharing his suspicions about what happened in the elevator was definitely not something to celebrate. Fortunately, Sharkey had grown accustomed to dealing with Troy's paranoia.

'Arturo's embarrassed,' he said. 'He let you down. Of course he's going to try to find excuses for his fuck-up.'

'Have a seat,' Troy said.

There was something about Troy's tone that irritated Sharkey. He couldn't count the number of times he'd wanted to pull out his piece and just shoot the motherfucker, get this assignment over with. But he'd always managed to restrain himself. And knowing that they were very close to closing the deal made it a helluva lot easier.

So he sat in the most comfortable chair he could find and waited for the lecture.

He didn't have to wait long.

'A man is only as good as the people around him,' Troy said. It was a sentiment he'd offered many times before, something he'd picked up from some corporate feel-good website no doubt, but Sharkey didn't believe he meant a word of it. 'And when I see breakdowns in efficiency like I saw today, it makes me wonder if we need a change.'

That didn't sound good.

'If a trusted employee comes to me with concerns about someone's loyalty, I think the best course of action to take is to confront the situation head-on.'

He was really starting to sound like a corporate executive now, but the greasy hair and cut-off sweats countered the effect.

'Confrontation's always good,' Sharkey said.

'I'm glad you think so. Because it's come to my attention that you may not be who you pretend to be.'

The raisin snail Sharkey had eaten earlier rolled over in his stomach. 'Say what?'

'I've been told we have a traitor in our organization. Would you know anything about that?'

Sharkey felt panic coming on. This wasn't part of

the script and he hadn't been expecting it. How could Troy possibly know about him?

All he could do was play along.

'That's ridiculous,' he said. 'Where are you getting your information?'

'Oh, from a very reliable source. A source that tells me that for the past couple of years you've been funnelling information about me and this organization straight to the Las Vegas Metro Police Department.'

Holy shit, Sharkey thought. How was this possible?

He tried to keep his cool. 'If there's a traitor in this organization, it sure as hell isn't me.'

'There's no point in denying it,' Troy said. 'I have living proof.' He gestured. 'Isn't that right, Detective Billingsly?'

'I'm afraid so,' a voice said, then to Sharkey's utter surprise, Captain Brad Billingsly stepped out of the doorway to Troy's game room.

Sharkey was too shocked for words, but Billingsly had no trouble filling in the gap.

'You see, O'Donnell, when I ferreted out our mole and I saw all the money in his bank account, I thought to myself: why him and not me? I want my own private island, too.' He paused. 'So I gave Mr Troy here a call this morning and offered him an opportunity to clean house.'

'And that's exactly what I'm doing,' Troy said. 'The Ghost has already taken care of our man in the LVMPD. Now he's off to Ludlow to handle the loose ends.'

'As for you,' Billingsly told Sharkey. 'It seems your assignment really has come to an end.'

And that was when Arturo came up behind the chair, brought his blade down and slit Ed 'Sharkey' O'Donnell's throat.

'Via con Dios,' he said quietly.

29

They took Evan to the emergency room at Ludlow County General.

Though conscious after the collapse, he was dehydrated and only semi-coherent, and they all agreed it would be best to put him under observation. Ronnie, who worked at the hospital as a staff nurse, called in to get the boy bumped to the head of the line.

They drove in silence, suffering from a collective shell shock, unable or unwilling to talk about what they'd witnessed.

Anna relished the quiet.

When they arrived at the hospital, she decided to stay in the Suburban as Pope scooped Evan into his arms, then carried him in through the automatic doors, Worthington and Ronnie moving alongside them.

She had a feeling this probably wasn't the first time they'd lived this particular scenario.

As they disappeared into the emergency room, Evan made eye contact and gave Anna a small, weak wave, breaking her heart into a thousand different pieces.

She was reminded of a moment shortly before college, when her cat, Zed, was diagnosed with a kidney ailment. She'd taken him to the veterinarian clinic to be put to sleep, and the last she saw of him was when he turned to look at her with those big sad eyes as the nurse carried him away.

There was no reason to compare the two, but Anna couldn't help herself. She had a sudden, vague sense that she might not be seeing Evan again, and she wasn't sure why. His condition was not life-threatening. Bringing him here was only a precaution.

Yet the feeling persisted. Resonated.

You're tired, she told herself. That's all. Tired and weak.

Pope had suggested she see the doctor as well, but she'd refused.

'I'll be fine,' she'd said, although 'fine' was a relative term, wasn't it?

The real reason she'd wanted to wait in the car was because she needed to be alone. To think. To wrap her head around what had happened.

There was no doubt now that Pope had been right. Jillian Carpenter was very much a part of her past and the details of that past no longer came to her in fleeting images. The last moments of Jillian's life were now a vivid part of Anna's consciousness.

She remembered everything.

The terror. The loss of power. The pain.

And amidst it all was the sound of her mother's voice. Calling to her. Singing that sad, familiar song.

To come out of her trance and find Evan beside

her, holding her hand, had been a shock, to say the least. But she had felt the connection. Knew that her mother had somehow used this boy as a vessel to contact her. To help her. And without that help, without her mother's call, Anna was certain she would have died right there along with Jillian Carpenter. Just as she would have died on that football field if Evan hadn't warned Pope.

All of which meant only one thing to Anna. And that one thing – despite all the blood and the horror she'd seen of late, despite being so drained of energy that she could barely move – filled her with an almost indescribable feeling of joy. Of hope.

Her mother was watching over her.

Worthington was the first to return.

'Ronnie's beside herself,' he sighed, as he climbed behind the wheel. 'Thinks this is all her fault.'

'*Her* fault? Why?'

'She thinks she should have kept better watch over Evan. She got up to use the bathroom and when she came back, he was gone. Says if she hadn't left . . .'

'I might be dead,' Anna said. 'And she had no more control over what happened than Evan did.'

Worthington nodded. 'That's what I told her, but she's a sensitive woman. Seeing this kid go through so much is tough for her. Stirs up a lot of bad memories.'

'I can imagine.'

'Truth is, she still blames herself for what happened to Ben, too.'

Anna was surprised. 'Why?'

'She's a nurse,' Worthington said. 'She thinks she should have seen the signs of Susan's illness. God knows Susan and Ben were at the house enough in those last few weeks.'

'I won't pretend to know all the details, but Ronnie's no more to blame for that than you are. Or Pope.'

'Hopefully she'll see that one day.'

He paused, lost in a memory, and Anna knew that he was deeply in love with his wife. He was a good man. And despite the toughness of his exterior, he was as sensitive as Ronnie was.

After a moment, he said, 'I think I owe you an apology.'

'For what?'

'While you were under, I said some pretty crappy things. Practically accused you of being a scam artist.'

'Relax,' Anna said. 'I was too far gone to hear you. And if I were on your end, I'd probably think the same thing.'

Worthington seemed to struggle with a thought, then said, 'I've never admitted this to anyone, but I'm not as much of a hard-core realist as I pretend to be. That story I told you about the cats? I was as scared as the rest of those guys. Maybe more.'

'I think I already knew that.'

His eyebrows raised. 'Oh? How?'

'Based on what you told me back at the Fair-weather house. That when you work a crime scene long enough, the victims start to talk to you. A hard-core realist wouldn't even think to say something like that.'

He smiled. 'Looks like I'm busted.'

She shrugged. 'I'm a trained investigator.'

'I used to think I was, too, until I saw what happened between you and Evan. There's no training on earth that can prepare you for something like that. I could chalk it up to a couple of nutcases feeding off each other, but I know that isn't true.'

Now Anna smiled. 'Welcome to the dark side.'

Worthington held a hand up in protest. 'I'm not quite there yet. Just dipping my toes in. But do me a favour and don't tell Pope. I hate it when he gloats.'

'Your secret is safe,' Anna said.

'Good. Because what I'm about to tell him is gonna knock him sideways.'

Her smile disappeared. 'What do you mean?'

His gaze shifted and he nodded towards the hospital. 'You'll find out soon enough.'

She turned and saw Pope exiting through the automatic doors, looking a bit glazed, undoubtedly another victim of the blame game.

He came up to the open passenger window. 'Ronnie's sticking around for a while. I'm thinking maybe I should, too.'

'Can't do that, Cuz. We've got someplace to be.'

'Why? What's going on?'

'Something I found out before all the craziness started. Climb in and I'll tell you on the way.'

'What about Evan?'

'Ronnie'll do what needs to be done. Now, come on, get in.'

Pope reluctantly opened the door and climbed in, pulling the seat belt across his chest. He turned, looking at Anna.

'You feeling okay?'

'I've been better,' she said, which was probably the understatement of the last few centuries.

'I don't know what happened today, but you scared the shit out of me.'

'Out of all of us,' Worthington said.

Anna grinned. 'Glad to be of service.'

They were on the I-15, headed towards the state line, when Pope said to Worthington, 'You wanna tell me what you're up to?'

Even with the air conditioner on, the late afternoon heat was oppressive, and Anna was slumped in the back, struggling to stay awake. A month in a feather bed would be bliss, she thought. With a nice ocean breeze and an unlimited supply of ice-cold tea.

Worthington glanced at Pope. 'You look a little nervous, Cuz.'

'That's because you're headed in exactly the opposite direction than the one I want to be travelling right now.'

'Don't worry, this doesn't have a thing to do with those two goons we've got locked up. I couldn't care less about them at the moment.'

'Then where are we going?'

'To see Susan.'

Anna could almost hear the scratch of the record. She sat up, fully awake. She couldn't see his face, but she could tell by the sudden stiffness of Pope's body that he wasn't happy. And the heat radiating from him had little to do with the desert sun.

'Are you trying to be funny?' he asked. 'Because there's not a fucking thing funny about what you just said.'

'Just hear me out,' Worthington told him. 'While you two were in the living room, I ran Jillian Carpenter's name through the system and came up with a major hit. The girl was ten years old, murdered by an unknown assailant in Salcedo, California, back in 1981.'

Pope looked surprised. 'Salcedo?'

'That's what I said.' Worthington reached into his shirt pocket and brought out a folded sheet of paper. 'I wasn't able to get access to the full file, so the details are sketchy, but take a look at this.'

Pope took it from him. 'What is it?'

'A list of witnesses who were interviewed by the Salcedo police.'

'And?' Pope said.

'Look at the first name on the list.'

Pope unfolded the paper and read the name, his entire body going rigid. He seemed unable to speak.

'What's wrong?' Anna asked. 'Who is it?'

They flew past a highway sign that read: WOMEN'S CORRECTIONAL FACILITY – 10 MILES.

'Suzie,' Worthington said. 'A.k.a. Susan Leah Oliver.'

Anna felt the hairs on the back of her neck rise. The little girl in that alley with Jillian Carpenter was Pope's ex-wife.

30

'Turn around. *Now*.'

Pope's mind was reeling. How could this be? He'd been married to Susan for over eight years and had dated her for four prior to that. How could he not know that she'd once witnessed her best friend's kidnapping?

This was a mistake. It had to be.

'You're the one who opened this bag of pretzels,' Jake said. 'We've got a perp out there who likes to kill little girls. And it looks as if he's been doing it for over thirty years. If Susan can shed any light on—'

'Turn this fucking car around.'

'You want to run away from this? Fine. There's the goddamn door. But don't expect me to slow down.'

'Then *you* talk to her. I don't want to have anything to do with that bitch.'

'Oh? Is that why you've got a room overlooking the goddamn prison?'

'That's as close as I ever want to get without a gun in my hand.'

And he meant it, too. One of his biggest fantasies

was to walk up to her in that prison yard and whisper, 'This is for Ben,' right before he pulled the trigger.

It made him sick to his stomach to think he'd ever touched that woman, or allowed her to touch him. Their entire history together had been tainted by her compulsive need for attention and the vicious acts it fuelled.

The damage she had done was irreversible. Unforgivable. And he wanted nothing to do with her.

Twelve years' worth of lies was more than enough.

Susan had moved to Ludlow from Salcedo in her junior year of high school. The shy girl who sat in the back of class. Who quietly ate French apple pie in the corner booth at the Hungry Spoon.

They didn't become romantic until many years later, when they bumped into each other at the University of Las Vegas. Susan was working as a research assistant and Pope was guest-lecturing.

The shy girl had turned into an equally shy, but beautiful woman and Pope felt the testosterone kick in the moment he saw her. It took him a while to convince her to go out with him, but she finally relented. It wasn't until that first date that he noticed a slight limp in her gait.

He hadn't mentioned it the first night, but when he finally did, several dates later, she told him she'd had an accident as a child, but didn't elaborate.

He asked her about it again, over the next several years, but she would never go into much detail and Pope hadn't pressed her. He saw no reason to make

her relive a painful experience she so obviously wanted
to forget.

But even as Anna told him of Jillian's final
moments, Pope never thought to equate little Suzie's
twisted leg with his ex-wife's limp. Why would he?

Yet there was no denying the name printed on the
witness statement in his hand.

And Susan was thirty-eight. Just the right age.

During the trial, when her lawyers tried to blame
her crimes on Munchausen by proxy, an expert witness
had testified that the causes of the syndrome were
largely unknown. But MBP was often considered a cry
for help, fuelled by anxiety and depression and feelings
of inadequacy.

Could Susan be as much a victim of this red-hatted
son of a bitch as McBride was? Had that moment in
the alley shaped her life forever? Warped her mind?

Even if it had, Pope didn't care.

None of it brought Ben back.

'Come on, Danny. You know we have to do this.'

'We? You're the cop. You deal with it.'

'She won't agree to see me. She never liked me
much in the first place, and after Ronnie and I testified
against her . . .'

'Forget it, Jake. It's not gonna happen. So you
might as well turn this car around right—'

'I'll go with you,' McBride said.

Pope swivelled his head, saw the intense look on
her face.

'If she knows something. If she can help us find this freak . . .'

'I wouldn't trust a thing she says.'

'We have to try,' McBride insisted. She reached a hand between the seats, squeezed his arm. 'You said yourself that you think he might be after me. That he might try again. If not me, then maybe someone else. Another Kimberly.'

'You don't know what you're asking.'

'I think I do. I saw the way you looked out that window this morning. I've seen the pain in your eyes. And, believe me, I wouldn't ask you to do this if I didn't think it was important.'

Pope said nothing. Didn't know what to say.

She kept her fingers wrapped around his arm, and he welcomed it, but she was asking too much.

Then he thought about little Evan shouting out her name in the car. He thought about her close call on that football field, and nearly losing her to a somnambulistic trance. He thought about Evan's little sister and what that fucker had done to her. And Jillian Carpenter.

How many more of his victims were out there?

McBride had asked him earlier if he believed in fate. Could this be fate giving him another opportunity to do what was right? To change his own destiny? To help change hers?

He'd worked so hard at shutting himself off these last couple of years. Pushing his friends away. His family. As if the only way he could avoid injury was to inflict a little damage himself.

Maybe it was time to put an end to that. No matter how repulsive the thought of seeing Susan in the flesh might be.

'Even if I agree,' he said, 'there's no guarantee she'll talk to me.'

'She will,' Jake told him.

'And how do you know that?'

'Because I remember the way she looked at you in that courtroom.' He paused. 'She's still in love with you, Danny.'

But Jake was wrong.

After they arrived at the WCF reception desk, a string of phone calls were made and word came back that Susan Pope didn't want to see anyone, including her ex-husband.

Pope silently celebrated.

Jake insisted that the guards try again, even threatened to call a friend in the governor's office (although Pope wasn't quite sure that such a friend really existed), and the deputy warden herself came out to explain that, short of a court order, there was nothing she could do to compel a prisoner to see them.

McBride flashed her credentials. 'This is important,' she said. 'Part of a federal investigation. Can you please try one more time?'

'I doubt it'll do any good. I'm told she hasn't been herself lately. Been showing signs of severe mental distress.'

'Tell her it's about Jillian Carpenter.'

The deputy warden sighed. 'All right. One last

time. But it's my understanding that she was fairly adamant about this.'

'Trust me,' McBride said. 'She'll change her mind.'

31

They were buzzed through half a dozen security gates before they reached the visiting room. The facility was decades old, smelling faintly of disinfectant and vomit.

This was Pope's first visit to the place, and the long hallways and grated windows reminded him, oddly enough, of high school – although he doubted they had much of a senior prom.

A prison trustee in an orange jumpsuit was dumping a trash bin when they entered. She regarded them warily, exchanged a look with the guard escorting them, then quickly finished her business and left the room.

Jake stayed by the door with the guard. Pope and Anna took seats in front of a Plexiglas wall that was divided into visiting stations, each with an intercom.

They waited ten full minutes before a door beyond the glass opened and Susan was escorted inside. She was also wearing a jumpsuit – this one red – her ankles and wrists shackled.

Pope's stomach clutched up the moment he saw

her – a simple reflex, triggered by an intense, uncon-
trollable feeling of hate. This was the woman who had
killed his boy. His Ben. That she was still walking the
earth was a crime in itself.

It took everything he had to keep his cool. He
kept reminding himself that he was here for McBride,
and for Evan and Kimberly and their dead mother and
babysitter.

He waited for Susan to make eye contact, but she
was oblivious to him. She kept her gaze on the floor,
her unkempt hair hiding her face as she shuffled over
to a chair opposite them and sat.

When she finally looked up, Pope was surprised.

Prison had not been kind to her. The beauty he
had once known was replaced by a haunted, dishevelled
wreck. He was reminded of photos he'd once seen in
a magazine – before and after mug-shots of meth-
amphetamine addicts. She seemed to have aged twenty
years.

The hatred he felt immediately morphed into pity.
Not sympathy, just pity. And it was laced with a contempt so strong he had trouble containing it.

Susan's brain finally registered who she was looking at. She blinked a couple of times, then – to Pope's
horror – broke into a smile.

'Danny?' she said, her voice distorted by the intercom. 'You came?'

Pope forced himself to reply. 'Hello, Susan.'

'I thought they were lying to me. Is it really you?'

'In the flesh,' he said.

'They always lie to me, you know. My lawyers.

Trying to get me to come out. But I don't want to come out. I just want to stay in my room. I've got everything I need there.' Her smile widened. 'Except you, of course.'

Pope was ready to offer his own contribution to the smell beneath the disinfectant, but Susan spoke in a kind of sing-song, far-away voice, and he was pretty sure the deputy warden had been right. She wasn't all there.

To prove it, she said, 'Where's Jillian? They told me Jillian was here. Was that another lie?'

'Jillian's dead,' Pope said. 'She's been dead for twenty-eight years.'

'Yes, yes, but I asked Ben and he said I should check anyway. Just to make sure.'

Pope felt his gut tighten again. 'Ben?'

'You remember Ben, don't you? Our boy? He talks to me all the time. Mostly in my head, but he's there. I know he is.' Another smile. 'He forgave me, Danny. He forgave me for what I did.'

All right. Enough of this. Choking back a curse, Pope started to rise, but McBride quickly put a hand on his knee and he sat back down.

That was when Susan noticed her for the first time. She stared blankly at McBride, but then her expression began to change, recognition spreading across her face.

'Oh, my God,' she said. 'It *wasn't* a lie. Jillian?'

Pope and McBride exchanged a quick glance.

'You look so different. All grown-up. But it's you, isn't it? I'd recognize those eyes anywhere.' She turned to Pope. 'The eyes are the mirror of the soul, you know. They really are.'

A chill ran through him. What had always been something of an innocuous saying suddenly took on new meaning. New weight.

This was all too creepy for words.

McBride, however, had the good sense to go with it. 'How are you, Suzie? I've missed you.'

Susan seemed startled by the sound of her voice. As if it were a slap to the face. Then she surprised them both by starting to cry.

'Oh, God,' she said. 'Oh, God . . .'

Pope and McBride exchanged another look.

'What's wrong, Suzie?'

'All these years,' she sobbed. 'All these years I've wanted you to come back so I could tell you how sorry I am.'

'For what?'

'It was all my fault. I yelled at you that day, but if it hadn't been for me, if you hadn't been trying to help me, the bogey man never would've gotten you. He would've gone away and left us alone.'

'Bogey man?'

'That's what he is, you know. They always tell you he hides in the closet and under the bed, but that's not true. He's everywhere. Always watching.' She paused and sniffed back her tears, wiping her nose on the sleeve of her jumpsuit. Then her gaze drifted towards the ceiling. With a surreptitious gesture to a surveillance camera in a corner behind her, she looked at McBride and said, 'You'd better be careful. He's watching you right now.'

This woman was completely unrecognizable to Pope. The Susan he'd once known was buried so deep, he doubted she'd ever come out again.

And he knew that they were wasting their time here. She could babble on for hours and they'd get nothing of value from her. All he wanted to do was leave.

But then she surprised him.

'I used to watch *him*, too,' she said. 'For a long, long time. Before I met Danny. Before Ben was born. I watched him for years and years and years. He's left a trail, you know, and I kept very good track of him.'

McBride leaned forward. 'I don't understand. What trail? How?'

'All I had to do was look for the sign. It wasn't easy, but I always managed to find it.'

'What sign?'

Susan lowered her voice conspiratorially. 'The wheel,' she said. 'The gypsy wheel.'

Pope and McBride exchanged yet another look.

'I saw it when he took you. On his neck? I've seen it over and over again. It's always there, but it changes.'

'Changes?' McBride said.

Susan nodded vigorously. 'Yes, yes. Eight spokes, twelve spokes, fourteen spokes. It's all there in the book. Every single bit of it.'

'What book?'

'I tried to get them to bring it to me. But nobody would listen. They all think I'm crazy.' She paused, turning to Pope. 'Do you think I'm crazy, Danny?'

Crazier than a goddamn loon. But he was intrigued now. Maybe there *was* something to what she was saying after all.

'Tell us about the book,' he said.

'It's all there. I kept it for years and years and years.'

'A book about the bogey man.'

'That's right,' she said. 'After he took Jillian, I was always afraid he'd come after me. But I was too young to do anything about it. So I stayed in my room a lot. Kept a light on at night. But when I got older, I started tracking him. Through every victim I could find. And I kept tracking him until one day I realized he wasn't interested in me at all.'

'How did you know that?' McBride asked.

'Because of the eyes. His victims all had your eyes.'

McBride was suddenly silent, and Pope could see that she was as creeped out by this as he was. And, despite Susan's obvious mental deterioration, they both knew that what she'd just said might not be crazy talk.

'What exactly is in this book?' Pope asked.

'I just told you. Everything. Everyone he hurt. It's all there. I tracked him for years.'

'And where can I find it?'

'I tried to get them to bring it to me, but they wouldn't listen.'

'Your lawyers? Do they have it?'

If Susan's attorneys were successful in their bid for a new trial, they might be able to use this book as evidence of a sustained diminished capacity. Although two minutes in a room with her would pretty much prove that.

'No, no,' Susan said. 'I hid it. A long, long time ago. Right before Ben was born.'

'Maybe I can bring it to you.'

'Really? You'd do that?'

'Just tell me where it is.'

'But if I told you, it wouldn't be a secret.'

'You can trust me,' he said. 'I won't tell anyone.'

Susan considered this a moment, but her thoughts seemed to wander to another time and place, and when they returned, she looked from Pope to McBride, then back to Pope again and frowned. Suspicious.

'How do you know Jillian? I never told you about her.'

No shit, Pope thought. There were quite a few things she'd left out. But he was losing her and needed to get her back on his side.

'Jillian came to me,' he said. 'She wants to help me. And you.' He paused, forcing himself to continue. 'To bring us back together.'

'Really?'

He watched as Susan's ravaged face lit up with such joy that he almost felt guilty.

Almost.

'The book, Susan. Where can we find the book?'

'What book?'

'The one about the bogey man. The one you hid.'

She smiled, suddenly remembering. 'I showed it to Ben, you know. I wanted him to see. To understand what kind of monsters are out there, watching us. The demons who prey on children.' She stared directly at Pope now. 'That's why I did what I did. To protect him from the monsters and the demons. You can understand that, can't you?'

Pope had to restrain himself from putting a fist through the glass. Unable to sit there any more, he stood, turning away from her. He couldn't stand the sight of her.

And even worse, he couldn't understand how he'd lived under the same roof as this woman and not known how truly twisted she was. He had loved her then. But what he'd loved was a fraud.

She was the demon. And he'd failed to see that. Just like he'd failed to protect his son from her.

'What's wrong, Danny? Did I say something wrong?'

He turned, his voice flat. 'The book, Susan. Where can I find the book?'

'Ahh,' she said and nodded. 'I put it in the attic.'

'Of our house?'

'Yes. Under a floor board. I marked it so I wouldn't forget where it was. Every once in a while I'd pull it out again and look at it. To remind myself of what can happen to us if we aren't careful.'

McBride leaned forward. 'What kind of mark?'

Susan looked at her as if this were the most idiotic question she'd ever heard. 'I swear to God, Jillian, sometimes you can be such a dumbo.'

Pope's patience was at an end. He wanted to get the fuck out of here. 'For Chrissakes, Susan, just tell us.'

He knew he'd spoken too harshly the moment the words were out of his mouth.

She looked stung. 'You don't have to get mad.'

'I'm not mad,' he said, softening his voice. 'I'm just anxious to get the book and bring it to you. You want it, don't you?'

Another vigorous nod. 'Yes. Very much.'

'Then, please, just tell me how you marked your hiding spot and I'll go straight home and get it.'

She said nothing, as if weighing whether or not she could trust him. Then, glancing around the room to make sure no one else was watching, she pressed a finger to the glass and made a small, tight circle.

A wheel, Pope thought.

She'd marked it with a gypsy wheel.

32

The Ghost did not consider himself a violent man.

To violent men, killing things is a form of therapy. A release of stress. A need to be fulfilled at regular intervals, as the pressure becomes too much to bear.

The Ghost felt no pressure.

He was a businessman. And because his business was violence, many of those with whom he worked believed that he enjoyed himself while carrying out that business.

Unlike Arturo, however, who was a brute disguised as a gentleman, he found no joy in killing people. Derived no pleasure from a slit throat or punctured kidney. Was not aroused by the smell of blood.

Certainly, he liked what he did or he wouldn't do it. But his emotional satisfaction came only from a job well done, a plan well executed, not from the infliction of pain. Unless his specific mandate was to elicit information, he tried his best to keep his target's discomfort to a minimum.

It was always easier that way. Less messy.

Unless, of course, it was *meant* to be messy.

Although he had been working for Anderson Troy for several months now, The Ghost did not feel like an employee.

This had nothing to do with Troy himself. Troy treated everyone like a slave and expected unwavering loyalty.

But The Ghost was, as he always would be, a free agent. He had no respect for his so-called master. Considered him something of a punk, in fact. A spoiled brat who had no business ordering anyone around.

But Troy had money.

And that, in a nutshell, was what The Ghost respected. That, in a nutshell, was what *all* of Troy's employees respected, save possibly Arturo, who wouldn't take a shit without Troy's approval and seemed to derive great satisfaction from the man's constant abuse.

So Troy may have been a spoiled brat, but he paid well. And because Troy paid well, The Ghost did as he was instructed and asked no questions. Even when he thought those instructions were ill advised.

Or downright stupid.

He did not offer advice or counsel. He did not pretend to be a friend.

He was a messenger. Pure and simple.

And his message, more often than not, was death.

The Ghost's first assignment of the day had been a trip to a Las Vegas casino parking lot, where he had arranged a rendezvous with one of Troy's law-enforcement contacts. Two minutes into the meeting, the contact had been eliminated with a bullet to the brain.

This was followed by a drive to the Ludlow County Sheriff's Department to assess any possible damage done by the twin defenders. Posing as their lawyer, he was able to learn that they were currently being held for assault and possibly attempted murder, but would not be formally booked until further investigation of the matter.

That investigation, however, was currently on hold because the department had its hands full with a multiple homicide across town. The family that Pope had told them about.

Despite this distraction – or perhaps *because* of it – The Ghost was granted a ten-minute private conference with the pair. And when he walked into the room, they reacted much as he suspected they would.

With immediate, undisguised fear.

The Ghost assured them that he meant them no harm, but had merely been dispatched to secure their guarantee that they would remain faithful to their employer. For a special bonus, of course.

Not surprisingly, they told him they would. What they didn't know was that they'd never have a chance to spend that bonus. But that was a project to be saved for a later date.

There was, unfortunately, the small problem of their cellphones, each of which had been programmed with Anderson Troy's private number. And a search of their tax records would reveal that they were security consultants for the Oasis. But none of this linked Troy directly to the incident in question, and as long as they stuck to their story, Troy was in the clear.

That story, it was decided, would involve a private poker game between the twin defenders and Daniel Pope. A poker game that had resulted in a significant amount of money owed to them by Mr Pope. They had merely been trying to collect their debt when the hypnotist attacked them.

Based on his conversation with the deputy who brought them in, it was The Ghost's understanding that Pope himself had yet to make a formal statement about the matter.

This was good news.

Because The Ghost's third assignment of the day was to make sure he never did.

His next stop was the cousin's house. It was located in a working-class neighbourhood, fairly empty this time of day. There were two cars in the drive. A grey Suburban and, to the right of it, looking like a pygmy in comparison, a red Toyota Tercel.

Parked at the kerb out front was an unmarked sedan with a small scanner antenna on top.

This would be the cousin's car.

The Ghost drove past the house twice, checking the windows, but the shades had been drawn and there was no way to see inside. The presence of the cars, however, was a fairly good indication that Pope was still here and wasn't alone.

Feeling the need to assess the situation, The Ghost parked under some trees near a vacant lot about two blocks north of the house.

The cousin was undoubtedly inside questioning Pope about his altercation with the twin defenders and the events that had led up to it. Pope had clearly threatened Troy over the phone, promising to spill his guts if he wasn't left alone, so The Ghost had to assume that that was exactly what he was doing. Which meant that a single mark had now become multiple targets, the number of which depended on how many people were in that house to hear what Pope had to say.

The Ghost would have to kill them all.

This did not make him happy. He considered, for a moment, simply driving away and telling Troy he was on his own with this one. It was Troy's own paranoia that had created this mess in the first place.

Instead, he picked up his cellphone and dialled.

A moment later Troy's voice was on the line. 'Talk to me.'

'You've put me in an impossible situation,' The Ghost said. 'He's not alone in the house and there's no way to know how much he's told or who he's told it to.'

'What are you suggesting?'

'Nothing. I don't make suggestions. You know that.'

'So, in other words,' Troy said, 'you want more money.'

'That would be gist of it, yes.'

'How much?'

The Ghost thought about it.

'Why don't we do it this way. Take whatever the hypnotist owes you and multiply it by five.'

'Are you fucking nuts? That's a lot of cash.'

'Do you want this situation contained, or don't you?'

There was a long beat of silence on the line. Then Troy said, 'All right. Whatever you want.'

'Make sure it's in my Cayman account by close of business day. I'll be checking. And if it's not there . . .'

'Relax. It'll be there. Just make sure you shut that son of a bitch up.'

'Consider it done,' The Ghost said. And as he clicked off, he couldn't help but smile. Troy's constant paranoia never ceased to amuse him.

Truth be told, Pope was not really all that much of a threat. He was a gambler and a womanizer and could easily be painted as an unstable, unreliable witness if it came down to that. And what he *didn't* know about Troy's business activities would probably fit in a small warehouse.

No one had to die over this.

All Troy had to do was make a few adjustments, shred a few documents, rely on his 'contacts' in the police department and federal prosecutor's office to grease a few wheels and make sure that Lady Justice turned a blind eye to his lawlessness. He was a rich man, and that's what rich men do. Always have.

But Troy was also a man who lived in fear. And The Ghost was more than happy to reap the benefits of that fear. A couple more scores like this and he'd be a rich man himself.

He was thinking about what he might do with all that money when he noticed movement down the street.

Grabbing his field glasses, he aimed them towards the cousin's house. The door was open and two men and a woman were moving quickly down the walkway, Pope among them, followed shortly by a another woman carrying a small boy in her arms.

The boy looked listless. Sick.

What was *this* all about?

They climbed into the grey Suburban, and before the tail lights lit up, The Ghost tossed the field glasses aside, uttering a curse as he started his engine.

Moving targets are always problematic. This assignment was getting far more complicated than he'd like.

It looked as if he was really going to have to earn his money today.

An hour and a half later The Ghost found himself parked, of all places, in a gas station just off the Oasis lot, his field glasses trained on the front gate of the neighbouring Nevada Women's Correctional Facility.

He could not fathom what these people were up to. A trip to the hospital had been followed by a straight trek out here, leaving the child and the second woman behind. He would not harm a child, but the woman was a loose end he knew he'd have to take care of at the earliest possible opportunity.

Following the Suburban, he at first thought they were headed to the Oasis to confront Troy directly, but rather than make the turn, they had continued on to the prison.

The only reason he could figure for this stop was a visit to Pope's wife. The child killer.

But why?

It made no sense.

Unless it had nothing to do with Troy at all. Unless they were up to something that was entirely unrelated to Troy's paranoia.

The Ghost had to admit he was curious. But when it came down to it, none of this made a difference. It was not his job to understand these people and their motivations. His only concern was logistics.

The assignment might have become more complicated, but it hadn't changed.

Troy wanted the spillage mopped up.

The situation contained.

And all The Ghost could do was wait for the perfect opportunity to strike.

33

It was growing dark by the time they left the prison.

Anna could tell that Pope was in no mood for conversation, so she sat quietly in the back seat of the Suburban, thinking about Susan's words.

And about her madness.

As much as she understood Pope's desire to see the woman dead or locked up here forever, Anna didn't believe she deserved either. What she needed was help. A long, heavy dose of psychological therapy. And even that wouldn't guarantee she'd ever be whole again.

Anna knew it all stemmed from that moment in the alley. If Susan's terror had been only half of what Jillian's was – or Anna's, for that matter – then it was more than enough to permanently damage her.

Then again, maybe Susan wasn't so crazy after all.

She believed that her son had visited her, had forgiven her for her sins. But if Anna's mother could pay a visit, why not Ben? Perhaps the dead return when we need them most. To reassure us. To guide us.

To save us.

If nothing else, Anna now knew that the world did not quite operate the way she once believed it did. There were entire levels of existence at play that most people never even knew about.

So where did she draw the line when it came to deciding who was crazy and who was not? Or what was real and what was merely fantasy?

Did spirits inhabit our homes? Were aliens among us? Did parallel universes exist? Were there tears in the fabric of time?

And, oh yes—

What about the bogey man?

Pope's house was located several miles north of the Las Vegas Strip, in an upper middle-class neighbourhood. Anna had grown up in Northern California, where most homes had wide green lawns, but the houses on Pope's street had front yards full of rocks and cactus.

Pope's was also full of weeds.

It was a two-storey, Spanish-style home that stood in the middle of a cul-de-sac. There was activity in both of the neighbouring houses, but Pope's stood silent, its windows caked with a year's worth of dust and grime.

'Never thought I'd see this place again,' he said, as Worthington pulled to the kerb out front.

'You never thought you'd be face-to-face with Susan again, either.'

'Thanks for that, Jake. It was a treat.'

'Don't mention it. You think she was telling the truth?'

'The part where she was completely off her rocker? Or the one where she was only mildly insane?'

'About her bogey-man book.'

Pope shrugged. 'Maybe you should've asked me that before we drove all the way out here. We don't even really know what we're looking for. Could be a book full of random gibberish.'

'So you're saying you don't believe her?' Anna asked.

'Who the hell knows? Right now you wouldn't have much trouble convincing me the earth is flat, so I guess I'm pretty much up for anything.' He popped his door open. 'But there's only one way to find out, so let's get this over with.'

Pope's house keys were in a drawer in his hotel room.

He'd seen no use for them when he fled the place, so it looked like they'd have to resort to some good old-fashioned B & E.

They decided to go in through the back and were surprised to discover that someone had beat them to it. The glass in the rear-door window had been shattered and the door was unlocked.

Squatters, most likely.

Both Jake and McBride shifted into law-enforcement mode and pulled their weapons. Jake brought out a flashlight, flicked it on, then gently pushed the door open.

'County Sheriff,' he called. 'Whoever's in there, identify yourself.'

Silence. No response.

'We have weapons,' he said. 'Identify yourself now or risk getting hurt.'

Nothing.

He and McBride exchanged glances, then stepped inside.

Pope took up the rear. One thing he had learned during his encounter with the twin defenders was that he was no hero. Let the people with the guns and expertise lead the way.

As he stepped through the doorway and took the place in, he was overcome by a sudden feeling of sadness.

The kitchen was on the right, with its chequerboard floor and double-wide refrigerator. There was a breakfast nook in one wall, where he and Susan and Ben had spent many a morning, slurping bowls of oatmeal and talking about the day to come.

Pope couldn't help but yearn for those days. The warmth he'd felt. The glow of family. As much as he hated Susan now, as blind as he'd been to her illness, he did remember those times with fondness. With love.

And it hurt his heart to know that he'd never see them again.

The spell was broken when he spotted the mess on the floor. Shattered plates and glass, rotted food. Whoever had been squatting here would not get the Good Housekeeping seal of approval.

They moved into the living room.

He'd left the place as is, but Jake and Ronnie had gone through and cleaned up, putting sheets over the furniture in the hope that he would one day return.

Some of the sheets were missing now and the furniture had been rearranged to suit the squatters. There was clothing strewn across the carpet, along with discarded food wrappers, some old magazines, faded newspapers.

Jake crouched down and shone his flashlight beam on one of the papers.

'Over a month old,' he said. 'I've got a feeling the occupants have moved on.'

Maybe so, Pope thought, but from what he could see in Jake's flashlight beam, they'd managed to do a pretty good job of destroying the place first. His plasma TV was missing. The carpet was stained and littered with cigarette butts. The decorative mirror Jake and Ronnie had given them as a house-warming gift had been ripped off the wall and discarded in a corner of the room.

The whole place reeked of stale body odour and vomit, and unlike the prison they'd just come from, there was no smell of disinfectant to cover it.

Pope had stopped caring about this place long ago, when he left it behind. But now his sadness turned to anger. How dare these people invade his home? His sanctuary?

This room was where he and Ben had watched *The Jungle Book*. Had played video games together. And now some thoughtless, desperate motherfuckers had taken that memory and turned it into this.

'Let's hurry up,' he said. 'I don't want to be here any longer than I have to.'

There was a small door with a pull chain in the ceiling above the second-floor landing. Pope pulled on it, and springs groaned as the door opened and a ladder unfolded, leading up to the attic.

Pope went first this time. McBride handed him a Maglite and he flicked it on, then climbed to the top of the ladder and shone it into the cramped space above.

Nothing had changed up here. By some miracle, the squatters had never ventured inside, leaving the boxes of old clothes, legal papers and discarded toys untouched. Pope had been up here a hundred times over the years, depositing unwanted junk, but he didn't remember ever seeing any marks on the floor boards.

Not that he'd been looking for any.

The attic walls and ceiling were unfinished, made of tar paper and two-by-fours. Pope shone the light towards a nearby stud and spotted the Stick 'N' Click light fixture he'd mounted there. The electricity in the house had been turned off months ago, but there'd never been a line up here anyway, and the Stick 'N' Click ran on a nine-volt battery.

Reaching over, he jabbed it with a finger and it came to life, illuminating the small room. Not well, but it was better than nothing.

Pope pulled himself all the way up, then shone the flashlight down the ladder.

'There's room for one more,' he said. 'That's about it.'

'You go on,' he heard Jake say to McBride. 'I've got some calls to make anyway.'

A moment later McBride was at the top of the ladder. 'Did you find it?'

'Give me a break,' Pope said, 'I'm still trying to get my land legs. This place wasn't built for full-sized human beings.'

As if to prove this, he pulled himself upright and nearly bumped his head on a cross-beam.

The floor was made of narrow wooden slats, and as McBride stood up next to him, he ran the flashlight along them, looking for Susan's mark.

Nothing there.

'We're gonna have to move some of these boxes,' he said.

McBride nodded and they spent the next several minutes shifting boxes from one pile to the next. But they found no marks of any kind, except for usual scuffs and scratches.

'I knew this was too much to hope for. Chalk it up to another one of Susan's—'

'Wait,' McBride said. She was staring at a nearby ceiling beam. 'Let me have that flashlight.'

Pope handed it over and she shone it towards the cross-beam, then moved in for a closer look.

'I found it,' she said. 'This is it.'

Pope was surprised. Stepping over to the cross-beam, he took a look for himself and, sure enough, etched into the wood with a knife or an ice pick or a screwdriver was a small, crudely drawn circle with several spokes – about the size of a dime.

The gypsy wheel.

He turned to McBride. 'This isn't right. She said she marked a floor board.'

'No, she said she *hid* it under a floor board. The wheel is just a reminder of where.'

Swinging the flashlight downwards, McBride shone it on the wooden slat directly beneath the mark, then touched it with her toe.

It wobbled slightly. Loose.

They crouched down and Pope stuck his fingers into the space between the slats, carefully prying the loose one free.

'Why do I feel like Geraldo Rivera about to break into Capone's vault?'

McBride shone the light inside, but they saw nothing, and Pope felt a twinge of disappointment.

'Maybe it shifted,' she said, then reached a hand in and patted the space between the floor joists. From the look on her face, she wasn't finding anything.

Then her expression changed.

'I've got it,' she said, then reached in further and brought out a thick, canvas binder. The kind they'd always used in school. It was crammed full of papers and news clippings, but instead of the usual hearts and flowers drawn on the cover, the typical 'Suzie loves Joey' adornments you'd find on a young teenage girl's notebook, this one was covered with gypsy wheels.

Some small, some large. Some crude, some intricate. Each one of them the sign of a serious obsession.

'I don't believe it,' Pope said. 'The goddamn thing is real.'

34

The Ghost had a problem.

After following his targets to this neighbourhood cul-de-sac, he had watched them disappear around the back of one of the houses. It looked to be a typical suburban two-storey, but on closer inspection, through his field glasses, he realized it was abandoned.

A moment later a flashlight came to life inside and he knew they had broken in.

It was, he'd thought, the perfect set-up. Go in quickly – *pop*, *pop*, *pop* – and the targets would be eliminated. And because the house was abandoned, it might be days before the neighbours got curious about the Suburban parked out front and decided to see if someone was home.

A minute or two passed, then a dim light went on in a window near the top of the house. The attic, most likely. Because they had been using a flashlight, The Ghost had assumed the place had no electricity. But apparently he was wrong, and working lights was a variable he'd have to figure into his strategy.

Unfortunately, before he was able to calculate his

angle of approach, the front door opened and the deputy, Worthington, stepped outside, a cellphone in hand.

Worthington being out in the open like this was the problem. The Ghost could easily take him down with a simple drive-by, but that left two targets inside, upstairs, and no way to get to them and get the job done without taking the risk of being seen or possibly even caught.

As is often the case, he had been presented with circumstances that were less than ideal. And while instinct told him he'd be better off walking away and telling Troy to go fuck himself, he kept thinking about the money.

Always the money.

And if he didn't act now, Troy might finally come to his senses and call the whole thing off, leaving The Ghost to argue with the fool about return of payment.

And such an argument would neither be pleasant nor beneficial to his career.

Training his field glasses on the small gap between the target house and its neighbour to the left, The Ghost focused on what he could see of the back yard.

Not much, but enough to tell him that access from the rear would not be difficult. The fence bordering the back neighbour's property was low and easily climbed, and there was just enough shrubbery along the side of both houses to limit his exposure to prying eyes.

A rear assault would also leave Worthington out of the equation until The Ghost was ready to deal with him – assuming he stayed outside long enough. And, based on Worthington's body language, it didn't look like he'd be heading back inside any time soon.

His mind made up, The Ghost set the field glasses down, started his engine and rolled down the street.

Estimated time of completion was six minutes and counting.

They weren't quite sure what they had when they opened the notebook.

Susan Pope's ramblings about tracking the bogey man had been promising at best, but there had been no guarantees that it would amount to anything substantial.

What they discovered was that this mentally ill woman, this shy research assistant from Salcedo, California, had spent a large portion of her life nursing an obsession. The notebook was filled with photographs, drawings, newspaper clippings, Internet print-outs and coded writings. It would take hours to sift through it all and decipher the language.

The first page held three faded photographs, under the handwritten caption, *For Jillian.*

A school portrait of a pretty young girl in a lavender blouse; a shot of the same girl wearing a pink one-piece at the community pool; a much younger version, holding a Jack Russell terrier in her arms.

'Mr Stinky,' Anna said, touching the photo.

'You remember?'

'Yes.'

Anna stared at the photographs and realized that

Susan had been right. There was no mistake that Jillian and Anna shared the same eyes. And based on these eyes alone, Anna would swear she was looking in a mirror.

But this wasn't the first time she'd seen them. She suddenly remembered an image from her trance. The locket dangling from the Rambler's rear-view mirror.

The girl inside that locket.

The gypsy girl.

She'd had the very same eyes.

The Ghost couldn't believe his luck.

The neighbours to the rear of the target house were not yet home, and slipping into their back yard undetected had merely been a matter of timing. The houses on either side were busy doing whatever families do, and he hadn't even had to throw on his Gas Company uniform to complete the task.

Within moments he was up and over the back fence and dropping to the ground in the target's back yard, which, from what he could tell, had seen better days. There was a swing set to his left and a sandbox full of abandoned Tonka trucks, and it suddenly occurred to The Ghost that this might be *Pope's* house. The very same house Pope had tried to sign over to Troy several times in the past.

Troy's refusal to accept it had always been a mystery to The Ghost. The man was certainly no humanitarian. But maybe he felt uncomfortable taking ownership of a house that had once been home to a nut-job and the boy she torched.

Even The Ghost felt a small chill of discomfort at the thought.

There was still light in the attic. Taking a pair of surgical gloves from his pocket, he snapped them on, then removed his weapon from his waistband and checked the magazine. He had considered using a knife for this assignment, but didn't want to be bothered with the clean up. Instead, he screwed a home-made suppressor onto the tip of his weapon, then quickly crossed the yard and slipped in through the open rear door.

He felt fairly confident that he hadn't been seen. Navigating the dark would be difficult, but he couldn't risk using a pen light.

Stepping past a kitchen doorway, he hugged the wall and worked his way into the living room, which was partially illuminated by light from the street.

He could hear Worthington out front, still on the phone.

But as he neared the stairs, The Ghost paused, slightly unnerved by the sudden sensation that he wasn't alone down here.

He turned quickly, surveying the room, but saw no one. Empty shadows. He was again tempted to use his pen light, but decided against it.

He stood there a moment, waiting, and nothing changed. The living room was still and quiet.

False alarm, he thought, then started up the stairs to the second floor.

*

'We need a brighter light and a pot full of coffee,' Pope said.

He was feeling claustrophobic. Needed to get out of here.

The sight of the notebook, the drawings, the scratchy, handwritten passages, served as a reminder of how little he'd known about Susan and how he'd failed her. And Ben.

She'd had an obsession that afforded no room for outsiders. And despite his animosity towards her, he couldn't help feeling as if he were invading her privacy. Peeking in on a part of her life that she'd never intended to share.

It would have to be done, yes – but not here. Not in this house. He needed to be far away from this place and the memories it held. The guilt he felt.

He suddenly realized McBride was staring at him.

'What?'

She closed the notebook. 'It's not your fault, you know.'

He just looked at her.

Was she a mind reader now?

'What are you talking about?'

'What happened to your son. It's not your fault.' She held up the notebook, shook it. 'It's *his*. *He* did this to Susan. The damage was done long before you even entered her life.'

Pope shook his head. 'I should've known what she was capable of. I should've stopped her.'

'How?'

'I don't know. I could've paid more attention.

Gotten her help. Not allowed myself to get so wrapped up in my work.'

'She was *hiding* from you, Danny. Don't you get it? She didn't want you to know about her dark side. She didn't want anyone to know. And even if you *had* known, there's no way you could've gone back and erased what happened to her and Jillian.'

'Doesn't matter. I should've protected him. I should've protected my boy.'

'From his mother?' Anna said. 'Think about that. There's no way you could have known she'd harm her own son. You did what a husband and father are supposed to do. You loved them unconditionally. No one could ever blame you for that.'

'It's not that simple.'

'Nothing about this is simple. But your blame is misplaced. It's *not* your fault.'

Her words hit home and Pope felt tears in his eyes. He started to turn away, but McBride reached up, touching his cheek.

'It's not your fault,' she said again.

Then she surprised him by leaning towards him and kissing his tears. And before he realized what he was doing, he turned into the kiss, pressing his lips against hers.

They stayed that way for a long moment, savouring it. And despite all the women he'd been with – the tourists, the showgirls he'd used to numb his pain – he'd never felt anything like this, the odd sensation of familiarity, as if this weren't the first time he'd kissed her. As if they were long-lost lovers, reunited at last.

When they pulled away from each other, McBride seemed embarrassed by her impulsiveness.

'Sorry,' she said.

'Don't be.'

Then he took the notebook from her, set it atop a nearby box and pulled her into his arms, kissing her again. He lost himself in it, all of his troubles melting away, taking the room, the house and the not-so-simple world with them. A feat that, until this moment, he'd thought impossible.

After a while he said, 'We need to get out of here. Find a nice, bright coffee shop and get to work.'

McBride nodded, kissed his cheek, then pulled away from him and picked up the notebook, carrying it down the steps.

Pope turned, taking a last look around the room, staring at a part of his *own* past life. A life he could never go back to. Then he doused the light and followed her.

But when he reached the bottom of the steps, McBride was nowhere in sight.

'Anna?'

No answer.

'Anna, where the hell did you—'

'Over here, Danny.'

But it wasn't McBride's voice.

Pope swung around and froze when he saw two figures step out of the shadows near the bathroom.

The Ghost.

Holding a gun to McBride's head.

35

'I've always liked you, Danny. I don't think I need to tell you that this wasn't my idea.'

Pope's mind was racing, but to his surprise, McBride seemed cool and collected. There wasn't even a hint of fear in her eyes.

'Let her go,' he said. 'I haven't told her anything.'

'That doesn't really matter at this point, does it? Normally, she'd already be dead, but I heard your little exchange upstairs and I've got a feeling love is in the air. And because I like you, I wanted to give you a choice.' He smiled. 'Who goes first?'

Pope stared at the gun in The Ghost's hand and felt helpless, wishing he still had Jake's Glock. There wasn't a whole lot he could do with a miniature flashlight.

'How much is he paying you?'

'More than you can afford, I'm afraid, so don't even go there.'

'You won't get away with this. My cousin's right outside.'

'Thanks for your concern,' The Ghost said, 'but

he's next on the list. Now, come on, Danny, decide. Or I'll decide for you. Time's wasting.'

'You motherfucker. You're enjoying this.'

'Not at all. Either you watch her die or she watches you. It's your choice.'

Pope looked at McBride. She was blinking at him, furiously. Then her gaze shifted to the flashlight in his hand.

It took him a moment to figure out what she was trying to tell him.

He looked at The Ghost. Tried to see the eyes behind those orange glasses. 'I can't do it,' he said. 'I won't do it.'

'Then I guess I'll have to decide for you.' He paused, then took the gun from McBride's head and pointed it at Pope. 'You first.'

Several things happened at once. Just as The Ghost started to squeeze the trigger, Pope brought the flashlight up and shone it directly in his face. The Ghost made a noise, squinting against the light, and the shot went wild as—

– McBride moved into action, simultaneously grabbing his gun hand and stomping down on his right foot.

The Ghost howled, but wasn't so easily dispatched. He made a quick turn and brought up his free hand, smashing the side of McBride's face, sending her sprawling.

Pope hurled the flashlight at him and leaped, taking him down with a hard tackle—

—but as they hit the floor, The Ghost brought a knee up into Pope's groin, and Pope felt his testicles implode, pain shooting up into his stomach as the wind was knocked out of him.

He rolled away, clutching himself, as The Ghost got to his feet and backed into the bathroom doorway, out of breath, his gun still in hand, pointed at Pope and McBride.

And, make no mistake about it. He was angry.

Very angry.

'You know something, Danny? I don't think I like you all that much any . . .'

He paused mid-sentence, his expression shifting, a startled look in his eyes. Then his fingers went slack and the gun fell to the floor, as he dropped to his knees and pitched forward, blood spreading across his back.

And standing in the doorway, knife in hand, was the man in the red baseball cap.

He spat on The Ghost, his voice full of disgust. 'Gadje scum.'

Anna's jaw was on fire, but the pain abruptly disappeared as she pulled herself upright and saw Red Cap staring at her.

Where had he come from?

Had he followed them here?

Without another word, Red Cap stepped towards her and she fumbled for her Glock, only to remember that the man on the floor had taken it from her when he grabbed her.

And as Red Cap moved closer, she suddenly realized that there was something different about him. His face was different from the one she'd seen in her visions. The misshapen half was no longer a hideous mess. It was still malformed, yes, but not nearly as bad – as if he'd had some sort of corrective surgery.

'Not to worry, Chavi. I would not let him hurt you. Not before you give me what is mine.'

McBride tried to get to her feet, but stumbled back and found herself pressed against the hallway wall, her gaze on the knife in his hand. 'What do you want from me?'

He seemed surprised by the question. 'What I always want, my darling. What I always—'

Anna heard a shout and suddenly Pope flew through the air towards Red Cap, knocking him to the floor. The knife went flying as the two rolled across the carpet, Pope pounding at him with his fists, landing blows to his face and chest.

Red Cap brought an arm up, blocking the assault, as his other hand dipped into a pocket and brought out the stun gun, jabbing Pope in the side. Electricity snapped and Pope jerked back, spasming violently as Red Cap threw him off and stood, about to bring the stunner down again.

Then Anna lunged, grabbing his wrist, slamming him against the wall—

—but he was strong, abnormally strong, and he twisted away from her and flung her aside. He turned and started towards her again as she stumbled back, losing her footing, and hit the ground hard—

—and just as he was over her, a shot rang out and he screamed, dropping the stun gun, grabbing his shoulder.

'Freeze!' a voice shouted and Anna heard Worthington pounding up the stairs.

Red Cap whirled, still clutching his shoulder, and threw himself towards the darkness of the bathroom as—

—Worthington fired again, the bullet gouging wood in the door frame as Red Cap disappeared from sight.

Then Worthington was at the top of the stairs, weapon and flashlight in hand. Stepping over the body on the floor, he pointed both towards the bathroom doorway.

'No place to go, asshole. Come out here. Now!'

But he got no response. No sound coming from in there at all.

Anna got to her feet and moved to Pope, who was no longer spasming. But his face was pale and he didn't seem fully coherent.

'What the fuck?' he groaned.

'It's all right,' she said, rubbing his arm. 'You'll be all right in a minute.'

Worthington took another step towards the bathroom. 'Get your ass out here right now, motherfucker, or I swear to Christ I'll let you bleed to death.'

He swept the bathroom with the flashlight beam and frowned. Moving carefully towards the doorway, he hesitated at the threshold, then stepped inside.

'Shit!' Worthington said, his voice reverberating against the bathroom tiles. 'I don't fucking believe it. He did it again. The son of a bitch did it again.'

36

The bathroom window was hanging open, blood on the sill.

Anna stared at it, amazed by Red Cap's agility. His ability to move so decisively in so short a time. And with a bullet in him, no less.

Her gaze shifted to her reflection in the mirror and she didn't like what she saw. Her hair was a sweaty and matted mess, there were dark circles under her eyes and her scar was inflamed. She looked at the tub and wished she could crawl in and soak for a couple of hours.

Hell, a couple of years.

Preferably in ice-cold water.

She heard pounding on the steps behind her and turned, moving into the hallway. Worthington coming back from outside.

He was out of breath.

'I looked up and down the block,' he said. 'No sign of him anywhere – although I did find some blood on the sidewalk.'

'Will someone please wake me up?' Pope said. He

was on the floor against the wall, looking as if he could use a long soak himself. 'I'm really getting tired of this nightmare.'

'Aren't we all,' Anna said.

Worthington gestured to the dead man near Pope. 'Would one of you like to tell me who the hell he is?'

'The Ghost,' Pope said.

'The what?'

'One of Troy's men. Just like the two you picked up this afternoon.' He sighed. 'It's a long story.'

'Well, it had better be a goddamn good one, because you're gonna tell it to the Vegas PD when they get here.'

'You called them?'

'No, but after all the noise we made, I can guarantee the neighbours did.'

And then, as if on cue, a siren wailed in the distance.

The lead detective was commander of the LVMPD Robbery/Homicide Division. Anna was surprised that such a high rank was running a crime scene, but maybe they did things differently out here in Vegas.

A couple of the responders knew Pope on a first-name basis, having worked with him in the past, but this one didn't seem to know much beyond the headlines.

They were standing on the sidewalk in front of Pope's house. The neighbours had gathered, the place quickly turning into the usual circus.

At the first mention of Troy's name, the detective

nodded to his car, a standard-issue Crown Vic. 'Let's talk in there.'

They all piled in, Worthington in front, Pope and Anna in the back.

Starting the engine, the detective turned his air conditioner up full blast, then looked at Pope. 'Okay, you got my attention. What do you know about Anderson Troy?'

So Pope told him his story, filling in the details about The Ghost, Sharkey and Troy and his connections to organized crime. It was a good story, and any law-enforcement agent would be thrilled to stumble into it. But this guy didn't seem all that impressed.

'Tell me about the assailant,' the detective said. 'The guy with the knife.'

This was when the truth got bent a little. They had decided to blame The Ghost's death on a squatter who had been hiding upstairs. The truth would only complicate matters and they'd be stuck here all night. Worthington said he didn't know if the guy was performing a good deed or was simply a wacko, but he'd just killed a man and was behaving erratically, so . . .

'You shot him,' the detective said. 'And it looks like you hit him.'

Worthington nodded. 'I thought I had him cornered in there, but he got away.'

'So what did this guy look like?'

'About six one, two hundred ten pounds, with short-cropped hair and a baseball cap. Red. It was pretty dark and I could be wrong, but I think he was a gypsy.'

'What makes you think that?'

'He fit the general type and had a tattoo of a wheel on the back of his neck. I've seen one similar on some of the Roma drifters I've busted.'

The detective shook his head in disgust. 'Fuckin' gypsies. We get a clan comes through every once in a while, but they usually get lost among all the other scammers and two-bit con artists in town. Looks like this one's a hero, though.'

'Looks like.'

'But one thing I don't understand,' the detective said, 'is what you folks were doing here in the first place.'

Pope took his turn again. 'Like I told you. This is my house.'

'Yeah, I get that, but it's been closed up for quite a while. Neighbours say you haven't been around in over a year. Why the sudden visit?'

Pope had an answer for that one, too. Not much of one, Anna thought, but it was all they could come up with.

'I've been consulting on a case for Agent McBride here. We came to get some papers I left behind.'

'This have anything to do with Troy?'

'Not at all,' Anna said. 'This is actually the first I'm hearing about him.'

The detective nodded, then lowered his head for a moment as if weighing a decision. Then he said, 'What I'm about to tell you can't leave this car.'

They all looked at him, curious, and he shifted his gaze to Pope.

'Your friend Sharkey's real name was Ed O'Donnell.

He was on a deep-cover assignment involving possible departmental collusion with Troy.'

'Was?' Pope said.

'Sharkey's dead. We found him in a dumpster behind Leroy's Bail Bonds downtown. His throat was slit.'

'Jesus,' Pope said, closing his eyes.

'We've got nothing that ties it directly to Troy, but we're working on it. Only a few people in the department knew about him, and I'm one of them.' He looked at Pope. 'And from what you've told me, it looks like you could wind up a star witness in all this.'

Pope opened his eyes now, and Anna could see that this proposition didn't thrill him.

'As you might assume,' the detective went on, 'this is still a highly sensitive case. So what I gotta know is if you've talked to anyone else about it.'

'Just the two uniforms,' Worthington said. 'The first responders. But not in any detail.'

The detective nodded. 'I'll be talking to them shortly. But when we leave this car, I need the three of you to keep your mouths shut. Just until we can get this whole thing contained.' He looked at Worthington. 'And I'd really like to get those two goons you've got locked up transferred out here. You think that can be arranged?'

'Consider it done,' Worthington said.

The detective turned to Anna. 'Does the Bureau have any interest in this?'

'Not as far as I'm concerned. I've got my own cases to worry about.'

'Then I guess all that's left to talk about is protection.' He looked at Pope. 'We need to get you someplace safe.'

'Forget it,' Pope said.

'This Ghost guy almost caps you and you don't think you need a detail? From what I know about Troy, he's not gonna give up easily.'

'I can take care of myself.'

'As long as there's a gypsy around, right? Look, I don't want to be an asshole about this, but it's in my best interest to make sure you stay safe.'

'And it's my right to refuse,' Pope said.

'I could take you in as a material witness.'

'Not if you want my cooperation.'

The detective studied him a moment, then shrugged. 'Whatever you say. But if it were me, I'd be asking for my own goddamn private island.'

'We'll keep him safe,' Worthington said. 'You need anything else from us?'

'Not at the moment. But like I told you, keep your mouths shut. Until we can get this thing sorted out.'

He dug a business card out of his pocket and handed it to Pope. 'For all our sakes, you be careful out there. You change your mind about that protection, just call the station and ask for Captain Brad Billingsly.'

37

'A little housekeeping before we get started,' Jake said.

They were sitting in a corner booth at Crandal's Coffee Shop, which was just far enough away from the glitz and glitter of the city to afford them a small amount of peace and quiet. The choice had been random, but it was roomy, well lit and air conditioned, and the waitress brought them coffee without asking. Pope figured they all looked like they needed it.

It was a little past ten p.m. They were exhausted by the events of the night, and Pope wasn't sure how much longer he could last on just a couple of hours' sleep.

'I talked to Ronnie before all the excitement,' Jake said. 'She told me Evan checked out fine and she was taking him to her mother's house for the night. They're both probably in bed by now.'

'Good,' McBride said.

'I also spoke to my forensics guy and he had some interesting things to say about our gypsy friend.'

'Oh? Like what?'

'He didn't get much from the shoe you managed to grab. Says it looks hand-made and fairly cheap. But it turns out the cigarette butts you spotted are a Slavonian brand.'

'Where the hell is Slavonia?' Pope asked.

'Eastern Croatia. It has a pretty good-sized gypsy population.'

'That would explain the accent,' McBride said.

'Yeah, but what defies explanation is how our guy got the cigarettes in the first place.'

'What do you mean?'

'The brand is defunct. The manufacturer went out of business over thirty-five years ago.'

'Must be a mistake,' Pope said.

Jake shook his head. 'The name is printed on the paper. So either this guy's got a helluva stockpile or he's smoking non-existent cigarettes.'

Pope thought he'd heard and seen just about everything at this point, but this new wrinkle only managed to deepen the mystery.

'None of which tells us who we're dealing with,' Jake continued, 'but maybe this will.'

He took a sealed baggie from his pocket and held it up. The gypsy's stun gun was inside.

Pope shuddered at the sight of it and felt a phantom jolt of pain in his ribs. He could only imagine what McBride was feeling.

'Soon as we're done here, I'm taking this baby back to the lab and putting a rush on it. If we don't get a match on this son of a bitch's fingerprints, I'll turn in my badge.'

'With our luck he doesn't *have* fingerprints,' Pope said.

It was a joke, but none of them laughed.

Pope shifted his attention to Susan's notebook, which lay on the table in front of them.

'Now that we've got that out of the way, why don't we get down to business? See what my darling little ex has to say about all of this.'

McBride nodded. 'My thinking exactly.'

The first thing they looked at were the newspaper clippings. There were at least a half-dozen of them, starting with the *Salcedo Daily*'s account of Jillian Carpenter's abduction and death.

The morning after the kidnapping she had been found by a jogger in Foster Park, her half-naked body nearly buried by fallen leaves.

When the leaves were cleared away, it was discovered that the killer had used Jillian's blood to draw something on the ground:

The symbol of a wheel.

The gypsy wheel.

Anna looked at the clipping. 'It says here that Jillian's left forefinger was severed and positioned inside the wheel to replace one of the missing spokes.'

Jake's eyes widened. 'That's pretty fucked-up. Why would he do that?'

'Because he's fucked-up,' Pope said. 'Why does he kill little girls? Why does he smoke cigarettes that're older than God?'

'Calm down, Cuz. It's a legitimate question.'

'You're right,' he said. 'But I feel like I keep having to hammer this point home: there's no rational explanation for half of this stuff. And the sooner we all accept that, the better off we'll—'

'Oh, my God, look at this.'

McBride had wisely been ignoring them and had moved on to another newspaper clipping. This one a stapled, two-page photocopy. She pulled the first page free and put it on the table in front of them.

It was a murky copy of an already murky tabloid photo. A teenage girl lying on a slab in the morgue, the victim of multiple stab wounds.

The headline screamed, WHEEL OF DEATH!

McBride read from the second page:

'Manhattan. Seventeen-year-old Mary Havershaw's lifeless body was part of a macabre crime scene discovered by a janitor in the gymnasium of the Columbia High School for Girls. The victim of multiple stab wounds, Havershaw was found lying next to a crudely drawn symbol of what sources describe as a chakra, or wheel, believed to be part of a satanic ritual. The symbol was drawn using Havershaw's blood.

'Police have zeroed in on a group of young girls who have been known to dabble in the occult at Columbia, but no suspects have been named and no arrests made.

'Friends of the victim, however, point to another possibility, claiming that Havershaw had complained of being followed in the days before her death.

'"She was really worried about this guy," said one friend, who wishes to remain anonymous. "She said he never got close, but he kept showing up all over the place. Outside school, on the subway, at Coney Island.

She tried talking to her parents about him, but they just thought she was being dramatic."

'When asked if Havershaw had ever described this man, her friend said, "Not really. Just that he looked like some kind of circus freak."'

McBride lowered the page and stared at them.

'What's the date on that thing?' Jake asked.

'September 3rd, 1971.'

'This guy's defying all the stats. Most serial killers usually get their jollies, then retire after a while. What does this put him at? Forty-something years?'

'Maybe longer than that,' Pope said. His gaze was on another photocopy in the stack, its protruding corner showing a handwritten date in the margin: 1954. He recognized Susan's handwriting.

Reaching across the table, he pulled it free and stared down at a two-paragraph article entitled POLICE BAFFLED BY BIZARRE RITUAL KILLING.

'Dayton, Ohio,' he read aloud. 'Police continue to be baffled by the bizarre stabbing death of thirty-year-old housewife, Anita Dallworthy, who was found on her living-room floor in what officials have determined to be a ritual killing. Her assailant or assailants used Dallworthy's blood to create a circular symbol on the carpet. Sources wouldn't confirm, but it's believed that one of the victim's body parts was incorporated into the symbol's design.

'Police are currently looking for what witnesses have described as a severely deformed man of possible foreign descent, who was seen lurking near the Dallworthy home just days before the incident. Their search, however, has so far proved fruitless.'

Pope looked up at them. 'It's dated January 14th, 1954.'

'This is impossible. It can't be the same guy.'

'Can't it?' Anna said. 'Take a look at these.'

She was holding a stack of photographs she'd taken from a small Manila envelope clipped inside the notebook. As she laid them on the table, Pope immediately recognized them as crime-scene photos – several shots of the victims in question.

Each one of them showed a savagely gutted victim lying next to a bloody gypsy wheel, a severed finger in place of one of the spokes. Pope was reminded of the photos of satanic ritual killings that he'd once seen when he took a class in cultural anthropology.

They all studied the photographs silently, then Jake said, 'How did Susan get hold of these?'

'I'm sure it took her years and a lot of determination,' McBride said. 'She didn't stop until she got what she wanted.'

Pope tapped one of the photos. 'Take a look at the date on this one.'

It was a high-angle shot of a young woman lying in the middle of an alley, her intestines exposed by lateral slashes across her stomach, another bloody gypsy wheel beside her on the asphalt – complete with severed finger. The legend in the bottom corner was written in a foreign language. Russian maybe. Pope couldn't be sure.

Slavonian?

Whatever the case, it meant the killings weren't limited to the US.

'1924,' McBride said. 'Thirty years before Dallworthy. And the MO's the same.'

Jake shook his head. 'This is bullshit. We're talking over eighty years ago. He'd have to've started this when he was kid, and the guy I shot was no goddamn senior citizen.'

'The evidence doesn't lie, Jake.'

'But what about Kimberly Fairweather? She still had all her fingers, and I didn't see any friggin' gypsy wheels near *her* body.'

'She was a mistake,' McBride said.

'A mistake?'

'That's what he told me before he grabbed me on the football field. He said he'd made a lot of mistakes.'

'Which means that these could be just the tip of the iceberg,' Pope said. 'There could be a lot more Kimberlys out there.'

'Exactly. It's like he's searching for someone special, but he doesn't always find her.'

Jake heaved an exasperated sigh. 'You people aren't listening to me. This is *not* possible.'

'No, you're the one who's not listening,' McBride said. 'Danny's right. We've seen enough craziness the last few hours to throw "possible" right out the window.' She paused. 'Check out the pattern in these photographs.'

'What pattern?'

McBride pointed to each of the crime photos.

'Look at the wheels. They're all incomplete, just like the tattoo on the back of his neck. 1924, it has twelve spokes, if you include the victim's finger. 1954, thirteen spokes. 1971, fourteen. And 1981, fifteen. Each one is a progression. Like he's working his way towards completing the wheel.'

Pope stared at the photos, stunned. He'd been too busy looking at the carnage to see the pattern. But there it was, as plain as can be.

But then another pattern began to take form in his mind. One that sent a chill rippling through his body.

'Look at the dates of each of these killings,' he said.

'What about them?'

'We already know Jillian died in 1981, the same year Anna was born.'

Jake frowned. 'So?'

'Check the others. Jillian was ten years old when he took her. Which means she was born in '71, the same year the high-school girl, Mary Havershaw, was murdered. Probably the same day.'

'Oh, my God,' McBride said. 'You're right.'

'Havershaw was seventeen, and seventeen years earlier, Anita Dallworthy was killed.'

'And Dallworthy was thirty. That puts her birth year at 1924, when the woman in the alley was found.'

'Which means what?' Jake asked.

'It's hard to tell from these photos,' Pope told him, 'but remember what Susan said when she saw Anna?'

'She thought she was Jillian.'

'Right. Because of her eyes. She said, "His victims all had your eyes." I thought she was just babbling at that point, but maybe she was trying to tell us something.'

'Wait a minute,' Jake said. 'You aren't saying what I think you're saying?'

'I'm afraid so. Every single one of these victims is Anna. One of Anna's past lives.'

The booth was suddenly quiet, McBride's gaze glued to the crime-scene photos, her face filled with alarm.

'I don't know how or why he's doing it,' Pope said to her, 'but that someone special he keeps looking for is you. And he's been killing you over and over again.'

McBride kept staring at the photographs, as the depth and magnitude of this pronouncement hit her full force.

And Pope wasn't sure if it was shock or the exhaustion that got to her, but for the second time that day she fainted dead away.

Part Three

WHEEL OF MISFORTUNE

38

She dreamed of wheels with spokes made of severed fingers.

Thousands of them superimposed on one another, turning like the gears of a clock.

And at the centre of it all was the face of a young girl. The gypsy girl from the locket. Her dark eyes shining in the light of a campfire.

'Who are you?' Anna asked.

'You don't remember me?'

'No. Should I?'

'Give it time,' the girl said. 'It will come.'

Another strange bed.

There were no stars on the ceiling this time, just a narrow slice of moonlight that came in from a nearby window, exposing a faint crack in the plaster.

Anna pulled herself upright, bed springs groaning, and realized she was in a motel room. And not a particularly nice one at that.

'You're awake,' a drowsy voice said.

She turned and saw Pope sitting in a chair by the door, her Glock in hand, as if he'd been standing guard. On the floor next to him was a flashlight and Susan's notebook.

'How long have I been out?' she asked.

'Not long enough. I think we both need about a year's worth of sleep.'

'Did *you* get any?'

He shrugged. 'I may have dozed a bit.'

She looked around the room. 'Why are we here?'

'When you passed out on us, I didn't want to take you back to Jake's house. Not with all this Troy business still hanging over me. This place was about a block from the coffee shop, so . . .' He gestured, as if to say: *here we are*.

'And Jake?'

'He wanted to get that stun gun to the lab. He still thinks we can find this guy through traditional police work.'

'And you don't?'

Pope looked at her as if he thought this was an unnecessary question. 'I'm beginning to think Susan's right. He really is the bogey man.'

Anna felt a knuckle of fear in her stomach. 'He's coming back for me, isn't he?'

'Unless he bleeds to death first – and I don't think that's gonna happen. I think the best we can hope for is that he's been slowed down a little.'

'But why me? What does he want?'

'I think that's pretty obvious, don't you?'

Anna thought about it, then nodded, remembering what Red Cap had said to Jillian.

I've come for what is mine, Chavi.

I've come to make it right.

'He wants my soul.'

'That would be my guess.'

'But if he killed me all those times before, what stopped him? Why hasn't he gotten it already?'

'That's what I've been trying to figure out.'

Anna swung her legs around and sat on the edge of the bed. It took some effort. She couldn't remember her body ever feeling this battered. Even after her screw-up in San Francisco.

Gesturing to the notebook on the floor, she said, 'You've been busy.'

Pope nodded. 'Trying to decipher Susan's writings. But it's all encrypted, and I've never been very good at puzzles.'

Anna stood up. 'Let me take a look.'

Pope held a hand up to stop her. 'You still need rest. We'll tackle this in the morning.'

She didn't listen to him. Crossing to where he sat, she bent down and started to reach for the notebook, but he caught her by the wrist.

'In the morning,' he said. 'We need clear heads and rested bodies.'

He set the gun on the floor and stood up, pulling her upright. They stood there for a moment, staring at each other, and Anna felt that same stutter of electricity she'd felt in the Worthingtons' living room, when he put his fingers on her arm. And, later, when he kissed her in the attic.

She nodded to the Glock. 'You've been watching over me. Protecting me.'

'Trying to learn from my own mistakes,' he said. 'Our gypsy friend doesn't have an exclusive in that area.'

She thought about that. 'Does it really matter? You say we have choices, can control our world, but maybe there *is* no controlling it. No changing what's happened, or what *will* happen.'

'I don't believe that,' he said. 'And right at this moment I feel more in control than I've felt in a long, long time.'

He proved it by kissing her, deeply, moving his hands to the small of her back, pulling her close. Anna forgot all about her battered body and leaned into him, crushing her breasts against his chest, moving her arms around him. And it all seemed so familiar to her. So right.

She turned her head, pressing her cheek against his, whispering in his ear.

'Why do I feel like I know you? That I've known you forever?'

'Maybe you have,' he said softly.

She awoke with a start.

She'd been dreaming again, but something – some noise – had pulled her out of it.

Fumbling for her Glock, which Pope had left

under the pillow, she sat bolt upright and looked around, willing her eyes to adjust.

But she saw nothing. No threat.

The room was quiet, except for the sound of Pope's breathing as he slept beside her.

The clock on the nightstand read four a.m.

She was about to settle back when she heard the noise again.

A small cry.

The cry of a kitten.

Climbing out of bed, she moved to the window, parted the curtains and looked out. A small, malnourished grey tabby stood on the walkway outside, tearing at a discarded burger wrapper.

Another orphan, she thought.

Worthington's wall full of cats came to mind and she smiled. Nothing to get excited about here, folks. Everybody's safe.

For the moment at least.

But then she remembered the photographs. All those poor, butchered women, who had shared her soul. A soul that this monster seemed to want.

But why *hers*? Why had she been singled out? And why was he killing her again and again and again?

Would it ever end?

If he were to kill her on the spot, to gut her right where she stood, would she move on to yet another life, only to be hunted down and killed again?

Chavi, he'd called her.

Chavi.

Who was this girl? What did she mean to him?

Was she the young gypsy from the locket? Had it all started with her? Another past life that had been snuffed out by this freak?

Anna turned from the window, feeling helpless and alone. She looked across at the gentle rise and fall of Pope's chest and thought about his kisses, his touch, the way their bodies had fit together so naturally as they made love.

He wanted to help her. Protect her. But for all his good intentions, what could he really do?

Would he be there in the next life? And the next?

Had he been there before?

A husband? A lover? A friend?

If so, he hadn't been able to protect her then. So what made this life any different? How could he protect her now?

Perhaps the only glimmer of hope in this mess was Red Cap's ability to bleed. To feel pain. If he could be slowed down by a bullet, maybe he could be stopped by one, too.

The trick, of course, was finding him before he found *her* again. But his apparent ability to appear and vanish at will would make that a difficult task.

An impossible one.

But then she shouldn't be thinking about possible, right? Isn't that what she'd told Worthington?

Maybe Susan had the answer to all of this. Maybe somewhere in that notebook of hers, that private obsession, she had discovered the truth about what drove this man.

And maybe that truth would help Anna.

Before he killed her again.

Cracking Susan's code took about three minutes.

The actual translation, however, took nearly an hour and a half.

Anna discovered that Susan had used a primitive form of cryptography called a Caesar cipher, which substituted one letter of the alphabet for another. If an A equalled a D, then a D would equal a G, and so forth down the line. The name Anna McBride, for example, would read, *Dqqd PfEulgh*.

Why Susan had felt the need to encrypt her writing was a mystery all its own. Most of it had little to do with the so-called bogey man, but was, instead, a tribute to her friendship with Jillian. A chronicle of how they'd met and time they'd spent together.

Their neighbourhood adventures. Their days at school. Their favourite teachers. Friends. Enemies. Crushes.

Through it all, however, Anna sensed an under-current of both envy and worship in Susan's words. Jillian was the pretty one, the popular one. Susan, the hanger-on. Yet despite that trace of envy, there was no malice intended. It was clear to Anna that Susan loved her friend.

And, as she read, Anna was surprised to find that she remembered some of the events and people Susan wrote about. Only vague glimpses here and there, but enough to fill her with a profound sense of loss.

Jillian had been taken away so young.

What would have happened if she had lived? What kind of life would she have had?

When Anna reached the passages chronicling those terrible moments in the alley and the discovery of Jillian's body in Foster Park, she had trouble breathing.

Susan's pain was so raw that all Anna could think about was how this one incident had led to so much heartache. A trail of devastation that could be traced forward to this very moment in time.

She looked across at Pope, still fast asleep. How different would *his* life be, if Susan had never suffered such a blow? Would they still be happily married, raising a beautiful son?

As she continued to read, Anna noticed a change of tone in the narrative. A darkness that had settled into Susan's words. This was where the passages became less coherent. A rambling screed against Red Cap. Part rant, part analysis, with detailed, but often confusing, commentary on the newspaper clippings and photographs.

She wrote of the failed police investigation. When the Rambler was found abandoned in the parking lot of Big Mountain – the same place from which it had been stolen – the police expanded their investigation to Allenwood, questioning neighbours near the amusement park. But none of them had seen the man young Suzie had described.

He was a phantom. A mystery.

But the police's failure to find this mystery man didn't stop Susan. As the years went by, and Susan got older, she spent hours in libraries, sitting behind micro-fiche machines, searching through decades-old news-paper articles, always looking for the same thing. Always hunting for that symbol of Red Cap's broken soul:

The gypsy wheel.

From what Anna could decipher, Susan's take on all of the material she'd gathered was much the same as hers and Pope's and Worthington's. The past lives, the chain of killings – all linked by that simple, circular symbol . . .

But then the notebook abruptly ended.

No further conclusions, no new observations, nothing.

A dead end.

Disappointed, Anna looked across at Pope again and thought she knew the reason. This had to have been the moment that Pope had entered Susan's life. The moment *she* became the centre of attention, the focus of his world.

And for many years she had managed to fake it, to repress her pain and play the loving, devoted wife. When their son was born, their household was undoubtedly filled with joy—

– until Ben started to overshadow Susan, getting most of his father's attention. Then old insecurities had surfaced and, coupled with the damage Jillian's death had done to her, Susan's illness could no longer be contained, morphing into something different now. Something deadly.

This was pure speculation on Anna's part, of course. A semi-educated guess. But she had a strong feeling she was right.

Unfortunately, none of it brought her any closer to finding Red Cap.

Depressed, she started to close the notebook when she spotted something. Inside the back cover was a small built-in pocket, normally used to store extra paper. Protruding slightly above the fold was the edge of what looked like a photograph.

Anna pulled it out, feeling a slight kick in her gut as she looked at it.

It was a photo of the young gypsy girl, staring solemnly at the camera. She looked about seventeen, with flawless dark skin, curly black hair and defiant, almost hypnotic eyes. A regal beauty in a long, patterned skirt and a stark white blouse, a shawl draped over her shoulders.

Chavi.

It was Chavi.

But where, Anna wondered, had Susan gotten this? None of her writings made any reference to it.

Turning the photo over, she read the caption in the upper left-hand corner: '*Roma Vjestica* by Jonathan O'Keefe.'

Just below this was a slightly smudged stamp that read: POWELL UNIVERSITY HISTORICAL ARCHIVES – DO NOT REMOVE.

Stolen apparently. Which meant it must have been very important to Susan.

Near the centre was a question mark, scribbled in

blue ink, and next to this were thirteen letters, written in Susan's precise handwriting:

Y LMXM WZAIE MXX

Another Caesar cipher.

But this time Susan had changed the key, and it took Anna a moment to decipher the code. When she was done, it translated to:

M ZALA KNOWS ALL

M Zala. Was this a source that Susan had found, but had never bothered to follow up on?

If so, what did he or she know?

Something about Chavi?

Red Cap?

Feeling energized, Anna got to her feet and started pulling on her clothes.

She needed to find a computer.

39

It took an eternity for the motel manager to come out of his office, which wasn't a surprise at four-thirty in the morning.

Anna stood at the front desk, ringing the bell, when the door behind it finally blew open and a kid who looked as if he were still in high school stepped out, bleary-eyed. His T-shirt read: P2P RULES.

'*What*?' he barked.

She showed him her creds. 'I need your help.'

He squinted at her ID, then looked up at her with surprise. 'You gotta be kidding me. You're a fed?'

'That's the rumour,' Anna said.

'Holy shit.'

Anna moved around the counter. 'I don't see a computer out here, do you have one inside?'

'Huh?'

'A computer,' she said. 'You know that little box with a keyboard and a screen?'

'Yeah, we got one, but what's this about? We ain't doing nothing illegal.'

'I need to use it for a while.'

'Why? You working for the RIAA or something? Think I'm downloading music?'

'I don't care if you're downloading Warner Brothers' entire catalogue. Just let me in.'

He eyed her defiantly. 'You got a warrant?'

Anna had reached the end of her patience. '*Move*,' she said, shoving him aside. She stepped through the office doorway into a cramped, untidy room with a desk, a chair and an old, beige desktop computer that was about the size of a small refrigerator.

Christ.

A fucking dinosaur.

The kid crowded in behind her. 'You got no right,' he said. 'You need a warrant before you can—'

'Call your congressman,' Anna told him, then took a seat behind the computer. 'Does this thing have an Internet connection?'

'Yeah, but it's dial-up.'

'Wonderful.'

When she touched the mouse, the screen saver disappeared and the monitor came to life, showing a web page with two drunken college girls exposing their breasts to the camera.

'Nice,' Anna said.

The kid eyed her sheepishly. 'That's the day man's computer, not mine.'

She gestured. 'Do me a favour and close the door on your way out.'

'Huh?'

'Get out,' Anna said.

The kid just stood there, staring at her until his

brain finally caught up with the command. Then he turned on his heels and left, closing the door behind him.

She went to Sentinel first, the Bureau's web interface for its automatic case-support system. But when she tried to log in to her personal work box, she discovered she'd been locked out.

Royer.

He'd probably spent the day convincing the brass that she was mentally unstable and couldn't be trusted. The lockout would be temporary, pending an INSD investigation, but that didn't help Anna much right now.

Next she went to the Powell University Historical Archives website and found their search page. Checking the caption on the back of the photograph, she typed in the name, *Jonathan O'Keefe*.

The search engine began churning the information, then transferred her to O'Keefe's bio page, which loaded so slowly that Anna could have taken a couple of bathroom breaks before the page filled the screen.

She hadn't used dial-up in years and remembered why she hated it. She started reading before the page had fully loaded.

Jonathan O'Keefe was an adventurer and photography pioneer, a young genius, fluent in several languages, who had started travelling the world when he was only sixteen, camera in tow. His collection of photographs was voluminous, much of which was believed to have been lost.

Until recently Powell had only owned a small sampling of the photographer's work. But thanks to persistence and a bit of luck, his entire library had been found in the possession of a private collector, whose family generously donated the work to Powell in 2007. The website now contained several of O'Keefe's collections, recently brought online by the Powell Preservation Project.

O'Keefe had died at a fairly young age, twenty-six, in 1882. He'd fallen victim, some claimed, to . . .

– Anna felt another small kick to the stomach as she read this—

. . . a gypsy curse.

Place of death was Osijek, Slavonia.

Slavonia, Anna thought. Home of the now-defunct cigarettes.

That single kick turned into a flurry of punches that intensified when O'Keefe's portrait finally loaded on the page. His face wasn't familiar at all—

—but his eyes were. Anna would recognize those intense dark eyes anywhere.

They were Daniel Pope's.

The collection she was looking for was called *The Nomads of Osijek*. It was O'Keefe's last work.

Clicking the link, Anna waited the interminably long time it took for the thumbnails to load. The text accompanying them said that O'Keefe had become fascinated by the Zalas, a Croatian gypsy clan, and had travelled with them in their caravan as they moved from town to town, following a travelling carnival troupe. At every stop the Zalas would pitch their tents and set up fortune-telling booths near the carnival.

It was unusual, it said, for an outsider, a gadje, to be allowed such access, but O'Keefe was known for his ability to get people to trust him.

When the thumbnails had loaded, over 200 in all, Anna studied shot after shot of the gypsy family – an assortment of young and old, some posed, some candid. Standing by campfires, wagons, in front of battered tents, telling fortunes to the locals. There was a haunted quality to many of the photos, as if these people had been trodden upon and had carried their pain for centuries.

Finding the one she wanted, Anna clicked the thumbnail and watched as a new window opened and a larger version of the photograph from Susan's notebook slowly loaded.

Roma Vjestica.

Chavi.

To Anna's surprise, the accompanying text explained that the word Vjestica was Croatian for witch or wizard. And, according to O'Keefe's biographer, the Zalas were believed by many to be a magical family, with supernatural and psychic powers. This claim, however, was not all that unusual among the Roma people.

Roma Vjestica.

Gypsy Witch.

Closing the window, Anna searched the thumbnails and found another shot of the girl.

This one was a less formal pose, Chavi showing a hint of a smile. Subsequent shots found that smile widening, the body language loosening, as if Chavi had begun to trust her photographer, to feel comfortable with him—

—just as Anna had become comfortable with Pope.

If Anna was right – that this young girl was another of her past lives, and O'Keefe was one of Pope's – then they had known each other for more than a century. Which would explain why their mutual attraction had been so immediate. Why Pope's kiss, his touch, seemed so familiar.

Chavi and O'Keefe had been lovers.

Anna went back to the thumbnails, clicking them at random, hoping for that sense of déjà vu, that vague stirring of recognition from one of the faces – the faces of her past. But no memories came.

Then, without realizing it, she found one. She almost missed it at first, glancing at the thumbnail but not clicking it, about to move on, when she realized it was another shot of Chavi.

Opening the larger version, Anna's body stiffened involuntarily as the photo filled the page.

This one was labelled: *Napasnica i raditi kao rob*. Chavi was standing at the rear of a wagon, doing what, according to the text, was forbidden in gypsy culture. A precocious look on her face, she was lifting her long skirt, exposing her legs.

A scandal, by Roma standards, apparently. But this wasn't the part of the photograph that had caught Anna's attention. Instead her focus was drawn to the back of the wagon, where the face of a teenage boy could clearly be seen. He was crouched inside, his unhappy gaze on Chavi.

His face was lopsided. Severely deformed. A dark bandanna covered his misshapen skull.

It was Red Cap.

The bogey man.

Something skittered through Anna, leaving an icy trail behind.

The accompanying text explained that the girl in the photograph was believed to be the Zala family's youngest daughter.

The boy in the wagon, however, was unknown.

According to O'Keefe's biographer, many believed – as Anna had suspected – that the girl and O'Keefe had been romantically involved, fuelling rumours of a gypsy death-curse against the photographer by one of her family members. These rumours had never been substantiated and the official cause of death was reported to be 'bleeding of the brain'.

Anna shuddered, staring at the photograph.

Staring at Red Cap.

Translated into English, O'Keefe's caption, *Napasnica i raditi kao rob*, read *Temptress and Slave*.

Anna's next stop on the Information Superhighway – which was still plagued by speed bumps – was a people-finder website.

There were dozens of them on the Internet, all claiming to have the most up-to-date databases. It was unlikely, however, that any of them were as accurate as the Bureau's own case-support system, but without access, Anna was out of luck. So she chose one at random and hoped for the best.

Typing the name *M Zala* into the search field, she clicked the 'Go' button and waited.

A minute and a half later a list appeared, showing full names and locations of more then sixty people around the country. Marion Zala, Manuel Zala, Michael Zala, Michelle Zala, and dozens of variations. But she was relying on instinct here, and none of them felt right to her.

Anna decided to widen the search to include only the surname, and got back twice the amount of entries. She carefully scanned the list, hoping one would pop out at her.

At entry number thirty-nine she got her wish.

Name: Antonija Zala.

Location: Allenwood, California.

40

'Wake up, sleepy head.'

Pope groaned. 'What time is it?'

'Almost seven. Come on.'

He groaned again. 'Give me a break. This is the best sleep I've had in a decade.'

'So that's how it is, huh? You have your way with me and now you want me to get lost?'

Pope stifled a laugh. Opened his eyes. If any other woman had asked him this during the last couple of years, he probably would have said yes. He'd been a walking zombie, thinking about nobody but himself.

Eat. Gamble. Get high. Fuck.

Oh, and make sure you spend as much time as possible letting everyone around you know how miserable you are.

This wasn't something he was particularly proud of, but in one day – and one unbelievable night – McBride had changed all that.

The sight of her now, sitting on the edge of the bed, fresh from a shower, her hair slicked back, a towel wrapped around her, made Pope want to reach out just to make sure she was really there. That she wouldn't disappear on him.

As crazy as it sounded, he was in love with her.

And it was a feeling he'd never felt this strongly before. Not even with Susan. A jump-up-on-Oprah's-sofa kind of feeling that he would've made fun of only a day ago.

But not now.

Now he understood.

And despite what they'd been through, he wanted *her* to understand, too.

'Come here,' he said, taking her hand.

She leaned forward and kissed him. 'That's more like it. But I wasn't kidding, it's time to get up. We have to go.'

'Why? You've heard from Jake?'

'No, but I've got a lead. At least I hope it's one.'

'What kind of lead?'

'I won't know until we get there,' Anna said, climbing off the bed. She went to a chair, tossed her towel aside and picked up her panties, stepping into them. It's funny what a night in bed can do to a woman's modesty.

Pope watched her and couldn't help thinking lascivious thoughts. She was breathtaking.

'Get where?' he asked. 'Where are we going?'

'Allenwood.'

He sat up. 'Allenwood?'

'It's near Salcedo, about a three-and-a-half hour drive.'

'I know. It's where the amusement park is. Big Mountain.'

'Was,' McBride said. 'The place has been closed down for nearly twenty-five years. The town couldn't afford to demolish it, so they just let it rot.'

'And you know all this how?'

McBride strapped her bra on. 'I took a little field trip while you were sleeping.'

'You what?' Pope got out of bed, approached her. 'Jesus, Anna, what were you thinking? That guy could be out there somewhere. Why didn't you wake me up?'

'And interrupt the best sleep you've had in a decade? I don't think so.'

She grabbed her blouse, slipped into it, but he took hold of her arm. 'Quit being so goddamn cavalier. I don't know if what happened in here last night meant the same to you as it did to me, but I don't want to lose you.'

She stopped, touched his cheek. 'Sorry. I'm sorry. I didn't go far. Just to the manager's office to use the computer.' She gestured to her Glock, which lay in its holster on the dresser nearby. 'And I took protection.'

Pope still wasn't happy. But what could he say? When it came down to it, she'd probably handled herself better with the gypsy than he had. The twin defenders, too.

He released her and let her button her blouse.

'I saw him,' she said.

'Who?'

'Red Cap. The gypsy.'

'*What?*'

'Relax. It was in a photograph. From 1881.'

1881? What the hell?

Pope was glad Jake wasn't around to scream: *bullshit.* McBride went to the dresser, picked up a photo and showed it to him. A young gypsy girl. A dark-haired beauty.

'I found this in Susan's notebook. It's the girl from the locket. I think it's Chavi.'

Then she turned it over, showing him a cryptic message written on the back in Susan's handwriting, with Anna's translation beneath it: *M Zala Knows All.*

Anna told him about an early morning spent searching the Internet and about an entire collection of photographs she'd seen online, one of which included Red Cap.

'You sure it was him?'

She picked up a sheet of paper and handed it across to him. 'He's younger, but it's him, all right.'

It was a computer print-out of another photograph. The quality wasn't the best, and the face looked even *more* deformed, but it was, without a doubt, the same man who had attacked them in Pope's upstairs hallway.

'I don't get it. How could he still be alive?'

'How does he do anything he does? Maybe Anton-ija Zala can tell us.'

'Who's that?'

She gestured to the name scrawled on the back of the photograph. *M Zala.* 'Hopefully someone who knows her.'

'There are probably dozens of Zalas all over the world,' Pope said. 'What makes you think this one's related?'

'Because she lives in Allenwood and I don't like coincidences. Besides, I've got nothing else.'

Pope thought about this, then nodded. 'I'll take a shower and get dressed.'

He started for the bathroom, but when he got to the doorway, McBride said, 'By the way, have you ever done any photography?'

He turned. 'Not really, why?'

'I saw a portrait of Jonathan O'Keefe – the one who took the photos? Rumour has it that he and Chavi were lovers.'

'So?'

'He had your eyes.'

Pope smiled, holding her gaze. 'That explains a lot,' he said.

41

Jake Worthington was about a block from home when his cellphone rang.

He groaned, hoping it wasn't someone from the office. After leaving Danny and McBride at the motel, he'd worked straight through the night on the Fairweather case, waiting for the crime-scene techs to send him the latents off the gypsy's stun gun. Then he ran them through the office's automated fingerprint identification system, waited a good three hours for the results—

—and got a big fat doughnut.

No matches. Nothing.

He had killed the time by filing reports and filling out the paperwork to facilitate the interstate transfer of the two goons who had attacked Danny, cursing his dumb-ass cousin for getting involved with these idiots in the first place.

The rest of the time was spent spinning his wheels, thinking about all the shit he'd seen in the last several hours and how his whole concept of reality had been stood on its head. By the end of the night all he wanted to do was crawl into bed and get a couple hours of shut-eye before it all started over again.

He dug his cellphone out of his pocket, hoping it was Ronnie. Married for eighteen years, they'd known each other since they were kids, and he never got tired of hearing her voice.

But it was Danny's name on the screen.

He clicked the receive button. 'What's up, Cuz?'

'You have any luck with those prints?'

'We got zilch,' he said. 'If this guy was ever printed, it wasn't in this century. Or the last one, either.'

There was silence on the line, and for a moment Jake felt as if he were in a cellphone commercial about dropped connections – except that he could hear Danny breathing.

'Did I say something wrong?' he asked.

'I wasn't gonna tell you this, but Anna found a photo of our guy in the Powell University Archives.'

Jake felt his pulse start to elevate. 'And why the hell wouldn't you tell me something that major?'

'Because I know exactly how you'll react.'

Jake made the turn into his driveway, noting the red Toyota that Danny had parked there. He knew it wasn't Danny's car, and wondered what poor fool was waiting for its return. A woman, no doubt.

'Don't you worry about how I'll react,' he said. 'Just get me a copy of that photo.'

'That was the Powell University *Historical* Archives, to be more precise.'

Jake shut off his engine and climbed out. 'And?'

'The photo was taken in the late 1800s.'

Jake stopped. 'Say that again.'

'In Slavonia,' Danny said. 'Sound familiar?'

Jake said nothing. Felt goosebumps travel from the top of his head down to his toes.

'It's true, Jake. You can check it out online yourself.'

He listened as Danny gave him the website information. 'This is nuts,' he said. 'Who the hell are we dealing with here?'

'That's what we're hoping to find out. We're headed to Allenwood.'

'Why Allenwood?'

'To follow up on a lead Anna found in Susan's notebook. Somebody we're hoping can shed some light on all this. Are you in?'

'Jesus, Danny, I'm running on empty right now. How solid is this lead?'

'On a scale from one to ten? About a four.'

Not very promising, Jake thought. He stood on his walkway trying to decide between a potential wild goose chase and some much-needed slumber. If he remembered correctly, Allenwood was a fairly good distance away, and the drive wouldn't be short. And if something more substantial broke here while he was gone, he'd have to run his investigation long-distance. Not something he wanted to do.

Besides, McBride was a professional. If this lead of hers panned out, he trusted that she'd ask all the right questions.

'Think I'm gonna pass, Cuz. I'm beat.'

'Sorry to hear that. But don't worry about it, we'll rent a car and let you know what happens.'

'Assuming you can wake me from my coma.'

They said their goodbyes and Jake clicked off, trudging towards the front door.

He was already inside, the door closed behind him, when he realized that somebody was sitting in his armchair.

Jake froze at the sight of him:

A small, Hispanic-looking man with two black eyes and a badly broken nose, wearing a neatly tailored suit. He was holding a Beretta 9mm, with a suppressor attached.

'Where are your friends?' he asked.

'Let me guess. You're not the owner of the Tercel.'

'I work for Mr Troy.'

'That would've been my next guess,' Jake said.

'Your cousin and the FBI woman. Where are they?'

'Sitting with a police stenographer as we speak, you stupid fuck. Which means your employer is shit out of—'

The Beretta went off with a small *pop*.

Jake felt a dull, burning thud in his chest as he flew back, hit the door hard, then slid to the carpet.

Something felt loose inside him. Loose and leaking. And as the light started to dim, he knew he was about to get more sleep than he'd bargained for.

Thoughts about past and future lives suddenly filled his head, and if Danny was right about all this nonsense, he wondered what the next life would have in store for him.

In the end, he supposed it didn't really matter.

Just as long as Ronnie was there.

'The deputy is dead,' Arturo said.

The voice on the line sounded thin and nasally. 'What about the others?'

'He was alone.'

'Shit!'

'You've only yourself to blame. You had them all in one place last night.'

'What was I supposed to do? Pop them in my car? Don't be ridiculous.' He paused. 'So where do we go from here?'

'Not to worry,' Arturo said. 'You have the ability to track a cellular GPS signal, yes?'

'I'll have to jump through a few hoops.'

'Then you had better start jumping and put a trace on Pope's cellphone.'

He recited the number from memory.

The voice on the line rose half an octave. 'This is all getting a little out of hand, don't you think? How many bodies do we have to pile up before Troy is happy?'

'As I recall, Captain Billingsly, *you* were the one who came to Mr Troy, looking for a handout. Are you dissatisfied with the arrangement?'

'I–I didn't say that,' Billingsly sputtered.

'Then stick to your commitment and don't ask questions. We don't like people who ask questions.'

'Sorry,' Billingsly said. 'I'll get right to work on that number.'

Arturo looked down at the dead man and smiled.

Compared to him, The Ghost had been a rank amateur.

42

In the end, it took them four hours to drive to Allenwood.

Anna rented the car, a Nissan Pathfinder, on her Bureau account, which, to her surprise, hadn't yet been suspended.

They took the I-15 past the Mojave National Preserve, then cut over to the 58, through Barstow and Boron and California City.

As she drove, Anna looked out at the desolate desert landscape and again wondered how people found themselves out here, living so far away, it seemed, from civilization. Yes, they had their shopping malls and their satellite TV, but the sun would bake you alive and turn your skin as rough as alligator hide, and she just couldn't fathom the attraction this part of the world held for those who lived here.

About halfway through the drive they switched, Pope taking the wheel for a spell. Anna settled back in the passenger seat, trying to get some sleep, but was too keyed up to manage it.

She knew that Pope was doubtful about this trip.

That he thought a visit to Antonija Zala was most likely a waste of time. And she appreciated his willingness to come with her anyway.

When she looked at him, sitting behind the wheel, his eyes fixed on the road ahead, she thought about how natural they were together. As if, without even knowing it, they had been searching for each other all of their lives. All of their *many* lives, perhaps.

She imagined herself as a seventeen-year-old Roma girl, posing for Jonathan O'Keefe's camera and, later, sneaking off in the darkness to be with him. To feel his hands upon her, just as she'd felt Pope's hands last night.

'I don't want to lose you,' he'd said to her this morning.

And although she felt the same, she hadn't been able to express it. Despite what they'd been through together, despite her complete abandon when they had made love, she couldn't commit herself beyond the moment, because she had no idea how all of this would turn out.

And Red Cap's success rate did not encourage her.

Unlike Pope, Anna *didn't* think this trip was a waste of time. Knew in her gut that Antonija Zala would have the answers she sought. Just as she'd known she was meant to be here.

She felt as if she were being guided by a sixth sense. Some sort of cosmic homing device had been planted in her brain and she was zeroing in on the signal. And no matter what anyone else might think, she had to follow that signal until she found its source.

The saw the amusement park well before they reached the city proper.

Its rusted, steel-framed roller coaster was easily visible from the highway, standing out in stark relief against the desert sky.

Close by stood the mountain itself, all plaster and peeling paint, the sign atop it missing several of its letters:

B G MOU T N

It was surrounded by a sagging, weather-worn aluminium fence, topped with several coils of barbed wire.

Anna was saddened by the sight of it. It seemed to represent hope gone sour. Someone's dream destroyed by time and indifference. A lifeless body lying on the side of the road, decaying in the hot desert sun, as the cars whizzing past paid little or no attention to it.

She thought about Jillian Carpenter and little Suzie Oliver riding that roller coaster, screaming in terror and delight as their car rose and dipped and turned. And in a way, this park represented them quite well.

One dead. One broken.

Pope pointed towards a highway sign. 'There's the turn-off.'

It read: ALLENWOOD.

'This is it,' Anna said. 'I can feel it. The place where it all comes together.'

Or falls apart, she thought.

It was an old, mid-sized city whose better days were behind it. Its population was well into the thousands, but was only half what it had been in its heyday.

Anna had looked it up on Wikipedia, which had described it as one of the fifteen poorest cities in the state. Big Mountain had been its stab at pulling itself out of a sustained economic slump. There had been an upturn in the beginning, but when the park ultimately failed, the fallout had been disastrous, leaving a city whose residents relied largely on welfare and public assistance.

Antonija Zala lived in the heart of what a dilapidated sign said was *Gypsy Town*.

'Not very PC,' Pope said as they drove past.

The streets were dusty and pockmarked, the store fronts in serious need of paint and repair. Some of the windows were boarded up. Others mended with masking tape.

'123 Bronson Avenue,' Anna said, consulting the directions she'd printed out. 'Turn left at the stop sign.'

Pope made the turn and drove slowly down a street that was more or less identical to the previous one – except for one major difference, which they nearly found out about too late.

'Shit!' he shouted, slamming on the brakes.

They came to a skidding halt just inches from a large sinkhole, and Anna felt her stomach lurch up into her throat. The hole – more of a trench, really – spread all the way across the street, making it impossible to go further by car.

Letting out a shaky breath, Pope backed up, then pulled the Pathfinder to the kerb.

'A few barricades and a couple of warning signs would've been nice,' Anna said.

Pope shrugged. 'We're probably the first traffic this place has seen in months.' He killed the engine and unlocked the doors. 'Looks like we're on foot.'

Fortunately the sidewalk was still intact. They climbed out of the Pathfinder and continued up the street, checking the addresses as they went.

Number 123 was set back from the street, not immediately visible until you were right up on it. It was a large, ramshackle Victorian, a remnant of an older neighbourhood, whose owners had apparently refused to cooperate when it came time to revamp and rebuild.

There was a sign in the front window and Anna felt a stab of disappointment the moment she saw it.

It featured a red neon palm with the words FOR-TUNE TELLER above it.

And beneath, in smaller print, it read:

MADAME ZALA KNOWS ALL

43

'Madame Zala knows all,' Pope said. 'So much for that lead.'

Anna ignored him.

Despite her disappointment, at least she knew she'd been right to come here. Her sixth sense was tingling now, telling her she was exactly where she was meant to be.

Either that, or it was warning her. She couldn't be sure which.

A set of dilapidated steps led to the front porch and a tattered screen door.

'You sure you want to do this?' Pope asked, eyeing the place warily.

'I'm sure.'

Without even realizing it, Anna grabbed his hand as they climbed. When they got to the porch, they stood there a moment, unable to see past the screen.

'Come in, come in,' a voice said. Female. Warm. Friendly. 'Madame Zala has been expecting you.'

'I'll bet she has,' Pope muttered, just loud enough for Anna to hear.

Ignoring him again, she pulled the screen door open and they stepped inside. With the store fronts on either side shading it from the sun, the place was dimly lit and it took a moment for Anna's eyes to adjust.

When they did, she saw a modest but tastefully decorated living room, full of furniture that had likely been there since the house was first built.

An ornate sofa faced the door, and an attractive, dark-haired woman of about forty sat smiling up at them.

Antonija Zala, no doubt.

For some reason – perhaps because of the photographs she'd seen – Anna had expected her to be wearing a shawl and a long skirt. But to Anna's surprise, she wore muted pink slacks and a bright-green tube top, looking much like a relic of the 1970s.

'You've come for a reading, yes?' the woman said. Her accent was vaguely European, just like Red Cap's.

Before coming here, Anna had wondered how she'd handle this. Show her credentials and question the woman like a suspect? Or simply let it play out naturally?

A direct confrontation, she'd decided, would only force Zala to put up her guard. Better to try to engage her in conversation, then ease into the subject of Red Cap.

In preparation, Anna had kept her Glock hidden under her blouse, nestled at the small of her back. She was just another tourist.

'Yes,' she said, in answer to the woman's question. 'Can you help me?'

'Help? Perhaps not. Advise? Yes.' The woman's gaze shifted between them. 'Just one of you? Or both?'

'Just me,' Anna said.

'But I'd like to sit in,' Pope told her.

The woman held out a hand, palm upturned. 'Fifty dollars.'

Anna and Pope exchanged looks, then Pope brought out his wallet and opened it.

'Twenty,' he said.

The woman frowned. 'Thirty-five.'

Pope pulled out a twenty and a ten and laid them on the outstretched palm. 'Take it or leave it.'

The hand closed with a snap, folding the bills, fingers tucking them into her tube top. She gestured to a nearby doorway with a beaded curtain.

'In there,' she said. 'I will be with you in a moment.'

They sat in silence at a small round table, covered with a lacy cloth, a single, unlit candle at its centre. The walls were blank. No photos. No paintings. No mirrors. The window to their right faced the crumbling grey brick of the neighbouring building, close enough to touch.

Madame Zala had been gone for more than a moment. Closer to five minutes, actually.

'Probably making sure the bills aren't counterfeit,' Pope said.

Then a toilet flushed somewhere inside the house and a few seconds later the curtain of beads parted with a rattle as Madame Zala returned, taking a seat opposite them.

She was carrying something wrapped in a blue scarf.

Anna shot Pope a glance, knowing he must be thinking that this was a waste of time. But she was convinced that Susan had written the name on the back of Chavi's photograph for a reason, and the least she could do was let this thing play out, for better or worse.

Madame Zala reached to a dimmer switch on the wall behind her and turned the lights low, then lit the candle and moved it to one side.

Placing the scarf at the centre of the table, she unwrapped it to reveal a deck of tarot cards, which she extended to Anna.

'Please shuffle them.'

Anna took the cards. There were twenty or so, but they were larger than normal and handling them felt a bit awkward. She did her best to shuffle them, then handed them back to Madame Zala.

The woman squared the cards. 'You have a question for me?'

'Question?' Anna asked.

'Most who come here seek answers, yes? Without a question, the cards cannot guide you.' She glanced at Pope then returned her gaze to Anna. 'Something about your love life, perhaps?'

'I just want to know my future,' Anna said.

'That could cover many things. Is there something specific you're concerned about?'

Anna thought about this. 'There's someone new in my life. A stranger. Can you tell me about him?'

Madame Zala nodded, then cut the deck and dealt several cards face up on the table, arranging them in an elaborate layout. Each card carried a number in the corner, along with daggers and swords and naked goddesses and New Agey symbols. Anna had no idea what any of it meant.

'The Major Arcana,' Madame Zala said. 'Each represents one of life's journeys.' She pointed to a card, showing a man with a wand. 'The Magician represents the journey of will. You have been weakened by recent events, only to gather strength and rally, your will growing stronger with each passing hour.'

She pointed to another card, showing an old bearded man. 'But the Hermit crosses before you, representing caution. Fear. Prudence. Ignore him at your peril.'

Then another card, this one showing a man hanging upside down from a tree. 'The Hanged Man,' she continued. 'The symbol of sacrifice. To achieve the goal you wish to achieve, your sacrifice will be great. Perhaps greater than you're willing to accept.'

'What does any of this have to do with the stranger?' Anna asked.

'Patience,' the woman said, then pointed to yet another card. A skeleton holding a scythe. 'Here is your stranger. The Death card. He is the cause of these things. The reason you have been put to the test.'

Anna sucked in a breath.

'But do not fear,' Madame Zala continued. 'This

card merely represents change. Transformation. Your life has been altered in significant ways, and you must adapt and change or suffer the consequences.'

Anna now wished that she had simply gone for the direct approach. She'd always thought of fortune-telling as a con game, designed to part unsuspecting fools from their money. What Madame Zala had just told her, however, was eerily accurate. Then again, it was also fairly generic and might apply to anyone who sat in this chair.

Enough of this, Anna thought. Time to get down to business.

Taking the photo of Chavi out of her pocket, she laid it on the table.

'What about this one?' she asked. 'What does she represent?'

Madame Zala froze, staring at the photo, then her head jerked up, her gaze meeting Anna's. 'Who are you?'

'A woman on a journey,' Anna said, then unfolded the *Temptress and Slave* printout and placed it in front of Madame Zala, pointing to the boy in the wagon. 'And this is the stranger I seek.'

Madame Zala's eyes widened. She jumped to her feet, nearly knocking her chair over as she backed away from the table. The candle wobbled, threatening to fall.

'Jozef!' she shouted. 'Jozef, get your ass out here! Now!' Her accent had mysteriously disappeared. 'Hurry, Jozef! It's her! She's here!'

They heard the pounding of heavy steps on a

wooden floor, then the beaded curtain parted with a sharp snap as a large, twenty-something lunk stuck his head into the room. In a dark alley, Anna might have mistaken him for Red Cap.

'What's wrong, Ma?'

'Get them out of here! Get her out of this house!'

Clenching and unclenching his fists, the lunk moved towards them aggressively, and Pope rose to meet him. 'Easy, pal.'

But the lunk ignored the suggestion, grabbing a handful of Pope's shirt as—

—Anna quickly reached back and brought out her Glock, pointing it at him. 'FBI! Let him go.'

The lunk's face went white at the sight of the weapon and he released Pope's shirt, stepping back to join his mom, who was now flat against the wall, her eyes narrowed in anger.

'What do want from us? Why did you come here?'

'The photo,' Anna said. 'Tell us about the boy in the photo.'

'I don't know anything about him.'

'Bullshit.'

'I swear to you, I've never seen him before.'

'Then why did you react that way? Like you recognized him?'

'You startled me, that's all. When I'm in the middle of a reading, I'm deep in concentration and—'

—A shout from the back of the house cut her off. 'Stop, Tatjana! Stop with the lies!'

It was a woman's voice, the interruption so unexpected that they all froze in place.

'Bring her back to me,' she shouted. 'I want to see her face.'

'But, Mother—'

'Don't argue with me, girl! What have I told you about that?'

Madame Zala, or Tatjana, or whatever her name was, lowered her gaze to the floor, then gathered herself, looking at Anna.

'You won't need the gun,' she said. 'It won't protect you from the truth.'

44

The old woman was the size of a small tent.

Sitting on a day bed in a poorly lit room, she was so enormous that it would take a crane to lift her off it. Anna had seen people like this on the news and in movies, but she wasn't prepared for the real thing.

The room had a gamey smell. A hint of urine. A walker stood at the foot of the bed, but Anna doubted it had been used in recent memory. The bedpan beneath it, however, obviously got regular workouts.

The sight made Anna's stomach churn with revulsion, and she was pretty sure her expression showed it.

'I am what I am,' the old woman said. 'Think what you will.'

She was close to eighty years old, with dirty grey hair and stark brown eyes. That she'd lived this long without succumbing to heart attack or some obesity-related illness was a miracle.

Glancing around, Anna saw that, unlike the previous room, this one was filled with framed photographs. On the wall, on tabletops. Photos of family and friends, including reproductions of some of the O'Keefe prints she'd seen online. But newer ones, too. A chronicle spanning decades. The old woman had surrounded herself with the history of her life.

And on the wall, just to the right of the day bed, was a framed blow-up of the photo of Chavi.

'My name,' she said, 'is Antonija Zala. Madame Zala to the gadje.' She lifted a finger and wiggled it at Anna. 'Come closer, child. I want to see your eyes.'

Anna glanced back at Pope, who stood near the doorway with the lunk and his mother. They no longer seemed to be a threat, having given themselves over to the will of the old woman. They were afraid of her. And Anna wondered if she should be afraid, too.

As if reading her mind, the old woman said, 'You've nothing to fear. Come closer.'

Anna hesitated, another wave of revulsion passing through her, then did as she was told. The old woman stared intently at her eyes as she approached, recognition spreading across her face.

'Ahhh, yes,' she said. 'I knew he had found you again. He wasn't certain at first, didn't want to make another mistake, so he held back. But he knows now. He knows you're the one.'

Anna couldn't quite believe what she was hearing. 'How could you possibly know all that?'

'I have the gift, child. How else?'

'And he *told* you this?'

'Not in words,' the old woman said. 'And not in this world. But in the nether. In the spaces between time.'

'I don't understand. What are you talking about?'

'That I can sometimes read Mikola's thoughts.'

'That's his name? Mikola?'

The old woman smiled. 'You have so much to remember, my dear.'

'Then quit being so goddamn cryptic,' Anna said, her frustration bubbling over. 'Tell me what's going on.'

'Calm down, girl. You have no enemies here.'

'Then answer my question.' She showed the old woman the printout, pointing again to the boy crouched inside the wagon. 'Is this him? Is this Mikola?'

The old woman didn't look at it.

Simply nodded.

'What does he want with me? My soul? Is that what he's after?'

Another nod.

'But *why*?' Anna asked. 'Who *is* he?'

'He's Roma,' the old woman said. 'Blood.'

'What do you mean he's blood?'

Antonija Zala smiled again, patiently, the folds of fat in her chins jiggling with the effort.

'He's family, my dear. He's your brother.'

Anna said nothing.

Feeling as if her legs might give out, she found a chair nearby and sat.

Her brain felt numb.

'Let me tell you a story,' the old woman said. She shifted on the bed, grunting with the effort. 'It's the story of two children, conjoined twins, you might say. But it isn't a body they share. No organs. No limbs. But something far more vital than any human shell could ever be.'

'A soul,' Anna said. 'They share a soul.'

Antonija Zala smiled again. 'That's right, my dear. They were born many years ago, to a family of Roma. Our family. The Zala family. The Zala clan had travelled for many a decade, then finally found their way back home to Slavonia, to a city called Osijek.

'When one of the daughters, my great-grandmother, Natasa, became pregnant by her husband Nikolai, there was much joy in the family. But at the moment of birth, those present knew something was seriously wrong.

'There were two children in Natasa's womb. One, the girl, was quite beautiful. Pristine, in fact. They named her Chavi.

'But the boy, he did not fare as well during the birth. He was small, sickly, with a deformed face and body. He was, they thought, possessed by demons, and those who saw him that morning did not expect him to live.

'He was taken into the forest and left to the elements, his father weeping as he lay the boy under a tree. And when Nikolai returned to camp, he found that little Chavi was crying as well, tears that had not stopped since her brother was taken from her side.

'She cried through the night, her little face red with anguish. But the deed was done. The boy had been given to the angels.

'Or so they thought.'

The old woman paused, shifting again on the day bed.

'When Nikolai returned the next day to the spot where he had left his son, he was surprised to discover that the boy was still alive. The temperature during the night had dropped below freezing, and Nikolai knew it could not be possible – yet there he was, crying angrily, just as Chavi had cried. And he knew that the boy had been warmed by Chavi's tears.

'Not knowing what else to do, Nikolai picked him up and carried him back to camp. At first the family celebrated. It was a miracle, given to them by God. But then the whispers started. Perhaps God did not have a hand in the boy's survival after all. Perhaps it was the Devil. The demons that possessed him.'

'But all Nikolai and Natasa knew was that their little beauty, their Chavi, was no longer crying.

'As the years passed, the twins became inseparable. It was said that they not only shared blood, but were two parts of the same wheel. The boy, Mikola, had trouble walking, but he would follow Chavi wherever she went. And while Chavi was doted on by members of the family and their friends, Mikola was often ignored, unless there was a chore to be done. A task to be completed.

'The Zala family had always been a powerful clan. Tales of their magic were known throughout the region, some true, some exaggerations of the truth. And as she grew into a lovely young woman, Chavi discovered that she had powers far greater than anyone else in the family.

'You must understand that it takes most Roma women many years to develop their supernatural skills. Some, like my Tatjana here, never develop them at all.

'But Chavi was different. Special. By the time she was seventeen, she was a full-fledged chovihani, a witch, respected and loved by all those around her.

'But Mikola was also special. It was unusual for a Roma male to develop any supernatural powers, but because he shared Chavi's soul, he also shared many of her skills. But rather than use those skills for good, as Chavi did, Mikola was drawn to the dark side and his days of tolerating insults were over.

'When several gadje children pelted him with eggs one day, he felled them all with a curse. When a carnival barker caught him trying to sneak into one of his sideshows, and threatened to flog him, Mikola rendered him mute, and the man was later found to have swallowed his own tongue.

'But the ultimate insult came from Chavi herself. When a young gadje photographer began travelling with the Zala family, Chavi found herself falling in love with the man and spoke of running away with him.

'This was not only against Roma law, it did not sit well with Mikola. Chavi belonged to no one but him. She was, after all, his twin sister, the second half of the wheel. How could she think to abandon him? To leave him behind?

'In an angry rage, Mikola put a curse on the photographer, who soon collapsed and died.

'Heartbroken and distraught, Chavi confronted Mikola, but his rage continued to burn, all the years of pain and frustration coming to the surface. Chavi had betrayed him. She was no longer his sister, but a thief. The girl who had threatened to take away forever what was rightfully his. The part of his soul she had already stolen at birth.

'And in a frenzy, Mikola grabbed a knife and stabbed Chavi, over and over again, then left her in the forest, under the very tree his own father had left him on the night of his birth.

'Mikola had expected her half of his soul to migrate to him, to bring him strength, to cure his deformities, but with her dying breath Chavi pointed a bloodied finger to the centre of his chest and said a single word:

'*Mine.*'

The old woman lowered her head as if weakened by the telling of the story.

Anna stared at her, waiting for more, but nothing came. It looked as if she had fallen asleep.

Then she stirred. 'This is, of course, a story that was told to me as a young child. There have been embellishments over the years, but the essence of what I've said is true.'

'But you haven't told me all of it,' Anna said. 'Where does it go from there?'

'I think you know.'

'Mikola went looking for Chavi and found her in the next life, taking what he felt was rightfully his.'

The old woman nodded. 'He was convinced that the last word she spoke was a final curse. If he didn't take his soul from *her*, she'd surely take it from *him*.'

'But how did he know where to find her?'

The old woman tapped her nose. 'He relied on his instincts. With every new life, our souls naturally seek out those we have known in our previous lives. If he couldn't find her directly, he would search for those who had been close to her. Like a lover. Or a friend.'

'The photographer,' Anna said. 'O'Keefe.'

'Among others.'

Anna turned, looking at Pope. Then she thought of Susan and it all made a kind of twisted sense to her.

He's always watching, Susan had said.

Could Mikola have been watching *them*? And what about the Worthingtons? Did he watch them, too? Had their lives somehow intersected with the Fairweathers, causing Mikola to zero in on Kimberly, thinking she might be the one?

It was like some cosmic game of hide and seek, and Mikola sometimes got it wrong. Perhaps the eyes of those chosen were close, so close that he had to take a chance, only to discover that he'd made a mistake.

I make many mistakes, he'd told her.

How many people, she wondered, had he killed? How many innocents? All of it on Chavi's shoulders. *Her* shoulders.

'I don't understand,' Anna said. 'If he wants my soul so badly, why didn't he just take it from me the first time and get it the hell over with?'

'Chavi's curse,' the old woman told her. 'Because of her refusal to let it go, he could take only a piece at a time. One new spoke for every successful kill. He started with eight, but he needed eight more to complete the wheel.'

Sixteen spokes, Anna thought. Hadn't Jillian Carpenter been the fifteenth? And didn't this mean that she, Anna, represented the only remaining piece?

'I'm the last,' she said.

The old woman nodded.

'But if he's been hunting me from life to life, why doesn't he get older? He should have been long dead by now.'

'Ahhh,' the woman said. 'According to the story, this is exactly what Chavi believed would happen. In that final moment, she thought she had outwitted him. But he began to study the black arts and came to know them intimately.' She paused. 'He grows older, just as any man would. But to you and me, he does not seem to age because he is not of our time.'

'What?'

'He spends much of his life moving in the spaces *between* time. As we might travel from continent to continent, he moves from year to year, decade to decade.'

'Wait a minute,' Anna said. 'Are you telling me he's some kind of . . .'

She couldn't complete the sentence. It was too absurd.

'Is it so hard to believe?' the old woman asked.

'Frankly, yes.'

'He's a powerful soul. And with each new spoke, he becomes more powerful.'

Anna felt lightheaded. This was too much information, too fast. She was still trying to assimilate this new world of blood rituals and gypsy witches and multiple lives. And this was one step she wasn't sure she was willing to take.

'But how?' she asked. 'How is it possible?'

'The mirrors,' the old woman told her. 'It's said that they are his pathway through time. That if he stands before them and looks beyond his reflection, when he ceases to see himself he sees the world, all the way back to its very beginning, and forward, to eternity.'

'Through the Looking Glass,' Anna said softly, remembering the book she'd seen in the Fairweather house. 'But how can that be? If all it takes is a mirror, he'd be popping up all over the place.'

The old woman shook her head. 'Not just one. They say he needs the strength of a thousand mirrors to make his passage.'

Anna baulked. Another ridiculous notion.

Then it hit her.

The *house* of mirrors. He had dragged her towards Dr Demon's House of a Thousand Mirrors.

And hadn't Jillian first felt his presence when she and Suzie were near the Miner's Magic Mirror Maze? And what about the previous victim? Mary Havershaw? Hadn't she mentioned seeing him at Coney Island?

That was how he was doing it. What other explanation could there be?

'When he was a child,' Anna said, 'the sideshow he was caught sneaking into. Was it the house of mirrors?'

The old woman nodded. 'Such places have always fascinated him.'

Anna stood up. 'I have to go to Big Mountain.'

'Yes,' the old woman said. 'That is where you will find him. And you must find him and kill him and take back your soul. But it must be you who kills him. Only you.'

'Why?' Anna asked.

'Anyone else, and the soul will move on to the next life without you, forever fragmented. And, as you must know by now, a fragmented soul is not a healthy soul.'

Probably better than anyone, Anna thought.

'But he's wounded and weak,' the old woman continued. 'Perhaps more vulnerable than he's ever been.'

Her eyes took on a far-away look, as if she were listening to some inner voice.

Then she smiled again. 'And he doesn't know you're coming.'

45

'I'm not so sure this is a good idea,' Pope said.

They were back in the Pathfinder, Anna staring at the sinkhole in front of them, wondering if it was a preview of things to come. It was certainly a commentary on her life. On *all* of her lives.

'Did you hear what Madame Zala told me?'

'Every word of it.'

'Then what choice do I have? We got exactly what we came here for, and if I don't go after this guy, he'll come after me again. I think I like the idea of being first this time.'

Pope took out his cellphone. 'At least let me get Jake in on this.'

'No. Leave him out of it.'

'Why? He has resources. He can—'

'No, Danny. This is my battle. Between me and Mikola. I have to be the one who does this.'

'That's easy to say, but have you ever killed a man before?'

'Yes,' she told him, and this stopped him cold. She gestured to her scar. 'The man who gave me this.'

Pope was silent. Put away his phone.

'So does this mean you want *me* to get lost, too?'

Anna rolled her eyes. 'Just back this fucking thing up and drive, okay?'

They asked the gun-shop owner how to get to Big Mountain.

Although you could see the place looming in the distance, they had quickly learned that the city was a jigsaw puzzle, and an access road wasn't readily apparent.

'Once you get to Marigold,' he told them, 'just take a left on Johnson, a right on Haywood and go straight. You'll find it. But the city don't like trespassers, and they sure as hell don't allow target practice.'

'I won't be practising,' Anna said.

Pope drove again, following the gun-shop owner's directions, and before they knew it they were travelling down a dusty, weed-infested road lined with bullet-riddled NO TRESPASSING signs.

It was a little past three p.m. when they reached the entrance, but for Anna, it might as well have been midnight. Darkness had settled into her heart, and into that single scrap of Chavi's soul that she still carried.

She was on a mission now.

She wanted what was rightfully hers.

The entrance to Big Mountain was blocked by a tall aluminium gate, topped with barbed wire. More bullet-riddled signs adorned it, warning people to KEEP OUT. DANGER. The gate was fastened by several heavy-duty padlocks, which would have been impossible to breach if Anna hadn't thought to buy a bolt cutter in the gun shop's HANDY HARDWARE section.

She snipped through them, then swung the gate open, and the two of them travelled by foot across a tumbleweed-strewn parking lot, Pope now armed with the Mossberg 590 shotgun they'd bought.

They came to a set of dilapidated ticket booths and rusted turnstiles that fronted the place. A sun-bleached sign above the turnstiles read: HAVE A NICE BIG MOUNTAIN DAY! – and if this was an example of the amount of imagination that had gone into the place, it was no wonder it had been a dismal failure.

The pavement was weather-worn and full of cracks, desert weeds sprouting up between them, some of which had grown waist-high. And just beyond the turnstiles was TRAVELLER'S TRAIL, or at least what was left of it, a crumbling yellow sidewalk that led into a wide tunnel carved into the side of a fake rock wall.

Sitting atop the wall, on rusted railway tracks, were the remnants of a three-car passenger train, THE BIG MOUNTAIN EXPRESS, scarred by neglect and the heat of many summers.

As they worked their way into the darkness of the tunnel, Anna kept the heel of her hand resting on her Glock, which was now holstered on her right hip. She was waiting for her sixth sense to kick in, to warn her of any danger ahead, but it never did. And as they emerged on the other side, they were presented with the full ruined glory of Big Mountain Amusement Park.

TRAVELLER'S TRAIL now split into two, wrapping around the enormous plaster mountain that stood at the centre of the park. Near the top of the mountain, a large hole was cut into its side, to allow the passage of sky cars, one of which hung precariously from a broken cable.

There was a faux log-cabin structure to the right, the words GENERAL STORE carved above it. A lone, empty postcard rack lay overturned in its doorway, a tumbleweed caught beneath it.

To the left, along the trail, was a sign that read LOGGER'S LODE, which, to Anna's mind, was an unfortunate name for a ride. But the structure itself was so overgrown with weeds that it was hard to tell what kind of ride it had been.

At the fork of the trail was a small kiosk made of fake logs. Mounted at its centre was a shattered glass case, a tattered and faded map inside.

The map was full of cartoon-like representations of the rides, showing their locations relative to where Anna and Pope now stood. All of the standard low-rent amusement park rides were there, but with new names to reflect the Big Mountain theme.

The roller coaster was called The Avalanche, the Ferris wheel had been renamed The Old Mill Wheel, and the bumper cars were Log Jammers. Even on paper this couldn't have sounded like much of an idea.

The Miner's Magic Mirror Maze was located at the north-east corner of the lot near the roller coaster, in an area labelled MINER'S COVE. Anna studied the map, then squinted towards the trail, trying to gauge the distance, and it suddenly occurred to her that, despite her bravado, she had no real plan in place, no specific approach to take.

'What do you think?' she said to Pope.

'This is your show, remember?'

She nodded and pointed to the map. 'Let's come around from the side here. That should give us a sweep of the area, then put us here, near the roller coaster, across from the entrance.'

'And then what?' Pope asked.

'Then I go inside.'

The Avalanche had looked big enough from the highway, but up close and personal, it was a rickety, rust-rotted behemoth that towered over everything in its vicinity. The cars, retooled to look like coal wagons, had been disconnected and piled up against the aluminium fence, home to at least one family of rats.

Anna and Pope were crouched nearby, in the thick weeds beneath the first dip, their gazes on the mirror maze, which stood in the shadow of the roller coaster. Another faux log-cabin structure, it was larger than Anna had expected.

A quick surveillance of the area behind the building had revealed a tear in the aluminium fence, just room enough for a man to fit through.

Parked beyond it, in an overgrown field, was a rusted-out Ford pick-up, which may or may not have been functional. There was a door in the rear of the building, but it was locked, and there was no way to tell if it had recently been accessed. They had searched for signs of blood, but found none.

Out front, the mirror maze's double-doored entrance was padlocked, more NO TRESPASSING and KEEP OUT signs adorning it. The words DANGER – BROKIN GLAS were spray-painted above them.

Anna and Pope stayed crouched there for quite some time, watching and waiting, but there was no movement, no indication that anyone was inside.

Keeping his voice low, Pope said, 'This is a waste. He isn't here.'

But Anna didn't believe that. Her sixth sense was kicking in now and she knew this was exactly where she was meant to be.

'He's here,' she said. 'I can feel him. But Madame Zala was wrong.'

'About what?'

'He's knows I'm coming. He's waiting for me.'

'Jesus,' Pope said. 'You're giving me the creeps.'

'He's hurt and he's weak, and he wants this over with as much as I do. One way or the other.'

'And you know this how?'

'I'm the gypsy witch, remember?' She tapped her temple. 'I have the gift.'

She was only half-kidding, but Pope gave her a look. 'You know I'm not gonna let you do this, right? I told you, I don't want to lose you.'

'This isn't your call,' she said, 'so don't even start.'

Pope said nothing, but she could feel his resistance. She touched his cheek. 'I love you, Danny. I do. But I've got to do this. You know that.'

'There's some other way. There has to be.'

She kissed him. 'You're not gonna talk me out of it.'

'Then at least let me go in with you.'

'No. I told you. It's between him and me.'

He gestured to the 590. 'Then what the hell did I bring this for?'

'Your own protection.'

She squeezed his hand and rose, pushing past the weeds until she was standing not thirty yards from the entrance to the mirror maze.

She turned, looking at Pope.

'Besides, if this all goes south and *he* comes out of there instead of me, I want you to take that thing and blow the shit out of him.'

46

She approached the building from the side, pressing her back against the wall as she inched towards the entrance. The padlocks were gone in two easy snips, then she dropped the bolt cutter to the ground and unholstered her Glock.

Trying to keep the noise to a minimum, she gingerly pulled the doors open just wide enough to slip through, then peeked inside.

Darkness.

Not surprised, she brought out her Mini Mag and hesitated. He could be waiting for her, right here, ready to pounce.

Sucking in a breath, she flicked it on and shone it inside.

No bogey men in sight. Just a wide hallway, littered with broken glass. Shattered light bulbs from the fixtures in the ceiling above.

Releasing the breath, she turned sideways, slipping in through the opening, skirting the glass as she moved into the hallway, each step making her cringe, certain he'd hear her and strike at any moment.

Sweeping the beam around, she saw the frayed remnants of a rope line and a few overturned stanchions, and realized she was in a lobby. A nearby set of double doors led to the maze itself, a faded sign above them reading: ENTER IF YOU DARE. But the doors were closed, guarded by another padlock.

Cursing herself for leaving the bolt cutter outside, she reached forward and jiggled the lock, surprised when it fell open in her hand.

Intentional?

Slipping the lock free, she pushed the doors open, expecting to see a maze of cracked and shattered mirrors, more glass on the floor. But a single sweep of her flashlight told her she was wrong.

Every mirror was intact, mounted between broad pillars that formed what looked like arched doorways, a dozen of her reflections staring back at her. Her flashlight beam was doubled and tripled and quadrupled, giving the illusion that there was more light in the room.

The sight was breathtaking. Someone – and she had no doubt who – had spent hours maintaining this place, keeping it pristine.

The angle of the mirrors made it seem as if there were several long corridors leading deeper into darkness, but she knew this was deceptive, designed to confuse. There would be only one true passageway, and finding it in near-darkness would be difficult, if not impossible.

Steeling herself, she moved forward, stepping through one of the archways. She was only able to go a few feet, however, before she hit a dead end.

Turning, she doubled back, tried another archway, and got luckier this time, moving several yards down the corridor before hitting another dead end. But when she turned to look behind her, ready to double back again, all she saw were more reflections and she couldn't determine exactly what path she'd taken.

A feeling of panic rose – a mild claustrophobia – but she tamped it down, telling herself to remain calm. The pathway was near. It had to be.

Pressing her back against the mirror to her left, she moved along it, using it as a guide, shifting from pane to pane, her progress slow but steady.

Then she turned, passing through another archway, moving deeper into the maze.

And that's when she heard it.

A shuffling sound.

Very faint, but unmistakable.

Anna clicked her flashlight off, knowing, without a doubt, that she wasn't alone.

Pope could barely contain himself.

Still crouched in the weeds, he gripped and regripped the 590, chastising himself fifty different ways for letting McBride go in there alone.

He was no hero – he'd proven that more than once in his life – but he knew he shouldn't have listened to her. Shouldn't have let her have her way.

He waited there, staring blankly at the building, wondering what was going on inside.

When he couldn't take it any longer, he stood up and headed for the entrance.

The maze was silent again.

Anna heard only the sound of her own breathing, and tried desperately to keep it under control. Leaving her flashlight off, she once again flattened against a mirror and moved slowly along it, shifting to the next and the next until she found the continuation of the passageway.

Turning, she passed under an archway—

—and another sound filled the room. A quick fluttering. The shuffle of feet.

She whipped around, peering into the darkness, then the sound came again and she caught movement in the mirrors. Something passing behind her.

Something red?

She turned—

—but he was gone. The room silent.

Backing against a mirror, she brought the Glock up and waited, heart thumping. Even in the darkness she felt exposed.

Suddenly thinking this had all been a colossally bad idea, Anna forced herself to move, inching along the corridor until she found another open archway.

Passing through it, she saw light ahead – at least she *thought* it was ahead – and moved towards it.

A moment later, she found herself standing in the centre of the maze, a tiny skylight overhead, letting in a narrow swathe of sunlight.

And here, in the middle of the room, was a set of wooden steps that led downwards, into a hole in the ground.

A wooden sign next to it read: MINER'S MAGIC MINE – ENTER AT YOUR OWN RISK.

Keeping her Glock up, Anna carefully approached the hole, peering into it. Candlelight flickered below, and there was just enough sunlight for her to see that the walls on either side of the steps had been decorated with spray paint.

She was immediately reminded of Susan's notebook.

They were covered with gypsy wheels.

Pope was about to slip through the gap between the doors when his cellphone rang, startling him.

Stepping back, he quickly dug for it, saw the caller's name.

Ronnie.

He clicked it on, keeping his voice low. 'Hey, Ron, this isn't exactly a good time.'

'Oh, God. Thank God.' Her voice sounded shaky. On the edge of panic. 'I've been trying to call you all day, but I didn't have your number – Jake's got it on his cell. Where are you?'

'Up near Salcedo. Why?'

'Is he with you?'

'No, what's going on?'

'Christ!' she said. 'I haven't heard from him since last night. He isn't home, he doesn't answer his phone, and nobody at the station house has seen or heard from him.'

'You know Jake. He probably turned his phone off to get some peace and quiet.'

'It's not just him I'm worried about,' Ronnie said. 'It's Evan.'

'Evan?' Pope's stomach tightened. 'Why? What happened?'

'We're at my parents' house. He was upstairs sleeping. I was going to let him sleep through the morning, but when I went to check on him, the bed was empty and the window was open.'

'What?'

'He's gone, Danny. He's been gone for hours. Either he ran away or somebody took him.'

'Took him? What makes you think that?'

'Jimmy Sanchez questioned the neighbours. One of them said they saw a car parked out on the street early this morning. One they've never seen before.'

'What kind of car?'

'An old Ford pick-up,' Ronnie said.

Pope didn't know if Ronnie kept talking after that. He had already dropped the phone.

Anna approached the steps, her gaze on that flickering candlelight, knowing it was a trap, that he was down there somewhere, waiting for her.

But what were her choices?

She could turn and flee, which wouldn't change anything. Wouldn't stop him from coming after her again. Or she could push ahead and hope for the best, even though her training warned her against it.

She looked into the mirrors, saw her reflection, could see the fear in her own eyes.

Do or die time, McBride.

Make up your mind.

But a sound made it up for her. Faint but unmistakable: a crying child.

And not just any child.

She'd recognize the sound of those tears anywhere.

Evan.

He had Evan down there.

Oh, sweet God . . .

Quickly stepping past the sign, Anna turned and moved sideways down the steps, keeping her Glock at the ready, the sound of Evan's tears growing louder with each step.

The room below was awash in candle light, dozens of them lining a long shelf and a small, squat table. There were more gypsy wheels spray-painted on the wall, the floor littered with stacks of newspaper and phone books and street maps, some new, some decades old.

And there, seated on an old army cot, a swatch of bloody bandages on his left shoulder, was Mikola. He held a blood-caked knife in his hand, precariously close to a crying Evan Fairweather, who sat at his feet on the cement floor.

Evan started to rise at the sight of Anna, but Mikola grabbed his collar, pulling him back.

'Do not move, boy.'

The sobs grew louder.

Mikola looked at Anna. 'He cries too much, this one. A small poke and he cries like an infant. Let him spend just one day in my skin and then he will find something to cry about.' His gaze snapped to Evan. 'Shut up, boy, or I cut your throat.'

Evan turned sharply, looking at him, and abruptly stopped crying.

Anna kept her Glock up, pointing it at Mikola. 'Let him go.'

'Of course,' Mikola said, calmer now. 'Once you have given me what I seek.' He paused. 'The boy is important to you, yes?'

'Let him go, goddamn it.'

Mikola shook his head. 'Such language, Chavi. I see you have been corrupted by the gadje.'

'I swear to God, I'll shoot you where you sit.'

Mikola swiped the knife through the air. 'And if you do, the boy will die. Is that what you want?'

Anna said nothing.

'You have only you and your friends to blame for this. It would not be necessary if the one on the stairs had not put this bullet in me. But no matter. I will get what I seek, yes?'

Again, Anna said nothing, her mind in turmoil, trying to figure a way out of this without getting Evan hurt.

'My terms are simple,' Mikola said. 'You for the boy.'

Anna wanted so badly to pull the trigger. A bullet straight to the neck would sever his spine, destroy his

369

motor senses and render him unable to use the knife. But what if she missed?

Evan would die.

'Do not disappoint me, Chavi. I've travelled far for this.'

'Through the mirrors,' Anna said.

'Yes, through the mirrors. A simple skill that so many have chosen to ignore. Even you.'

'Me?'

'You are the greatest chovihani the Zala family has ever seen, yet your fear of the black arts is amusing. What is the harm in simply looking into the mirrors and asking that they take you where you wish to go? Look what it has done for me.'

'Allowed you to kill a bunch of innocent people. Let's all celebrate.'

'You are mistaken if you think I enjoy the killing. But to get what I seek, I will not hesitate to use this blade.'

'But for what?' Anna said. 'All those people dead for a piece of my soul?'

'Not just a piece this time. This time I become whole. I become you. The thing I worshipped for so many years. Look at me now. Look how much stronger, how much more beautiful I've become. You are the last spoke on the wheel, Chavi. The tattoo will be complete.'

'But to get it from me, to get this last piece of my soul, you have to kill me, right?'

'Yes.'

'And it has to be you. No one else.'

'Yes,' he said. 'So put the gun down, and I will release the boy.'

For a long moment, Anna didn't move.

Then she raised the gun higher. Put it to her temple.

Mikola's eyes went wide. 'What are you doing?'

'My terms are simple,' Anna said. 'Let the boy go, or I shoot myself.'

He scowled at her. 'You are a mad woman!'

'What's mine is mine, brother. It isn't much, but it'll be lost to you forever if you don't let him go.' She looked at Evan.

'It's okay. He won't hurt you. Go upstairs.'

But Evan didn't budge. Just stared at her, his body shaking.

'Go, Evan. Now!'

The boy finally got to his feet, Mikola making no move to stop him. But as Evan started towards the stairs, Anna made the mistake of following him with her gaze, and before she caught herself—

—Mikola sprang from the cot, diving into her, slamming her to the floor.

The impact knocked the wind out of her and the Glock went flying, Mikola straddling her as he brought the knife up, ready to plunge it into her chest—

—but as his hand came down, Anna twisted beneath him and the knife sank into her shoulder instead.

Hot white pain shot through her, more pain than she could ever remember feeling, as—

—Mikola pulled the knife free, bringing it up again and—

—Anna dug frantically into her back pocket, trying to grab hold of the back-up weapon she'd bought.

Then she had it and brought her hand up, jabbing the business end of a stun gun into Mikola's side, sending 100,000 volts of electricity through him.

He howled, rolling away from her, and she hit him again, then again—

'Run, Evan! Run!'

—and Evan didn't need any more encouragement. He tore up the steps as Anna searched frantically for the Glock, wanting to get this over with once and for all. But she couldn't find it. Not enough light.

But then she spotted the knife on the floor and dived for it—

—but just as the fingers of her free hand brushed the blade—

—Mikola grabbed the handle and brought the knife up, swiping furiously at her. The blade caught her cheek and she dropped the stun gun, reaching for her face, blood gushing between her fingers.

But Mikola was still trembling from the shock of the stun gun and dropped the knife before he could do any more damage.

Anna jumped to her feet and kicked at him, connecting with bone, then turned and ran for the stairs, her shoulder and cheek on fire, blood leaking from the wounds. She took the steps two at a time and saw Evan standing in the centre of the mirror maze, staring at hundreds of his own reflection, not knowing where to go.

Anna grabbed hold of him and swept him up into her arms, heading for the maze as—

—Mikola roared behind her, running up the steps, about to go into a diving tackle, when—

—a shotgun blast rang out, shattering a mirror, shards flying and—

—Anna threw herself to the floor, covering Evan with her body, as—

—Pope stepped through the hole he'd made and fired again, sending a charge straight into Mikola's chest.

The gypsy flew backwards, tumbling down the hole, his greasy red baseball cap fluttering onto his lifeless body.

47

'It's wrong,' McBride said. She seemed delirious. 'It's all wrong.'

It had taken two more shotgun blasts to get them out of the mirror maze quickly.

When they reached the lobby, Pope took Evan from McBride's arms and set him down, then yanked his shirt off, bunched it up and shoved it against her cheek, which was bleeding pretty badly.

The shoulder would have to wait.

'You weren't supposed to kill him,' McBride said.

Pope tucked the 590 under his arm. 'Give me your phone.'

When she didn't respond, he reached into her pocket and pulled it out, dialling 911.

A moment later the operator came on the line. 'We have a shooting death,' he said, 'at the abandoned Big Mountain amusement park in Allenwood. And another person down with major injuries.'

'It was supposed to be me,' McBride said. 'I was the one who was supposed to kill him.'

'We're near the roller coaster, in front of the

house of mirrors. Get an ambulance out here right away.'

He hung up, McBride still babbling. 'You remember what Madame Zala told me? It isn't over. His soul will move on to the next life.'

'Maybe she's wrong.'

'No, no. He's evil, Danny. This isn't over. He's still—'

Pope grabbed her shoulders. 'I can't worry about what might happen twenty years from now. He's dead and you're alive. That's all that matters to me. You're alive. And so is Evan.' He released her and took Evan's hand. 'Now let's get out of here.'

They moved to the entranceway doors, and Pope pushed them wide, stepping into the sunlight, which seemed brighter than before. Then he turned, looking at McBride's shoulder.

'It's a clean puncture, not bleeding too bad. The ambulance should be here any minute.'

'I'm afraid that will be too late,' a voice said.

Pope turned sharply.

Standing in the shade of the roller coaster, his nose broken, a pistol in hand—

—was Arturo.

'I saw the phone on the ground and thought I had lost you,' he said. 'But all good things come to those who wait.' He smiled. 'Mr Troy sends his regards.'

And as Pope reacted, fumbling for his shotgun, Arturo pointed the pistol at him and pulled the trigger.

*

Anna saw the bullet hit in slow motion.

It tore into Pope's chest, spinning him sideways. Blood erupted and he went down hard as—

—the stranger shifted his gaze to Anna and—

—she dived towards Evan, knocking him aside, reaching for the Mossberg 590, which hadn't yet hit the ground, as—

—the stranger squeezed the trigger, the bullet blowing past Anna and Evan, hitting the pavement behind them.

Anna's hands grabbed the 590, which wasn't a light and easy weapon to handle by any means, as—

—the stranger adjusted his angle and squeezed the trigger a third time, and—

—Anna rolled, narrowly avoiding the hit, then pumped the barrel and came up firing, knowing the Mossberg only held five rounds, and that four had already been expended. If this shot didn't connect, she was dead – and so was Evan.

The shotgun roared, bucking hard against Anna's already wounded shoulder, pain reverberating through her body as the charge flew, and she had no idea if she'd hit anything, until she was on the ground and realized the stranger had stopped firing.

Fighting against her pain, she scrambled to her feet and saw him lying about five yards away.

Half of his face was missing.

Motherfucker.

'Evan?' she shouted, and the boy started to cry again.

Anna turned and saw him sitting on the ground nearby, banged up, but still in one piece.

Then there was a groan behind her and she spun around, moving to Pope, who lay on his back on the mottled pavement, his chest bloody, his breathing ragged and laboured, his eyes staring blankly at the sky.

'I think I'm hit,' he said, and she fell to her knees beside him, grabbing his hand—

—oh, God, oh, God—

—but there was nothing she could do for him, he'd be gone soon, and tears flooded her eyes as she looked down at him, not knowing what to say, wanting desperately to rewind the clock, to take it all back—

—and then his eyes shifted slightly, as if he'd seen something in some far-off place.

He said, 'Ben?'

—then stopped breathing, stopped moving, all the gears grinding to an abrupt halt.

Anna just sat there, tears falling, not quite believing what had happened here, not wanting to let go. Evan was still crying, too, but she couldn't find the strength to move, couldn't go to him, as sirens wailed in the distance, signalling that help was on its way.

But what did it matter?

Pope was gone, Evan's family wiped out, Susan in jail, little Jillian Carpenter taken long before her time, and all Anna could claim in return was a small scrap of her gypsy soul.

Red Cap had won. He may have been lying at the

bottom of those steps, but he still had most of their soul and would carry it on to another life, another time.

And when he realized who he was and what he needed to do, it would start all over again. She would never be free.

Never.

But then it suddenly occurred to Anna.

Time.

What if she *could* rewind the clock?

What if she *could* take it all back?

'What is the harm,' Mikola had said, 'in simply looking into the mirrors and asking that they take you where you wish to go?'

Just like Peabody and Sherman. Her own personal wayback machine.

Was it possible?

Could it be done?

She was, after all, Chavi Zala, the gypsy witch, one of the most powerful chovihanis the Zala family had ever seen.

All she had to do, Madame Zala had told her, was to look beyond her reflection and, when she ceased to see herself, she'd see the world, all the way back to its beginning, and forward, to eternity.

And suddenly Anna knew where she needed to go. What moment in time. The only moment where she knew he was certain to be, a part of the past that could be replayed and retooled and would change everything that came after.

Getting to her feet, she shuffled over to Evan, crouching beside him, putting her arms around him.

'It'll be all right, hon. Everything's gonna be all right. You hear the sirens?'

Evan wiped his face, nodded.

'They're coming to help you,' Anna said. 'To take you away from here. But I can't go with you. I have to go back inside.'

'No,' Evan whimpered, grabbing hold of her arms. 'Don't go.'

'I have to, dear. But I promise I'm going to make it better. Everything will be better. All your hurt will go away forever.'

'No,' Evan cried, clinging to her, but she pried herself loose and stood.

'I'll make it better,' she said. 'You'll see.'

And then she turned, shuffling back towards the entrance to the building.

Back towards the magic mirror maze.

Back into the past.

48

'What are you doing?' Suzie Oliver asked, sounding a little nervous.

Jillian Carpenter moved down the street, approaching the Rambler parked just outside Carl's Liquor Store.

'I wanna look inside,' she said.

'What?' Suzie sounded alarmed now.

'Just a quick look,' Jillian said. 'I'm not gonna get in or anything.'

'What if somebody catches you?'

'I'll tell him we thought it was your uncle's car.'

Moving up to the driver's window, Jillian peered inside, cupping her hands for a better view, then crouching down a little to look at the locket dangling from the rear-view mirror.

Then Jillian moved to the Rambler's rear passenger window, staring into the back, before something in the rear windshield caught her attention.

A parking sticker.

'Come on, Jillian, let's *go*,' Suzie said. 'Somebody's gonna come.'

Jillian turned, looking at her friend, then headed back and grabbed Suzie's hand.

'Race you home,' she said, then they broke away from each other and ran.

As they tore past Carl's, Mikola Zala stepped out of the liquor store, and watched them intently. Taking a last drag of his cigarette, he tossed it aside and crossed to the Rambler, quickly unlocking it and climbing inside.

This was Anna's cue to move.

Opening the Honda Civic's door – the Honda Civic she'd stolen from the Big Mountain parking lot – she got out and crossed the street towards the Rambler.

'Excuse me,' she said, waving her hand at Mikola.

He started the engine, paying her no attention.

'Excuse me,' she said again, and he turned, scowling at her, rolling down his window.

Anna knew she must've been a sight, with her wounded shoulder and the gash in her cheek.

But Mikola didn't seem to notice. 'What do you want, woman?'

'You don't remember me, Mikola?'

He looked surprised. 'How do you know my . . .'

Then the surprise turned to recognition as he looked into her eyes.

'Chavi?'

'That's right, motherfucker.'

Anna raised her Glock, touching it to his chest. Before he could react, she said, '*Mine*.'

Then she pulled the trigger.

Part Four

CONTINUITY

49

On April 14th, 1981, Anna Elizabeth McBride ceased to exist. There are no records of her birth to be found.

Two weeks later the girl who carried Anna's soul celebrated her eleventh birthday at the Big Mountain amusement park, with her mother Delilah, her step-father Craig, and her best friend, Suzie Oliver.

Later that night, as a special surprise birthday present, Craig gave Jillian a puppy, which she promptly named Stinky, Jr.

During a poker game, at approximately two a.m. on November 16th, 2007, the Desert Oasis Hotel-Casino owner and reputed organized-crime figure Anderson Troy bit into a slice of peperoni and onion pizza and began to gag.

When those around him failed to administer the Heimlich manoeuvre, he promptly choked to death.

Three weeks later Troy's loyal manservant, Arturo Medina, was arrested for the murder of the hotel chef who had prepared Troy's pizza.

An undercover investigation into Troy's illegal activities was promptly abandoned.

On May 12th, 2009 Evan Fairweather and his little sister Kimberly attended the wedding of their mother, Rita, who married a visiting certified public accountant named Hans Crawford, whom she had met at the bar where she worked three nights a week.

The family moved away from Ludlow to Santa Barbara, California, where Crawford lived on an acre of land. He later filed papers to adopt the children, both of whom took his name.

The children's biological father never attempted to find them and his whereabouts are currently unknown.

50

Jillian Carpenter was sitting on a bench in the middle of the Midstreet Mall in northern Las Vegas when she saw her.

'Oh, my God,' she said, getting to her feet. 'Suzie? Suzie Oliver?'

The woman, who was standing outside Kern's Drug Store, turned, a startled look on her face.

Then her eyes registered recognition. 'Jillian?'

Within seconds the two women were hugging each other, Jillian having a bit of trouble, because of the beach ball attached to her abdomen.

She was seven months pregnant.

'This is unbelievable,' Suzie said. 'How long has it been?'

'Since freshman year in high school. I'll never forgive you for moving away.'

'Oh, God, remember that last night, when we were both crying like crazy?'

Jillian nodded. 'I think my mom had to go out and buy more Kleenex.'

They laughed, then Suzie looked down at Jillian's belly. 'How many months?'

'Seven,' Jillian said. 'I'm way too old to be doing this, but it was now or never.'

'Congratulations.'

'What about you? Do you have any kids?'

Suzie smiled, digging into her purse. 'Uh-oh, out come the pictures.'

She brought out her cellphone, flicked a button and showed the screen to Jillian. Two attractive teens stared up at her. 'James and Lisa. Thirteen and sixteen.'

'They're gorgeous,' Jillian said.

'Fortunately they look just like their father.'

'Oh, stop it. You're as beautiful as ever.'

Suzie laughed and shook her head. 'God, I've missed you, Jills. I think about you all the time.'

'Me, too,' Jillian said, feeling a hitch in her throat. 'Oh, crap, I think I'm gonna cry.'

'That's just the hormones.'

'No kidding. I've got 'em to spare.'

They laughed again, and a voice rang out behind them. '*There* you are. We've been looking all over for you.'

Jillian turned.

'Oh, good,' she said, 'you're just in time. I want you to meet my best friend in the whole world, Susan Leah Oliver.'

'Fenton,' Suzie corrected. 'I left the name Oliver behind a long time ago.'

'Well, Susan Fenton, this is my husband Danny, his cousin Jake and Jake's wife, Ronnie.'

They all shook hands, then Susan frowned. 'This is gonna sound strange, but I think we went to high school together. You're Danny Pope, right?'

'You're from Ludlow?'

'Yes and no,' Suzie told him. 'When my family left Salcedo, we moved to Ludlow, but we only lived there for about four months. But I remember, you used to work at the Hungry Spoon. I'd go in there once in a while and get a slice of pie.'

Danny nodded. 'That's right, I remember now. French apple, right?'

Suzie laughed. 'Right.' She looked at Jillian. 'So how did you two meet?'

'In college, actually. We both had the same major, so we shared a lot of classes, and it was pretty much love at first sight. I don't know, but the minute I saw him, I felt like we'd known each other forever. Right, Danny?'

'Like it was destiny or something.'

'That's wonderful,' Suzie said.

Jillian nodded, grabbing Danny's arm, pulling him close. 'Then later we both got certified and went into business together.'

'Oh? What kind of business?'

'We have a hypnotherapy clinic downtown,' Danny said. 'Jillian does the chronic smokers and bedwetters and I specialize in forensics.'

'He works with the police a lot,' Jillian said.

'Hypnotherapy, huh? I'll have to look you up sometime and you can put me under, discover all my deep, dark secrets.'

They all laughed and Suzie checked her watch. 'Oh, crap. I've gotta go. But it was great seeing you, Jills.' She touched Jillian's stomach. 'Is it a boy or a girl?'

'A boy,' Jillian said. 'We're thinking of calling him Ben.'

'Great name. I almost used that one myself, but my husband overruled me.' She smiled. 'Anyway, I'd better get out of here. Give me your number and I'll call you.'

They exchanged numbers, gave each other a hug, then Suzie said her goodbyes and headed for the exit.

'Nice girl,' Danny said, watching her as she walked away.

'Keep your eyes in your head, buster. You're taken.' She looked at the bags in his hands. 'Did you buy me anything?'

'Fat chance,' Danny told her. 'You'd only return it.'

'Don't worry,' Jake said. 'I bought you something.'

'Oh?'

'Well, not really for you. But for Ben, once you pop the little bugger out.'

'What is it?' Jillian asked. 'Let me see.'

Jake dug around in his bag. 'It was actually Ronnie's idea. We saw it in the Babies R Us window and couldn't resist.'

'*He* couldn't resist,' Ronnie said. 'I had nothing to do with it.'

'Well, come on, spill.'

Jillian watched as Jake dug around in the bag some more and finally found what he was looking for.

When he brought it out, Jillian felt another hitch in her throat and tears in her eyes. The hormones kicking in again.

'Oh, my God,' she said, 'it's perfect.'

She took it from him, giving him a kiss on the cheek. Then she turned it in her hands, thinking how cute her baby boy would look wearing it.

It was a baseball cap.

A little red baseball cap.

Visit **www.panmacmillan.com** to read more about all our books and to buy them. You will also find features, author interviews and news of any author events, and you can sign up for e-newsletters so that you're always first to hear about our new releases.

www.panmacmillan.com

| GIFT SELECTOR |
| YOUR ACCOUNT |
| WISH LIST |
| WAITING LIST |

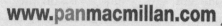

| HOME | ABOUT US | IMPRINTS | TRADE/MEDIA | CONTACT US | ADVANCED SEARCH | SEARCH | GO |

| BOOK CATEGORIES | WHAT'S NEW | AUTHORS/ILLUSTRATORS | BESTSELLERS | READING GROUPS |

Coming Soon...

Reading Groups

Competitions
Feeling Lucky?

Extracts
Sneak Previews

Interviews

Events
Meet Our Stars

Reviews
What The Critics Say

News & Awards

Editor's Choice
What We're Reading